CORMACK

Black Ops Romantic Suspense/Military Romance

NEMESIS INC.
BOOK 2

ANNABELLA STONE
BELLA STONE

CORMACK

NEMESIS INC.

NEMESIS INC, BOOK 2

Editing:
Crowder Editing

Proof Reading:
Julie Deaton
SN & NM Proofing

Cover Design:
LK Graphics

Cover Photo: JW Photography and Covers
Model: Darrin James

ACKNOWLEDGMENTS

NEMESIS INC.

I'd like to thank the following people who have been a part of my journey:

Thank you to my guy, for always having my back. You have owned my heart for over two decades and you will always be my hero. You and our amazingly sweet kiddos, Potterhead and Pottermonkey... you all make this crazy life worth it.

Thank you to my soul sister, North. Without your help in researching and developing the plots, these stories would lack some of the extra sparkle and glitter you bring to the table. I will never be able to thank you enough for all you have done and all you continue to do. Love you!!! Thank you for being my rock and providing the required boot in the ass when needed.

Thank you to my family, who read this story as it was written, answering all my military questions and helping ensure my information is as factual as possible. Any mistakes I have made are mine. Thank you for the middle of the night conversations and virtual smacks upside the head that were needed to keep me on track.

I have to say a huge thank you to Riley, she booted my butt and kept me writing all the way through this story. Without her I may have given up. Thank you, Ri, I owe you so many more packs of Taytos, it's not funny.

I'd also like to take this opportunity to thank the god who discovered that Coffee is an amazing way to keep my eyelids propped open when the characters in my head are yelling out their stories at 3 AM... Without the aid of the coffee gods these stories would not exist.

#NEVERFORGOTTEN

For the 31 heroes of Extortion 17 .

Brothers don't always have the same mother.
Until we meet again to feast in the halls of Valhalla.

Lieutenant Commander (SEAL)
Jonas B. Kelsall

NEMESIS INC

NEMESIS INC.

#0.5 LINA.

Will their surprise wedding be their downfall, or will it bring them a love that lasts a lifetime?

Navy SEAL Dalton Knight only wanted a night of drinking with his team brothers. The last thing he expected was to meet the other half of his soul.

Lina Maxwell knew she should have stayed at home. Drinking and dancing is so not her jam. When her drink is spiked, a knight in shining Kevlar insists he marries her to protect her from the demons who haunt her nightmares. Will their surprise wedding be their downfall, or will it bring them a love that lasts a lifetime?

#1 DALTON

The war on terror tore them apart. Will a terrorist bring them back together?

. . .

FORMER NAVY SEAL, Dalton *Nemesis* Knight thought he had it all. A Navy career he loved. His Seal Team brothers, and her... his Lina. The war on terror proved him wrong. It cost him everything, including his wife. With his trust broken, he'd had to find a new way forward and a new system he could believe in. Eventually, he picked the shattered pieces of his broken heart up off the floor and built Nemesis Inc. from the ground up. Now he makes the rules, he signs the checks, and his heart is off the table for good. Nobody is ever going to get close enough to destroy him again.

For years, Lina Maxwell has watched him from the shadows. Cheering his successes and mourning his losses. He's always been hers; she's always been his. Neither anger nor distance can change that. The time has come to gather her courage and fix the wrongs of the past. In leaving him, she protected him the only way she could, Lina needs Nemesis to see that she did not betray him, that she still loves him with everything that she is. Her bosses and her mission will not allow her to make contact. Her whole life is an illusion. She no longer has an identity, no longer has a name. As far as anyone, including her husband, is concerned, she never existed at all.

Just when Lina is ready to ignore her orders and step silently out of the dark, a terrorist wages war on Eastern Europe. With Nemesis running headfirst into danger, she will use every contact and source in her network to protect him. Will showing him she's still alive destroy not only their memories but any chance they might have had of a future?

Will this mission be the bandage to fix two broken hearts, or will it finally destroy them both?

#2 CORMACK

His happy sunshine girl didn't deserve to be pulled into his world of fire and brimstone. All he could do was hope like hell he found her in time.

As a Black Ops Contractor for Nemesis Inc. Cormack *Jeep* Ford, has seen the worst humans can inflict on their fellow man—in some of the shittiest hellholes on earth. With a twenty-year military career under his belt, he's not one bit sorry when Nemesis Inc. relocates from Kabul to Montana. Maybe now his boots are firmly on US soil, he can peruse a happy ever after with woman who calls to his soul.

To Willow Black it feels like she's waited a lifetime for her soldier to come home. Who'd have thought a connection made over emails and letters would lead her to the man who makes her heart and body sing. With Cormack moving back to the US full time, she can't wait to see if the connection between them can withstand the test of time spent in the same freaking time zone. Just when she's starting to believe he may be her happy ever after, a terrorist destroys everything she trusts in— dragging her into the terrifying reality of the world's underbelly.

A man forged in fire and brimstone—a woman made for sunshine and roses—and a terrorist determined to make them pay. Can Cormack convince Willow her life's not over? Can she convince him to let her go? Or will their hearts have the final say?

Coming Soon in Nemesis Inc:

Logan

Rory
Aria

PROLOGUE

Nemesis Inc. Headquarters, Montana.

CORMACK *Jeep* Ford leaned against the wooden porch post and watched Dalton *Nemesis* Knight and his wife Lina *Mamba* Maxwell-Knight, walking toward him from the pond, with the sun at their backs, and their heads together as they laughed at something the puppy bouncing around them had done. His boss had a reputation for being an asshole. Dalton ran his paramilitary organization, Nemesis Inc., with an iron fist and a balls to the wall, get the job done attitude. Not that you'd know it to look at him today. Any one of the many terrorist organizations they'd taken down would have shit a full-grown cow to see Nemesis playing the big goofy idiot like this.

"Who'd have thought a tiny ass woman and a mini excavator with four paws, a tail that never stops waving, and who shits on the floor, would bring him to his knees?"

He jerked at the sound of Logan *Sensei* Winters' voice and spun around to face him. "Perfect picture of a happy ever after, isn't it?"

"Yeah." Logan handed over a bottle of Bud and twisted the top off his own. He studied Dalton and Lina for a couple of seconds, took a swig from his beer, and swallowed before asking, "Do you think he's done?"

"No." Jeep swallowed down the beer and shook his head. "No, I think now he has her back, her protection is going to be his number one priority, and he'll be even more of a hard bastard. He's not gonna stop until the threat to his wife is gone."

"I think the same." Logan sat on the porch step, leaning his back against the railing as if he didn't care either way. But Jeep could see something about his boss was bothering his brother in arms. "How long before he takes the fight to them?"

Ah, there it was. He'd bet someone ten bucks that Logan was bored as hell. "Not long." He studied Sensei as he picked at the label on his bottle. "Why? You bored?"

"Yup, I agreed to fight out of a forward operating base in the sandbox or any other hell hole we could find," Logan muttered. "I didn't agree to be based here on a ranch in the back ass of Montana."

"Here has one hell of a setup," Jeep reminded him. "This ranch offers us a lot more than Kabul. A full tactical operations center, a firing range, and the training facility is top-notch, better than most I've seen in the military."

"Agree." Logan shrugged and took another sip of his beer. "But happy families are not my jam." He jerked his thumb to where their boss rolled on the ground wrestling with the malamute puppy. "You think you could ever give up the rush of going out full time?"

"Nope." Jeep snorted. "Not a chance in hell. I'll stop going out when they put me in the ground."

"Damn straight."

He opened his mouth to ask Logan what brought all this on when his cell vibrating in his ass pocket distracted him. He pulled it out and frowned at the screen. He didn't answer private numbers. He tapped the screen to send it to voice mail. "Fucking call centers."

"Assholes," Logan agreed. "But at least they're earning an honest living."

"True." He scowled at the phone when it beeped indicating he had a message. "Why don't you call these ones back and offer them a dick pic just for shits and giggles?" He hit play on the message.

"Cormack, help me."

He stared in shock at the low husky whisper coming from the speakers of his cell. "What the fuck?" The sounds of one hell of a fight filtered to them along with the distinctive *pop, pop* of suppressed gunfire and return fire from what sounded like a Glock.

"Shit." Logan got to his feet. His eyes were trained on the phone in Jeep's hand as if it would strike out and bite them.

"I'm not going to hold them off," the woman's voice whispered. "If you get this, Cormack, you come looking for me. Do you hear me? You found me once, you can do it again." Her whimpers were muffled as if she'd stuffed her fist into her mouth, followed by a hitch in her breathing before an ear-piercing scream echoed down the phone.

"Fuck." He fumbled with the phone, searching for the recent calls. "Damn it, no number. Fuck."

"Boss!" Logan yelled for Dalton and waved. "Jeep has a woman, and she needs our help, stat." He took the beer bottle from Jeep's hand and placed it on the floor with his.

"On it!" Dalton yelled back.

Jeep hit replay on the voice message; this could not be happening. "She was at home safe at her family's house."

"Who?"

He understood Logan's confusion, but he didn't have time

to give him that information, he was too busy tapping through the screens, looking for the number. It had to be there. Why the fuck was she calling him from an unlisted number? "I can't find the number."

"Hit reply on the message." Logan reached for the cell, but dropped his hand when Jeep swung it away from him.

"It's a voice message, remember?"

"Then press number five."

He followed Logan's instructions and growled in frustration when nothing happened. "It's not work—" He cut himself off when the phone in his hand rang again. "Willow?"

"I have your Willow." The mechanical voice turned his blood to ice. "You bring me your boss's wife, and I'll give you your woman back."

"I don't give a fuck who you are, who you work for, or how powerful you think you are," he snarled into the phone. "Let Willow go, or there is nowhere on the planet you can hide from me."

"Make me."

"I will find you, asshole," he swore the promise into the phone. He had to hope Willow was close enough to hear him. "Everything you do to her; I will make sure you pay for it a thousand times over." Manic laughter was the only response before the line went dead. "Fuccck."

"What happened?" Dalton's boots pounded up the steps of the porch.

"Fucking King has taken my girl to trade for yours." He had to work hard to keep the accusatory tone out of his voice but failed. He also failed on an epic level at suppressing even an ounce of rage. He was going to rip that asshole, King, apart with his bare hands. Just as soon as he had his sunshine girl back. "Help me find her."

"Always, brother." Dalton's fingers buried into Jeep's

shoulders. "I swear to you, we'll burn the world to the ground to get her back." He shook Jeep softly. "Do you believe me?"

"Yeah." He did believe him; he believed in his team's abilities, too. He'd trusted Nemesis to have his six. He trusted him and their brothers in arms to help him get Willow back. But swap Nemesis's woman for his own? Hell no, that was never going to happen.

"Then let's get to work." Dalton dropped his hand from his shoulder and turned to bark out orders.

All Jeep could do was swallow down the bile and the rage. His happy Sunshine Girl didn't deserve to be pulled into his world of fire and brimstone. All he could do was hope like hell he found her in time.

CHAPTER ONE

HE CLAMPED down on the inside of his cheek, hard. This was the fourth time Trev had replayed that fucking message. Every second they spent relistening to it was a second he wasn't gearing up or heading out on the run to find her. But fuck, there was no way he could get from here to her tiny house on the east coast. By the time they got there, there would be no trace of her. He knew it, but it didn't mean keeping his ass planted in this room was easy. She called him. Him. He would not fuck this up. He would find her, and fucking King was gonna pay.

"Cormack?"

Yes, she'd called him… Cormack. She fucking called him and here he was relistening to her message for round number goddammed four, or maybe it was round number five, or even six. Counting wasn't important, what mattered was he was here instead of out there looking for her.

"Cormack."

"Jeep."

It was only on hearing his name called for the third time

that it sank into his brain, it wasn't Willow's voice calling him, it was Nemesis, his boss. "What?"

"Snap the fuck out of that shit," Nemesis ordered. "We'll find her, but in order for us to do that, you have to give Trev the intel we need. What's her full name?"

He knew Trev needed the information. It pissed him off to have to tell anyone about her. If it wasn't so damn important, he didn't know when he'd be in the right place to share. But tough shit, that choice was taken out of his hands the second King put his goddamn dirty paws on her. "Willow Ebony Black." On screen he could see Trev's fingers moving on the keyboard. Based on experience, he was probably running Willow through all his databases and probably a couple he shouldn't have access to. Damn it, his Willow shouldn't be on anyone's fucking radar. For now, he was going to ignore the raised eyebrow from his boss, in about five minutes flat, the reason he'd kept Willow, and who she was to him, in the shadows, would become apparent and Dalton would lose his shit.

"Date of birth?"

"April first nineteen ninety-five." He made a point of scanning the room and meeting each one of their eyes. If any fucker had something to say about the huge difference in his and Willow's ages, he was going to toss them out the window. Rory *Mokaccino* Costa opened his mouth, but a sharp nudge in the side from Lucifer *Devil-Man* Brady had him shutting it again. Smart choice.

"Address." Trev dragged his attention back to the screen.

This was it, shit hit the fan time, but Willow was more important than the bruises Dalton would dish out. He refused to be the reason she didn't get to come home. "2528 Dellwood Drive, Virginia Beach."

"Shit," Nemesis growled softly.

"Don't even fucking say it, brother," Cormack warned. "Now is not the goddamned time."

Nemesis's growl was the only warning he had before his boss bodily grabbed him by the shirt, dragged him out of the room, and slammed him against the wall across from war-room number two. He didn't need a translator or subtitles to read the rage on his face. Hell, Dalton had every right to be angry. If the boots were on the other foot, he'd be pissed as fuck.

"She's Eli's daughter?" Dalton pulled him forward and slammed him back again for good measure. He didn't wait for Jeep to respond; he could probably see the truth in his eyes. "I should kick your ass."

"But you won't." Jeep understood the anger. Fucking around with a team guy's daughter was asking for trouble. Doing it with a team brother who was feasting in the halls of Valhalla, that was way over the line of right and wrong and exactly the reason he had told nobody about Willow.

"Don't fucking count on it."

"Could you stay away from Lina?"

"Do. Not. Bring. My. Wife. Into. This."

"She's already fucking in it, Nemesis, King took my Willow because he couldn't take Lina."

"Fuck you." Dalton palmed his knife and pressed it under his chin. "We are not fucking even going to consider..."

"I'm not asking you to," Jeep interrupted and flattened his hands against the wall he was pressed against. Punching or making an attempt to disarm Dalton when he was this pissed would likely result in a hell of a lot more blood than what was currently dripping down his throat. "Life's fucking complicated. She makes it less crazy in my brain."

"Fuck." Dalton spun away from him and threw his K-bar down the hall, hard. It slammed into the oak frame of the door into the living space. No doubt Lina would give him shit about that later.

Cormack took the opportunity to press his finger under his throat. He pulled it back and looked at the drop of blood there. The cut didn't sting yet, but he knew it would later. "I'm not going to apologize," he warned Dalton. "She's as much mine as Lina is yours."

"I'll find her for Eli," Dalton muttered. "He was a brother." Dalton's face darkened with a brief flash of grief before he shook it off and pointed at him. "I watched that kid go to her first day at school, damn it."

"What's the matter, Nemy? Does it make you feel old?"

Well, that was someone he hadn't expected to be on his side. Lina. Dalton hadn't either if the fingers pinching into his eyes was any indicator. "She was over age when stuff happened between you two?" Lina asked. "Right?"

"Yeah."

"Then my husband will quit being an overprotective asshole and get his shit together to help you find her," Lina said the words all matter-of-fact like, but even he could hear the steel behind them. And this right here was exactly why he would never do the exchange King wanted.

"Boss, Jeep, Trev's got street cameras and shit."

Sensei's reminder of what was important cut off any more of the dick measuring contest going on between him and Dalton. There would be time enough for that shit later. After they'd found Willow and put the assholes who'd taken her somewhere about six feet south of a flowerbed.

"We'll be discussing this," Dalton growled softly in his ear.

"Count on it."

Dalton pushed past him into the war-room, coming to a

stop in front of the screens. "Hit it, Trev, show us what you got."

"I managed to pull some footage from the security cameras on the front door of the house across the street." Trev minimized his own picture until it was a tiny box in the lower left corner of the screen. The rest showed black and white footage of what could be any street in any suburb in the US.

But Jeep knew it wasn't just any freaking suburb. This was Willow's... He recognized the paint job on her trash can across the street. She'd spent most of a Saturday painting that snow scene, while he'd cleaned the gutters and fixed the loose shingle on the porch roof on his last visit to see her. God, had that only been a couple of months ago? If he hadn't had to leave to dig Dalton's ass out of the shit... Nope. He cut off that thought before it could get a foothold. He would not blame anyone... well, anyone but himself.

"The time we're interested in is coming up in, three, two, one..." Trev's warning snapped his focus back to the screen and the camera footage. He watched as a dark colored panel van almost drove past Willow's house before reversing into her driveway, knocking over the trash can. He winced; she'd been so damn pleased with her paint work on that can. If they'd scratched it up, he'd have to come up with some creative way to make the fucker pay.

They watched as two men jumped out of the front while the sliding door opened to reveal three more. King, the asshole, sent five men after his tiny Sunshine Girl. "What a dick."

Trev hit pause on the footage.

"You know them?" Dalton asked.

"No, King's an asshole. Who the fuck sends five men after one tiny woman?" he muttered. "Five!"

"We know he wants her alive," Lina said. When she saw

his confused look at her comment, she added on, "He didn't send a snake."

"Jesus, a fucking snake." He pinched his fingers into his eyes deep enough to hurt. He needed the bite of pain to keep himself from jumping across the table to shake information on King's methods and his goddamn snake named assassins out of Lina. She'd know all about them, wouldn't she? Considering before she and Dalton had reunited, she'd spent years as one of King's murder harems of snake assassins. "Play it," he spoke through gritted teeth. He didn't dare open his mouth fully to voice the words, as he couldn't be sure a scream of frustration wouldn't escape.

They watched as the men fanned out around the front of the house, two of them climbing the step to ring the bell. Even though he knew what would happen, in his head he silently begged Willow to not answer the door.

Don't open it, Sunshine, don't answer the door.

The front door opened, and he caught his first glimpse of her, her dark hair spilling free over her shoulders. In her usual attire of cutoff shorts and a band tee. Even with the grainy footage from the camera across the street, he could see a welcoming smile across her face. How many fucking times had he told her to check the peephole? To not answer the door to strangers. He growled low in his throat when the asshole closest to her grabbed her arm and tugged.

His internal protective caveman snarled with rage when the smile on her face fell. Along with her foot. Not that a bare foot against a booted one would be much help. But his little spitfire went straight for the eyes, just like they'd practiced. The one holding her dropped her and she bolted into the house. From there he could no longer see her.

But in his head, he replayed her message. He imagined

her racing for the kitchen and the Glock he kept in the lockbox over the fridge.

Four of the five men barged in the door and disappeared into the house.

Trev paused the video. "Watch for the flashes. I'm assuming those are the gunfire we heard on the message." He hit replay again once Jeep had nodded his agreement.

He physically jerked for each of the three flashes which indicated shots fired. From the sound he remembered from the voice message, he was guessing they came from his Glock and the suppressed fire from the guns the thugs had brought with them. He tried to match up the voice message which now played in a loop in his head with the footage, but despite counting the steps from the front door to the kitchen and maybe the pantry or out into the back garden, it didn't quite make sense.

"Hey, Trev?"

"Yup?" The video paused again.

"Can you overlay the audio from the voice message starting from about ten to fifteen seconds before they enter the house?" He needed to figure it out in his head. He had to be able to visualize what was happening.

"Lemme match up the sounds of gunfire with those flashes and see what that gets us."

"Whatcha looking for, Jeep?" Mokaccino tilted his head to one side and studied him like a bug under a scope.

"I need to visualize where she was in the house. And what's happening."

"Makes sense."

"Okay, I got it as close as I can," Trev said. "Want me to rewind to the start or just when they enter the house?"

"When they go in the door is fine." He knew they would

replay this video multiple times before Nemesis's plane was ready for takeoff in the next hour or so.

"You got it, bro." Once again, the video filled the main screen, this time from the point where Willow bolted through the door. He retraced her steps in his head. Down the hall, turn right. Swing step behind the kitchen door and pull the Glock from its place on top of the fridge, grab her phone off the table, and bolt for the pantry door. Call him and get fucking voice mail. Then *pop, pop, pop*. That was the suppressed gunfire, the fuckers were shooting at her. Followed by the boom of the Glock, twice.

That's my girl; make every shot count, Sunshine.

On screen less than a minute later, two men came out the front door, dragging her between them. "Pause it." The video footage stopped. He went closer to the screen. Tilting his head this way and that, memorizing every feature on those two assholes' faces. "Those two fuckers are mine." He didn't give one single flying fuck that he wasn't the one who called the shots. That was Nemesis's role. In this he would not be denied; these were the two bastards who'd dared put their hands on his sunshine. When he was sure he could recognize those two he stepped back. "Go on, Trev."

They watched as the men dragged Willow to the van and tossed her inside. They saw them slam the sliding door and the lights flash as someone hit the auto lock. Less than a minute later, Willow bolted from the door on the other side of the van and disappeared. "Shiiiiit. Get me a fucking plane. Now!" She'd escaped; holy fucking shit. Where the hell was she? He was already running for the door and the ready room. "Weapons, I'm gonna need big ones. Move your asses. Come. On."

"She killed one, or at least put him down!" Trev yelled from the computer.

"What?"

"They're carrying one out." If he wasn't mistaken, Trev sounded proud as fuck. Jeep spun around at the door and watched the scene unfold on the screen. The tangos hitting the locks, opening the van to put their downed comrade into it, and realizing Willow was gone. The panic he'd had to work so hard to suppress receded. Now a different urgency slammed into him as the assholes spread out around Willow's neighborhood, obviously searching for her. He had to find her first.

CHAPTER TWO

As soon as her butt hit the floor of the van she was thrown into, she bounced up into a crouch, just as she did during her dancercise class. Who freaking knew dance torture would come in useful in a life-or-death situation? She was never, ever whining about going to her dance class again. Ever. She frantically reached for the door which they'd just slammed shut, second-guessed herself, and scrambled over the bulkhead into the driver's seat. "Please let there be keys." But under the steering wheel her fingers met nothing. She wasn't waiting, despite having heard the locks engaging when they'd closed the door, her fingers were already reaching for the door handle. Thank you, sweet baby Jesus, for fail safes in case of an emergency, the door opened. She jumped down and softly closed it behind her.

Ducking low she scrambled through the hole in the hedge made by the neighbor's dog yesterday. That hole that she'd been so freaking annoyed by was now saving her butt and giving her a chance to escape whoever these thugs were. She raced across the Callaghans' patio and around their pool. Their mixed breed thankfully wasn't in the yard and he for once didn't bark at her intrusion into his space. Letting herself out of her neighbor's yard, she turned toward the track she walked along every other day. Her feet knew where she was going, and automatically avoided the loose shale which would slice her bare feet. She raced for the park. If she made it there, she could disappear into the city and call Cormack again.

She ran along the trail and over the foot bridge. Who were those people? Was it someone her father had pissed off at some point? Or maybe Cormack? God, was Cormack in trouble? "Think, you ninny, you've got to get yourself somewhere safe, then you can figure stuff out." Trying to run and think was almost impossible. Most conventional thinking was women were good at multi-tasking, she snorted in her head; there was nobody on the planet who'd say that convention applied to her. She had her own way of doing things. Method-ically, and one at a time, in a linear fashion.

Behind her she heard voices, and she put on a spurt of speed. The muscles in her thighs and butt protesting at running where she normally walked. She was never, ever again going to complain about Cormack and his backup training plans for every freaking thing.

"God, you're an idiot." If she hadn't been running, she'd have slapped herself for not thinking of it in the first place. "Get your butt to the bunker." She swerved off the trail at a place between two trees where hopefully her path couldn't be picked up by any decent tracker. Her breath sawed in and out of her lungs so hard, she was sure those men would be able to hear her from back at her house.

Don't panic, Sunshine. Get to the bunker.

As clearly as if he was running right beside her, she heard Cormack's gruff tone in her head.

Panic will get you dead. If they aren't in sight, slow down and move slowly so you don't make noise. Do not draw attention to yourself.

She glanced over her shoulder and couldn't see anything but trees and more trees. She forced herself to stop running. Pressing one hand against a tree, she bent over almost double with the other hand pressed against her chest.

Good girl, now breathe for me.

She had no freaking clue how this was working. Had no idea how she could hear him so clearly in her head. But dang it, she could question her sanity later. If crazy got her out of this, then she'd happily be freaking crazy.

Slow your breathing down, Sunshine. In for four, hold for a count of four.

She squeezed her eyes tight and fought with her instincts to do as he'd taught her. Inhaling slowly sucked; it hurt her chest. Her lungs wanted to snatch as much air as possible in case it was restricted again. Hold that first breath for a count of four seconds, that was worse than inhaling slow and deep. But she did it.

Exhale for four seconds, Sunshine.

She did what the voice in her head told her to do. Was told the correct word? She had no freaking clue, but the voice in her head sounded like Cormack so she would listen. If it got her killed or she died from lack of oxygen, she could haunt him for the rest of his days. Move stuff in his packs and bags and, oh boy, the fun she could have driving him nuts by throwing stuff around the kitchen. He'd lose his mind.

Focus, Sunshine, the voice in her head chided. *Do it again, four square, come on, breathe for me.*

Jeez Louise, even made-up Cormack was a bossy-boots. But she followed his instructions anyway, and after two more rounds her heart finally decided it really didn't need to climb out of her chest through her rib cage. Maybe now she could move on and find where she was supposed to go.

Get your bearings. Figure out where you are and what direction you need to go.

She could do this. She looked around. Could she have a signpost? An arrow? How about a big flashing neon sign that said go this way? Of course, she couldn't, that would be too freaking easy. "Which way?" She cocked her head to one side as if listening. But despite how she'd heard him so clearly in her head a few minutes before, there was no such help coming now. Of course not, magic wasn't real. People did not talk in other people's head in real life. She looked over her shoulder. "Think. Be logical."

In her head she snorted at her own whispered comment. "Logical my butt." Those men were behind her, so she would go the opposite direction. Away from them was good. If she heard them, she would hide.

Walking and watching sucked, she stubbed her toe... multiple times and had to bite down hard enough on her lip to keep from crying out. This had to be why most people wore shoes all the time. It had to be why they didn't enjoy the feel of grass between their toes and even wore them in the house. Heathens. From now on she was never, ever leaving the house without shoes.

As she wiped silent tears from her eyes, a rock formation caught her eye. "I know you... rabbit rock." Excitement started to build and bubble up inside her. She knew that rock. Didn't she? If she was correct and this was the same rock where she and Cormack had seen momma rabbit and her babies, then she wasn't far from his bunker and his stash of weapons.

"Think." Now which way had they gone from the rock? She got as close to it as she could while avoiding the brambles and sticky plants. Then turned her back to rabbit rock and tried to play back the scene in her head. She squeezed her eyes shut, sucked in a breath, and let it out slowly. "Left." She went left around the blackberry brambles and frowned when she didn't recognize anything. Not a single tree or plant looked familiar. This would teach her to pay attention and to not be distracted by the baby animals.

Oh, who was she kidding? Baby animals were always going to be a distraction to her. She couldn't help herself. Baby animals were squishy and cute and there was never going to be a time when she didn't want to watch them tumble and play.

She retraced her steps back to the front of the rabbit rock before going the opposite direction. "This way." She had to pick one way, this one went further away from the trail, so it had to be the way, right? Lord, she hoped so.

She scrambled over the scattered fallen logs which blocked her way, skinning both her knees on the bark, but when she landed on the other side, she was sure she was on the right path. Not that there was a path. A path would be both a blessing and a curse. It would make it easier for her to get where she was going, but also easier for the men to find her.

Her toe caught on something, and she felt herself falling. She tried to stop it, but face-planted right into the dirt, just like she did that time she tried platform shoes to add some extra inches to her five-foot-four height and attempted to run across the lawn. "Dang it." She got her arms under her and glanced up. "Yes!"

If she hadn't needed her arms to scramble to her feet, she'd have done a fist pump. But klutzy as she knew she was, she didn't dare. She recognized that deer stand. Now she just needed to find the oak among all these trees. She half ran to the broken-down wooden ladder and around it until she was under the structure. If this thing fell on her head, it would be a craptastic end to her day.

Straight ahead, one tree back is the oak, two trees left, and at the roots of the third is the trap door. She couldn't see a freaking thing in the waning light. But she was going to trust the voice in her head. Trust it and follow its instructions. She pushed her way through bushes until she emerged at the tree line and stepped behind the first tree. Then walked to the second. Those scalloped edges on the leaves meant it was an oak... right? How in the name of everything sacred could she live this close to the forest and not be able to tell an oak from a pine tree? She put her right hand on the tree she hoped was the oak, then carefully placed her sore feet into the leaves. The two steps to the next tree were a lesson once again on why she should have worn shoes as the bumpy, rough nuts under the oak dug into her feet. No, acorns, they were acorn-husks and not nut shells. At the third tree, she dropped to her hands and knees, her fingers skimming through the leaves, searching the forest floor looking for the hook.

"Come to momma." The tips of her fingers met metal and she pulled up the padlock. "Of course, it's freaking locked." Argh, she'd come all this way, only to find it locked. Now what was she to do? She peered at the combination dial on the padlock. What number would a man like Cormack use? She tried his birthday. Then the date he'd told her he'd joined the military. The date she'd replied to his email for the first time, and every other date she could think of until she could feel the scream of frustration building in the back of her throat.

Your birthday, Sunshine.

If this number didn't work, she'd have to move. She couldn't stay here. Those men had to be still looking for her.

They had no reason to stop looking, and they obviously had wanted her badly enough to try and kidnap her in broad daylight. No, she didn't dare wait, waiting would be stupid which was something she tried not to be very often. If this safe spot didn't work out, then she had to find another one fast or make it to a police station. Her fingers fumbled over the numbers, and she had to readjust the second one twice until she got it to the nine. Holding her breath as she rolled the last dial, she almost didn't hear the click of the lock opening over the rushing sound in her ears. She stared at it for a couple of seconds in disbelief, not fully comprehending that she'd done it before she unhooked the lock from the hoops. She jumped to her feet, pulled up the trap door enough so she could slide inside, and shut it behind her, plunging her world into darkness.

CHAPTER THREE

HE PAUSED in front of the cage which held his weapons and squeezed his eyes shut. Had he done enough to prepare her? Did she remember the lessons he'd disguised as hiking trips? Fuck he hoped so. His sunshine had a tendency to get lost in her own thoughts. Daydreams and small animals distracted her like nobody's business. She'd happily spent an hour running around chasing a damn butterfly, while he'd sat his ass on a tree stump watching her, for fuck's sake. It drove him nuts that she didn't see danger as he did, but her joy in life and the simple things around her also dragged him deeper into her web of innocence and he wouldn't trade that for the world.

Except to have her safe. He'd trade everything he owned for her to be driving him nuts as she skipped through the woods, pointing out pretty leaves and daisies. He tapped in the code for his cage and pulled out his weapons as the rest of the team filtered into the room.

"Local LEOs are on site," Dalton called from the other side of the metal gun lockers, which backed up to each other separating their cages.

Jeep grabbed his guns, faced the wall with the muzzle down, racked it, cleared it, and laid it on the small table before doing the same with the next two. He grabbed boxes of ammo and his flak jacket. He didn't need camo, he was already wearing it, camo was his go-to way to dress.

"Are you going to answer me?"

Shit, had he missed a question? He didn't think so, he replayed Dalton's words in his head and still couldn't find the question he was supposed to answer. "Sorry, Boss, what am I answering?"

"I said." Dalton stuck his head around the gun safe and scowled at him through the wire. "Local LEOs are on site."

"I don't hear a question."

"Fuck." Dalton scrubbed his hand over his head. "Are you going to be obtuse, or are you gonna get your head in the game?"

He reached for a go bag and started filling it with shit he may not need, but just in case he added them anyway. Med kit, bangs, frags, mags, MREs, and anything else which may be useful. "My head's already in the game. I will find her." He zipped the bag shut and slung it over his shoulder. She had to be safe, she just had to be. The alternative didn't bear thinking about. "Ready?"

"Yeah, almost," Dalton muttered. "Two minutes."

"I'll be at the truck."

As he walked through the door, he heard Rory ask Dalton, "He knows the plane can't leave without the rest of us, right, Boss?"

He didn't wait to hear Dalton's response. He couldn't allow himself to stop or to wait, he had to do something, even if it was to go stare at the damn plane, or he'd lose his damn mind.

"How are you doin'?"

He'd just pushed through the door into the kitchen when Lina's voice made him jerk. "Damn it, make a little noise."

Lina had the audacity to smirk at him before her face softened. "You know she got free, and we have no evidence that says they caught her again."

"Except King's message."

"There wasn't enough time." Trust Lina to grab onto the thread he was hanging onto like a lifeline. "In the two minutes it took you to listen to the voice message and call back, she was already running from the van," Lina said. "You know this." She reached out one finger and tapped on his chest. "You know it right here."

"I hope so." He tilted his head to one side and studied her. "You aren't coming?" He totally wouldn't be opposed to having another weapon in their arsenal, when it came to finding his girl, he'd take all the help he could get. Lina had worked for King, if anyone knew how he worked, it would be her.

"I promised the sailor I wouldn't put myself in King's path for a while." Her face twisted into a scowl. "I regret that promise now."

"You're pregnant, your ass stays here, Princess," Dalton growled from behind them.

Shit, no, not shit, where the hell were his brain cells? He should be happy for his friends... he *was* happy for his friends... "Congratulations." He grabbed Dalton's hand and tugged him into a bro hug. Being a dick, with urgency riding him hard, could wait for five seconds. "I'm happy for both of you."

"Thanks." Dalton dropped his gear on the ground at his feet and turned to his wife. "You will behave." He tugged on her hand, pulling her close to him.

"You met me... right?"

"Princess." Dalton folded his arms around her and rested his chin on her shoulder, his nose buried into her hair.

"I know. I know. Don't pick up anything heavier than a coffee mug."

"You shouldn't be drinking coffee."

"And you shouldn't use Google." Lina snuggled into his chest. "Google lies or freaks you out, then I have to find ways to piss you off because I don't follow Google's orders."

"Damn it."

Listening and watching their exchange made him feel like a peeping Tom. He turned away, not wanting to intrude, but also because it made his chest ache. Would he get the chance to do this with Willow? Would he find her in time? He immediately gave himself a metaphorical boot in the ass. It was stupid to tempt fate, he knew better. He would find her before King's goons did, end of discussion. He quietly turned away and stepped out onto the front porch. Even the stunning views which had always soothed his soul didn't have its usual impact. The colors were somehow muted. His world was now just a tiny bit darker.

"Do you have any idea where she'll go?" Logan slammed through the door with his usual force. The man had never met a door which could be closed softly. Every single one had to bang shut behind him or it wasn't closed. "She's near the base at Virginia Beach. Will she go there?"

"No." Jeep scratched the back of his head. "She may go to the bunker." God, he hoped she remembered the way and didn't get lost. He had to believe he would find her there.

"Bunker? What bunker?"

"Um, you know me, my folks were preppers. It's built into my DNA to have a bunker." In his head he could travel the path, take the shortcut and make it to the bunker in less than ten minutes. But his sunshine didn't follow directions well unless it was a recipe, and even then, once she'd mastered it, she tweaked and played around with it until it had her own unique twist, making it hers alone. She couldn't tell north from south and needed a left or a right. Would she be able to remember the way and make it there? Fuck, he hoped so. He mentally kicked his own butt, he knew better, had his childhood and his time at war not taught him the importance of training. As soon as he found her this was something he was rectifying, stat.

"Yeah." Logan tilted his head to one side, studying him like he'd never met him before or he was a potential tango in the sandbox and he was trying to figure out if Jeep's face was on a most wanted list somewhere. "Do you have one here?"

"That's for me to know and you to find out."

"Can I see?"

"Hell no." There was no way in hell he was showing his stash to Logan. The asshole would use it for that poker game on Thursday nights which he was trying to persuade everyone they should attend.

"Boss," Logan whined to Dalton as he came through the door. "Jeep has a bunker and he won't show me."

"You mean you don't have one?" Dalton nudged Jeep with his elbow as he passed him to head down the porch steps to the trucks. "What kinda merc doesn't have a backup bunker?"

"A dumb one," Jeep muttered. See, the boss got it. He at least understood the need to have a couple of stashes here and there.

"You got a bunker in Virginia?" Dalton tossed his go bag into the bed of the truck and jumped into the driver's seat.

"Yeah."

"Smart." Dalton switched on the truck, then winced and scrambled to turn down the music which blared out of the speakers, loud enough to make them both wince. "Will she make it?"

"I don't know." He wrapped his hand around the 'oh shit' bar and braced for takeoff as Dalton gunned the engine. Hitting his head off the windscreen would suck. His brain was already running at a million knots an hour, he didn't need a headache on top of it. "I hope so."

"Then let's go find your girl."

"PULL IN OVER HERE." Jeep pointed out the turnoff. "We can go through the woods."

"You don't want to go to the house first?"

"Hell no, I'm not dealing with cops if I don't have to." He pushed open the door and stood out of the truck. Forcing himself to stand and wait for the others. That took more effort than he'd expected, but he planted his boots into the dirt and stayed put. He wanted to bolt into the woods and go straight to the bunker, but he wouldn't be an idiot, he'd use his brain cells and follow his training.

The five minutes it took for everyone to be out of the trucks and ready to move lasted forever. He could feel his gray hairs multiplying by the second. Wasn't it a good thing that Willow insisted she found the gray in his beard sexy as hell? She'd have a least a couple of dozen more to swoon over if they didn't get their asses in gear fast. Finally, he was leading his brothers into the woods. Mission Find My Sunshine Girl was officially a go.

I'm coming, Sunshine, I promise.

CHAPTER FOUR

COULD it get any darker in here? It had to be nighttime now. She had no concept of how much time had passed, minutes and hours all seemed to run together. "This is what happens when you don't wear a watch." Muttering to herself made her feel better. She thought she'd been here for hours at this point. Was it dark enough to leave? "Don't be stupid, stay in place, Cormack will come."

She'd never been afraid of the dark before. The walls had never closed in on her either, but now they were. She was fully convinced those dirt walls were an inch closer every time she lifted her head out of her knees. She may not want to admit it, even to herself, but it was official, she was now scared and no matter how many times she tried to do the four-square breathing thingy that Cormack had taught her in an attempt to calm herself, it only lasted a couple of minutes. Or maybe it was an hour. She couldn't freaking tell. "You're being a ninny, get out of here and go to the base or to the cops."

She didn't even know if Cormack had gotten her message, or if he was out on a mission. He might not get her voice message for days or even a week. Waiting here was ridiculous. She couldn't stay buried in a freaking hole in the ground forever. She should go to the police station. The cops would help keep her safe, right?

Talking herself into doing something was also taking longer than it should have. As much as she didn't want to stay here with the spiders, she also didn't want to go out there where the men who'd attacked her in her own home may be waiting for her. She wrapped her arms around her knees and buried her face into them again. Hopefully hiding in her legs would keep the spiders off her face.

Snakes, too.

OMG. Snakes.

Shut up, brain.

Snakes. Hissss. Rattlers, copperheads....

Noooo. Brain, stop it.

A shuffling noise filtered into the bunker from above. She strained her ears listening, and when she heard it again, her head jerked up from where it had been hiding against her knees. She sucked in a breath and held it. She'd slammed the bolt home when she'd come down here. Right? It was solid, it wouldn't break. Cormack didn't do flimsy.

Her eyes stared into the dark, trying to make out the shape of the trapdoor. Her ears straining to hear something, anything over the sound of the rattling of the door.

"Blow it."

Blow it? Oh my God.

They had explosives. She was going to die in this box in the ground. She didn't want to die, she had so much to do first, and a lot of life she wanted to live. She wanted to visit Europe. Wanted to ride a camel in Morocco. She wanted to kiss Cormack again, wanted to have kids, get a dog, have the white picket fence and all that jazz.

Knock, knock.

She shrank back, trying to melt into the wall when the knocking sounded above, as if doing so meant whoever was out there wouldn't be able to see her when they opened the hatch.

"Sunshine?"

Sunshine? That's what Cormack calls me. Have they caught him?

Her brain took off at a million miles an hour, worst case scenarios flashing behind her eyelids. She swiped at the wetness pooling in her eyes. Cormack. They couldn't have him.

"Sunshine, it's me."

This had to be some kind of trick. Right? She wanted him to come get her so much that she was imagining what she'd convinced herself was possible was actually happening. That her man would come save her and now her mind was funning her. Cormack was either in Montana with his team or out on a job. Whoever those men were, they couldn't have him. He couldn't be here already; it was way too soon. Right?

You called him, he'll come. It's him.

"IKYAS, Sunshine."

It took a couple of heartbeats for the code to filter into her brain. "I'll. Kiss. You. Again. Soon. Sunshine." She whispered softly to herself. "Cormack." Jumping to her feet she bolted for where she thought the ladder was. There was no way anyone could force that code out of him. It was how he signed off on his emails and letters. It was their code. How he told her he was going out on a mission. It had taken her forever to figure it out what he was saying when he'd sent it in the military alphabet. India. Kilo. Yankee. Alpha. Sierra. Sunshine.

Her outstretched hands bumped off the wall, and she

widened them, feeling with her fingers for the boards screwed into the dirt. "Yes."

"IKYAS, Sunshine."

"IBW." I'll be waiting.

"Open the hatch, baby."

"I'm trying." Her fingers slipped twice as she made it up the ladder and she fumbled with the bolt until it finally gave and slid free of the latch.

The trapdoor opened over her head, she blinked against the light, her arm coming over her eyes to protect them from the strong beam from a torch.

"Sorry." The light went out, leaving only the dim light from where the moon filtered through the treetops. Cormack's voice had never sounded so freaking sweet. Although how she could call that deep growly tone sweet shouldn't be possible. But to her ears it was the sweetest sound she'd ever heard. She threw herself up the ladder. The second his massive arms wrapped around her she could finally breathe without her breath hitching. He shifted to put one hand under her butt, and she jumped, wrapping her legs around his waist. Climbing him like a tree was her goal and she was going to hang onto this tree like a dang monkey. "You came."

"I'll always come for you, Sunshine." One hand stayed under her butt, providing her with a ledge to sit on. The other brushed the hair back from her face. "Are you hurt?"

"No, I swear."

"Willow."

She squeezed her eyes shut and hid her face against Cormack's neck. Logically she'd known if he came, he wouldn't come alone and he'd bring the others as backup. This was so not how she'd wanted them all to find out about this thing between her and Cormack. Maybe if she hid here, breathing him in, she could avoid what was to come for another few seconds.

"Willow…"

"Don't touch her."

Cormack spun on his feet, turning them away from the voice she knew only too well. She inhaled deep, sucking his scent deep into her lungs, before lifting her head to peer over his shoulder. "Hi, Uncle D."

"Don't, Uncle D, me." Dalton Knight, one of her father's best friends from Teams, scowled at her. "Explain…"

Well, he could just take the overbearing hillbilly, redneck growling stuff he had going on and put it where the sun didn't shine. She was a grown ass woman, not the five-year-old who'd traipsed after him with a barbie tea-set and paint-brushes.

"Let's move," Cormack interrupted whatever Dalton had been planning on saying. She was going to kiss him for that later when there was no busy-body pseudo uncle to chop important bits like his… er… hands… she was totally going to use hands here… off.

"I'm letting this go for now," Dalton warned. "But I will have an explanation."

"The only explanation you need is Willow is mine."

"Boys," she interjected. She knew both of them too well to not know that they were going to be measuring body parts and while she absolutely adored Cormack's penis, there was no way on earth that she wanted to see her uncle Dalton's on display. That would just be totally ick.

Cormack brushed her hair back from her face and peered down at her as if he was trying to read her mind. She managed to force something she hoped resembled a smile to her face, but when his mouth tightened, she knew she'd failed miserably. "Come on, Sunshine."

"I can walk."

"I know," he spoke against her head. "I want to hold you, but I also need my hands free." Just like that the safety which had surrounded her by having him here dissipated. Poof, like magic it was gone. Knowing the reason he needed his hands free was to access his weapons if he needed to use them was a sobering thought. She wriggled in his arms. "I can walk."

"You're not wearing shoes," Cormack pointed out. "Swing around onto my back, I'll take you for a piggyback ride."

"Crap." She tightened her arms around his neck and huffed out a breath.

"I have thick socks if that's any help?" a man's voice said from her left.

"I have one better," a woman's voice, who she knew could only be Snow, the team's sniper, said. "If you wear size eight or if an eight will work, I've got a pair of flip-flops in my pack."

"You bring spare shoes?" the first voice asked.

"Flip-flops aren't shoes, they're comfy soles."

"I can wear an eight," she cut off any more of the bickering which she knew was bound to happen. You didn't grow up around these kinds of people and not know that they bickered and argued like cats and dogs or siblings. She peered over Cormack's shoulder at the blonde woman. "You're Snow, right?"

"Yes." Snow shifted her rifle on its sling and pushed it to one side. She swung her pack off her back and unzipped one of the side pockets. "Sorry they're rolled up." She took off the hair tie which held the flip-flops together and handed them to Willow. "They've been in there about two years, but it's better than nothing at all."

"I appreciate it." Somewhere she managed to scrounge up

a smile for Snow and wriggled to let Cormack know she wanted to get down. He grabbed one of the flip-flops from her and put it on her right foot before lowering her to the ground. She balanced against him while she put the other one on. Something poked into the underside of her foot, but she could ignore that long enough to get to the house... right? "Thank you, Snow."

"You're welcome."

"Let's move," Dalton growled. "I don't want to be out here all night."

"Boss, you're an asshole," Cormack muttered softly. He swiped a thumb down her cheek, gave her a soft smile, then stepped in front of her. "Stay behind me, okay?"

"Sure." She could do that. He knew where he was going, she didn't. The others fell in around them and they started walking. After a couple of minutes, she didn't recognize anything, not a single tree or rock. They all looked exactly the same. It was a good thing she hadn't attempted to make her way out of the forest or she'd have gotten lost for sure. She looped her hand into the back of Cormack's belt and felt him stiffen at the first touch of her fingers before he relaxed again. "It's okay to do this?"

"Yes, Sunshine. Keep your hand there, so I know where you are."

Was that relief in his voice? She thought it was. She had to work at ignoring the stabbing into her foot from whatever was stuck there as she walked. But she'd do it. Soon they'd be at her house, she could check it then. Whining about it now would be stupid. She opened her mouth to ask how far it was, but then shut it again, as 'are we there yet?' was not the most important question which needed answering tonight. Who had tried to kidnap her and why?

CHAPTER FIVE

CORMACK BLEW out a slow silent breath. For the first time since he'd heard her voice message, the panic which had fought for dominance inside him retreated. He'd found her, she was safe. He was taking her back to Montana with him until they figured out what the fuck was going on. Maybe while he had her there, he could convince her to stay.

The slight pull of her fingers against the back of his pants reminded him with every step that she was okay. He'd take it. He kept one eye on Mokaccino as he ranged out in front. Normally, he'd be point position. But there was no way in hell that anyone else was leading his girl out of here. If that made him a caveman, then he'd wear that damn badge with pride.

They were almost to the point where they'd parked the trucks when Mokaccino stopped with one hand lifted and his fist closed. Jeep immediately froze mid-step. "Drop," he whispered softly to Willow and crouched down. A fast glance over his shoulder told him Willow had listened and was crouched behind him where he could protect her if needed. With Dalton at her back, she was as sheltered as she could be, so why the hell were his guts screaming at him? He kept his eyes on Mokaccino, Rory's body language would tell him if he needed to cover Willow. When he saw his friend's shoulders relax, and his hand signal to move on again, he huffed out a silent breath he hadn't known he'd been holding.

They stepped out of the tree line and into the clearing where they'd parked the trucks. He knew the second Willow realized they weren't anywhere near her house. The slight tug on his belt when she stumbled told him all he needed to know. In his head he started counting off seconds, one of the many things he adored about his girl was she wasn't shy about giving him her opinion. One. Two. Three. Fou—.

"Why are we here?"

"Because going back to the house would be stupid until we know if it's being watched or not."

Thank you, Boss. Dalton's firm voice had saved him. Not that he wouldn't have gone toe-to-toe with Sunshine when her safety was in question, there was no line he wouldn't blow straight through. She was his to protect, even if it was from herself. "Sunshine…"

"Don't you Sunshine me, Cormack…"

He felt the loss of her hand on his back the second she removed it.

"…Why are we not going back to my house?"

That this was the question she was asking told him she was smart enough to figure it out. It also told him she didn't like the answer she'd come up with one little bit.

"Because it's not safe." He spun around and reached for her, but the little minx side-stepped him and stayed just out of reach.

"We have to move." Dalton hit the locks on the truck and pulled open the door. Out of the corner of his eye, Jeep could see him start the engine and hit the button for the aircon.

"Gimme a minute." He took one step toward Willow, and she took two back. Damn it, he didn't want her to be afraid of him. Although by the fire flashing in her eyes, he was going to presume she was mad and not afraid. Good, because while a healthy dose of fear was good for everyone, mad lit a fire under your ass and got you getting shit done.

"We don't have a minute," Dalton replied.

"Give me a minute." He knew he was repeating himself, just as he knew growling at Dalton was never a good idea. But he just couldn't find it within himself to give one flying shit about it. He was more concerned about getting Willow somewhere safe and having that happen as fast as possible. He watched her like a wolf watches a fawn, waiting to see if it moved or ran. Like the wolf, he, too, was a predator... if she ran from him... he'd chase her, and he would catch her.

He saw in her eyes the second her temper won and her stubbornness set in. Fuck, she was glorious. He bunched his muscles, waiting for her to move. Her weight shifted and he readied himself. "Don't do it."

She arched an eyebrow at him and bolted.

"Damn it." How the fuck could one tiny ass girl run so fast in fucking flip-flops? He'd thought he'd catch her in two steps, maybe three at the most. But as his fingers skimmed off her shoulder, she changed direction on the fly like a damn hare and took off to the right instead. Just as she reached the trees, he put on a burst of speed and grabbed her around the waist. His momentum carrying them forward, he twisted in midair, and they tumbled to the ground, with her landing on top of him. Thank fuck, if he'd landed on her he'd have squished her like a bug for sure.

"You're a bully." She glared into his face.

"Yup." He had to force the word out. Breathing was difficult when you had a whole person sitting on your chest.

"I want to go home."

"I know." He was taking it as a good sign that she wasn't struggling. He wrapped his arms around her waist and stroked up her back. "I know you want to go home, Sunshine. It's just not safe yet."

"But…"

"Do you trust me?" His heart winced when she didn't answer immediately. It was only because she'd had a rough day. At least that was what he told himself. But he wasn't entirely sure he believed it. He waited a couple of heartbeats before repeating the question. "Do you trust me, Sunshine?"

She huffed at him and shifted to look into his eyes. "You know I do."

Nope, no, that he hadn't known for sure until right this minute. But knowing it sent a burst of satisfaction and happiness bubbling through his veins. "Then trust me when I tell you it's not safe."

He didn't think she would listen. He could see she didn't want to believe it. He understood it, that house was her sanctuary. It was where she retreated to when the world was too much to handle. "It's not forever," he coaxed. "I promise, I'll take you back there as soon as it's safe for you to go." If it killed him, he would keep that promise. As soon as this shit with King was done, he would take her home.

"You promise?"

"Yes."

"Okay." The word was spoken on a sigh. "I believe you." She scrambled to her feet, nearly taking out his balls in the process, then turned back toward the trucks. "Coming?" she called over her shoulder.

He could see the others laughing at him. Snow didn't even bother to hide it; she laughed out loud and walked toward Willow.

"I think," Snow said softly. But not soft enough that he didn't hear her. "I think I may like you." She held the door of the truck open for Willow to climb in the back seat, then followed her in, leaving the front for Cormack. He swallowed down the irrational growl which threatened to escape his mouth. Aria had no reason to believe he would change where he sat in the truck. But, damn it, he wanted someone else to ride shotgun so he could sit next to Willow.

"Nemesis, she's going to need clothes."

"I'm not going shopping," Dalton muttered. "Last time I went shopping for women's clothes, a freaking sniper pinned us down for a fucking hour."

"Then we'll have to swing by the house."

"Fuck no." Dalton hit the gas, speeding up. "We ain't doing that either." He thought about it for a couple of seconds. "Text Rexar, he'll go."

Fucking fabulous, another one of Eli's team to give him shit about having a relationship with a team brother's daughter. Damn it, could he not catch a break? But there was no way in hell he was mentioning that. The less he reminded Dalton of it the better. "Sure." He shifted in his seat to pull his cell out of the pouch on his flak jacket, turned it on, and flipped through the screens until he found the number he wanted.

Text: Rex, you at home?

Text: Yup, what's up?

Text: Can you do me a solid and go to Eli's house and pick up clothes and shit for Willow?

Exactly six seconds later the phone in his hand vibrated with an incoming call from a blocked number. Logic told him it was probably Rexar, but still his fingers hesitated before he pressed answer. He tilted the phone to show Dalton the screen.

"Answer it," Dalton ordered. "Put it on speaker."

"Roger." He hit answer and tapped the microphone button, then held the phone between them. Turning, he glanced at Willow and held one finger to his lips, asking her to remain silent. "Go."

"What happened to Willy?" It was a relief to hear Rexar's deep baritone and not the nasally pitch of King's voice. "Where the fuck am I going, and who the fuck am I killing?"

"Nobody," Dalton replied to Rexar's last question before Jeep could. "Yet."

"Sitrep," Rexar demanded.

"King sent someone for her."

"How the fuck does King know about her? Does he know who she is?" In the background, noise rose and fell as if Rexar had moved from the bar into one of the back rooms, probably into his office.

"That's what we're trying to figure out."

"Bring her here," Rexar ordered. "I'll make sure she's safe."

"Hell no." The words were out of his mouth before he could stop himself. "She's coming home with me." He was going to ignore the solid poke Willow gave his shoulder and the snickering from Snow as she witnessed it.

"Excuse me?"

Even he could hear the warning in Rexar's tone, and he got it. Willow's father had been a friend to Rexar. But there was no fucking way he was ever going to be afraid of Rexar Mitchell. "She's coming home with me," he repeated. "And we don't have time for bullshit and dick measuring. Can you go and get the clothes or not?"

"Shut it." Dalton elbowed him, while keeping his other hand on the wheel. "What Jeep means is he and Willow have a thing and he's got a bunch of overprotective hormones ruling his brain cells."

"I'll kill him."

"Get in line," Dalton agreed.

"Assholes."

"No, you won't, Uncle Rexar," Willow said. "You either, Uncle D. I'm a grown woman, and I get to decide."

He pressed the fingers of one hand into the corners of his eyes and winced. He'd entered the damn twilight zone. How the fuck were they having this conversation right now? "Can you do it or not, Rex?"

"Of course, I can do it," Rexar grumbled. "Tangos are still on site?"

"Nope, LEOs were there as of a couple of hours ago." Jeep quickly filled him in on the details.

"Roger that, then it's safe to bring my ma." He could hear the shudder in Rexar's voice. "There is no way I'm going through my niece's underwear drawer."

"Thank you, sweet baby Jesus, for small mercies," Willow whispered softly.

"My ma will take care of the cops if they cause issues, too," Rexar carried on as if Willow hadn't spoken at all. "I think every cop in town is afraid of her wooden spoon."

"Thanks, man."

"No worries. Where will I meet ya?"

Jeep rattled off the address for the private airfield. "Our plane is there; we'll clear you through security."

"You need me to come to HQ with you?"

"You bored, Rex?"

"Fuck, yes," Rexar grumbled. "I'm going insane, pulling pints and serving shots is not my jam."

"I hear that," Dalton said. "Bring your shit," he ordered. "I told you I have a place for you at Nemesis Inc."

"If it's riding a desk, stick it up your ass."

"Language, Uncle Rex."

"Sorry, Willy."

"Don't call me that."

"I gotta go." Rexar apparently refused to be pulled into the old squabble between himself and Willow over the nickname he insisted on using. "I'll be at the airfield in under two hours."

"See you then, bro."

LESS THAN AN HOUR later as they loaded onto the private jet, Jeep couldn't shake the feeling that there were eyes on them. It crawled up his back like a fucking spider. He could feel every one of its eight legs as goose bumps rose along his skin. He didn't have to be able to see his back to know it was happening. After having spent so many years living and working in war zones, he knew what a sixth sense was, thank you. "Nemesis?" He turned in a slow circle. He didn't give one flying fuck if the asshole out there saw him do it. In his head, he automatically broke the airfield into quadrant squares and started analyzing.

"Something's off?"

"Yup." He'd known he wouldn't have to say much more than Nemesis's name for his boss to understand what he meant. They'd worked together long enough that they could nearly hear each other think at this point. "Something's off," he agreed.

"Snow, stay with the package."

"Yes, sir."

"If it's a sniper, he could be a mile away and we'd never

see him." He maneuvered himself into cover next to one of the trucks.

"I know but keep looking anyway."

He snorted, as if he was going to stop looking. If there was a threat out there, it wasn't just against his team. This time it was against Willow, too. Probably even more than against his team, and that pissed him off, add in that he hadn't been able to kiss Willow since they'd found her in the bunker. He hadn't had two minutes to check every inch of her to make sure she was okay, and his me man, you my woman, side was rioting inside him like it was going out of fashion.

"Nem, we have incoming from the gate," Sensei warned.

Jeep's head spun around so fast, if it had been in the movies, he'd have looked like that freaky ass scary doll. As soon as he saw the beat-up Chevy, the adrenaline which had started its march through his veins receded. "Rexar."

"Thank fuck," Dalton muttered. "Get Willow on the plane."

"Yes, sir." He reached for the door of the truck and motioned for Snow to slide out, then leaned in to reach his hand out to Willow. "When we get out, I'm going to spin you around and tuck you into my body." He explained what was going to happen as he didn't want any hesitation. If Willow picked now to have another independent streak flash to life and insist she could do it herself, that might leave her exposed. Exposed could mean dead. *Not on my watch*, he promised himself.

"Okay." Willow placed her small hand in his and when he wrapped his fingers around hers, she lightly squeezed his hand. Christ, was his sunshine trying to comfort him? Un-fucking-believable.

"Good girl." He tugged gently on her hand, and she slid across the seat toward him. He used his body to block as much of the doorway as possible while she stepped out onto the small space he'd left for her. As soon as she straightened, he wrapped both arms around her, pressing her back into his chest, and carefully spun toward the steps of the plane. Using his body to protect hers, he ushered them both up the steps and didn't breathe until they were out of view of the doorway.

He tightened his arms around her. Now that they were out of view and couldn't be seen through the blind-covered windows, he allowed himself a second to inhale her scent. His eyes closed as he breathed in deep. The others could get the gear. For once he was going to slack off on his duties and just take care of his girl. He needed it. She needed it. And fuck knows after the day they'd both had, they'd earned it.

Willow wriggled in his arms, and he loosened his hold. He wasn't ready to let go yet. He was so freaking tempted to beg her to wait another couple of seconds. Just five more, maybe ten. But she didn't try to pull away, instead she twisted in his hold until she faced him and wrapped her arms around his waist. Her face buried into his chest. Everything which had rioted inside him calmed when she tilted her head up and kissed the underside of his chin. "I'm sorry I scared you."

Was she insane? She was the one who'd almost been kidnapped. It was her who'd run through the fucking woods looking for his bunker and the chance of escape, and she was worried about scaring him? Un-fucking-believable. That word was rapidly becoming his freaking mantra at this point.

"Sit down, dumbass, you're blocking the way."

"Shut it," Willow muttered against his chest.

He more felt than heard the words, but Sensei was right, they were standing in the middle of the plane and with how narrow the aisle was, it was better if they moved. "Let's sit." He reluctantly unfolded his arms and stepped back.

"Which seat?" Willow looked around the plane and chewed on the corner of her lip, telling him she was nervous. He couldn't blame her for that, she'd had one hell of a day.

"Pick one." He smiled at her and knew it was the right thing to say when her face lit up. If one of the guys had an issue with her being in their seat, he'd strap the fucker to the wings for the ride home.

"Any seat?"

"Yup." She'd been on planes before, so why was she acting like this was the first time she'd flown?

"Next to the pilot?" She clapped her hands together.

Oh, hell no, there was no freaking way she was going anywhere near the cockpit. "No." He shook his head, and while he felt a pang of sympathy when her face fell again, he refused to be swayed by a pair of pretty blue eyes. "Somewhere I can sit next to you," he told her softly. "Please."

"Okay." She slid into one of the comfy leather double seats and scooted next to the window.

"Don't open the blind until we're in the air, okay?"

"Now I'm getting more scared."

"I know." He did understand it. He hated that she was scared, it pissed him off. But he didn't dare let any of the control he was working so fucking hard to keep in place slip. If he did, then he'd rage and need to hit something. Which would fucking scare her even more. "But we'll be in the air soon, and we'll figure it out, I promise." He slid in next to her and rested his head back against the seat. Just as she had a million times before on her comfy couch, she kicked off her flip-flops, stashed them in the pocket of the seat in front of them, pulled her legs up under her, and curled into his side with her head on his shoulder. He lifted his arm so she could snuggle into his chest and wrapped it around her shoulders. He took a second to nod at Snow as she passed them, going toward the back of the plane and the next time he looked down, Willow was fast asleep with her fingers bunched into his shirt.

"Dickhead," Rexar muttered as he paused next to them, his face softening when he glanced from Jeep to Willow.

"She's mine."

"I see that," Rexar whispered softly. "But that doesn't mean I think you're good enough for her."

"Me either, bro, me either."

Rexar slid into the row of seats in front of them. "Her shit is in the hold."

"Thanks, man."

"I did it for her, not for you." Rexar turned and peered at him through the seats. "You and I will be talking about this."

"I know." And this right here was why he'd said absolutely nothing to anyone about Willow and him. They were a bunch of overprotective uncles. Both Dalton and Rexar had served with her father. Now that Eli wasn't around to protect her, they were going to take their uncle roles to the extreme. He felt it in his bones. It didn't matter a fuck what they thought though. He was keeping her as long as she'd allow him to. He closed his eyes; he had time now to rest them for a second. Right?

CHAPTER SIX

"Sunshine?"

"Mmh." She was having the best dream. Cormack in her dreams sounded even more like himself than he normally did. She rubbed her cheek against the palm which cupped her face. "Another few minutes."

"We don't have a few minutes, Sunshine." Cormack's scruff rubbed against her ear as he spoke. "We're hitting a rough patch and I need to get your seat belt on you until we land, as it's storming so it's gonna get bumpy."

Land? Huh? Were they not curled up in her bed? She blinked her eyes open, then shut them again fast when the lights made them sting. "Turn off the sun."

"Shit, sorry." She felt Cormack reaching up. What the heck? He couldn't reach the sun and pull a fricking string to turn it off. She squinted and dared to raise one eyelid just a fraction, but all she could see was his arm. The world dimmed around them a little, just as the bed dipped and rolled under them, making her clutch at his arm and squeal.

"Shh, s'alright, Sunshine, it's just some turbulence."

She was losing her mind, or this dream had gotten hella

weird really fast. She pinched herself on the arm hard. That was what you were supposed to do to wake yourself up from a nightmare… right? But all it did was hurt like a wasp sting. "Ow." Once again, the whole bed shook, rattled, and rolled. Was that an earthquake? Okay, apparently dreams had earthquakes now, too. Wonderful.

"You awake, Sunshine?" Cormack asked. "Come on, I need you to put on your belt."

Was she supposed to be awake? It was nighttime, right? She was in bed curled up with her man, which was the only time she actually had a decent night's sleep. Finally giving in to the inevitable, she opened her eyes fully and they widened when her surroundings slammed into her. The memory of what had happened hit her so hard, she had to swallow down the cry which thankfully got stuck behind the lump in the back of her throat as the plane once again hit a rough patch of turbulence and rapidly dropped a couple of hundred feet.

"Fuck."

Oh, that could not be good, Cormack swearing softly under his breath in that tone was so not a good thing, she was sure of it.

"Are we going to crash?" If they were going down, then she wanted to know. She wanted to be able to tell Cormack something important before she went splat all over the ground in a tangled mess of metal and jet fuel.

"Nope, not happening."

His words were meant to comfort her, but his tone… that needed a heck of a lot of work before she'd believe him. "It sounds like we are."

"We're not going to crash, Sunshine." Cormack, may the gods bless him, was trying to reassure her. But the plane was determined to make a liar out of him, and it chose that exact moment to drop the oxygen masks.

They both stared at the orange dangling devices, then looked at each other. She could see the concern in his eyes. Did he think she couldn't hear the swearing from the others around them? She was ditzy, and a little bit klutzy, but stupid had never, ever been something she'd associated with herself. Well, maybe she had somewhere in the dark of the bunker, but it wasn't something she normally liked to think she was. Yet here she was in a tin can with wings, staring at the oxygen masks and trying to decide if she should put it on or not. The masks had dropped for a reason, that meant she should put one on...right? Was there an air hostess on this flight? She didn't think so. Dang it, if they survived this, she was going to smack the life out of Uncle D for not having an air hostess to tell her what to do.

The intercom crackled to life and the pilot, at least she thought it was the pilot, spoke. "Put your damn masks on and get your fucking chutes ready," he ordered. "Get ready to bail if I call it."

"Balls." The man in the seat in front's voice was muffled as his head disappeared from view. It was only when his head reappeared that she realized it was Uncle Rexar. "Put her chute on, dumbass," Rexar called between the seats.

Oh, was he talking to Cormack? He was, wasn't he? Yes, if the way Cormack exploded into action and was now pulling life vests and parachutes out from under their seats were anything to go by. She braced her hands on the arms of the seats and tried not to get in the way. If you were going to have to bail out of a plane at stupid number thousand feet, then having a former Navy Seal as your tandem jumper was the way to do it. She couldn't freak out now. If she did, it would distract Cormack from everything he had to do. So, instead she kept her death grip on the arms of the seat and squeezed her eyes shut, *Daddy, if you're up there, now would be a good time to call in any favors you're owed. Okay.*

"Arm." Cormack slid the harness over her hand and up to her shoulder. She leaned forward so he could push it behind her back and onto her other side. Once he was happy with the placement, he buckled the strap and pulled it so tight she could hardly breathe. "Good?"

She nodded in response, as the plane shook hard, doing its level best to break apart around them. But someone must have used the strong duct tape during maintenance this week and it held. That, or her daddy was taking her silent request to heart and was calling in favors in Valhalla.

"I see a hole in the clouds," the pilot called over the intercom. "It's going to be rough as blue balls at church on Sunday, but if we hit it right, we can be clear in a couple of minutes."

"And if we don't hit it right?" She watched Cormack reach for the oxygen mask and copied his movements to don hers.

"Then we jump." Cormack turned the hand closest to her over and turned his palm up. "Hold my hand?"

"Yes." She wrapped her fingers around his and squeezed them hard, pressing their skin together as tight as she possibly could. His grip bruised her fingers but there was no way on earth she was going to complain about it now. If this was how she was meant to die, then she would go with this man by her side and know that she was loved. Not only that but she would know that she... "I love you."

"I know, Sunshine." He pressed a kiss to the top of her head. "But you save that for when we're safe on the ground."

"No." She knew her voice was sharp when his eyes widened. "If..." She cleared her throat. "I couldn't bear it if you didn't know I love you."

"I know you love me, Sunshine," he whispered softly. "Just as I love you. You are the sun in my sky and the lighthouse on the coast that guides me home. I love you, Willow, don't doubt it, ever."

"And now he's a god damned poet."

"Shut up." If it hadn't meant pulling herself out of Cormack's arms she would have reached between those seats and smacked Rexar upside the head, just like her daddy would have done. But if this plane was going to go down, then the only thing she was doing was going down in Cormack's arms. Until he got them out the door to freefall into nothing.

"Hold on to your balls, ladies," the pilot warned them the poop was going to hit the fan. "Shit's gonna get real." As if the plane had been waiting for the man's orders, it completely did an Elvis and shook, rattled, and rolled. It dropped into a steep nosedive, but before her stomach could find its way out of the boots she wasn't wearing, the pilot somehow got it level again and they started climbing.

"How are you so fricking calm?" She tightened her fingers around Cormack's. If this plane rolled another time, she was going to throw up. But he said he loved her; he would just have to deal with a little puke until they got off this ride. She was giving it zero stars, do not recommend. As soon as her butt was on the ground, she was posting on Instagram telling anyone who'd listen to never, ever fly with Nemesis Inc.

"Baby." He lifted their hands to his lips and pressed a kiss to the back of her fingers. "Until you've seen an RPG chasing your tail across the sky, there's no reason to panic about a little turbulence."

"We're going to have a discussion about your definition of little, mister."

"I like her," one of the men said from behind them. "Sensei, we're gonna need so much popcorn for the show that's to come."

"Are you bringing the good pops?" the one who must be Sensei asked. His voice sounded muffled, so she knew he was probably wearing an oxygen mask, too. She had to strain to hear the conversation over the sounds of the storm and her rapidly beating heart.

How in the name of all that was holy were they teasing and carrying on a normal conversation? Planes were not meant to act like a bucking bull at the PBR World Finals. Even the freaking bulls stopped bucking after eight seconds.

"Yup," the first man answered. "I found some Snickers covered popcorn and Twix, too."

Their conversation took her mind off what was happening. Even she had to admit to herself that Snickers popcorn sounded way beyond awesome. Not that there was any way she was telling these men that. Or they'd surely find a way to tease her about it. She'd grown up around men like these. She knew their standard operating procedure. Tease, make crazy, and tease some more.

The plane dived again, and she had no idea how the pilot managed to level it off. Thunder crashed so loud the whole plane vibrated. She squeezed her eyes shut against the flashes of lightning, until finally the shaking stopped, and everything went quiet enough to be the inside of a church during reflection.

"And that's a wrap, ladies, we're clear."

She wasn't imagining the relief in the pilot's voice. She knew she wasn't, just as she also knew she wasn't going to acknowledge it. Doing that meant they'd come way too close to dying.

"Hooyah." Cormack pulled off his oxygen mask and

whispered softly against her hair, "How you are doing, baby?"

"I'm never flying with you again." She definitely did not recommend this plane. She'd sit on Cormack's lap any dang day of the week, but getting on a plane with him, that was going to need some seriously big bribery on his part.

"I wasn't flying the plane, Sunshine."

"You're on it, and I'm never flying again."

"Good, that means I get to keep you."

Wait… what? She didn't need to look at him to hear the smirk in his voice. "Keep me?"

"Yup." Cormack grinned at her. "You said you're not flying again, so that means you're staying in Montana." He paused a second then tagged on, "With me."

"You're impossible."

"Nope." He leaned his head back against the headrest and turned to grin down at her. "Just statin' a fact."

She didn't have time to figure out a response, and even if she had, she didn't think she'd be able to come up with one. Her brain was refusing to work. It was on strike, called out sick, or maybe it had gone on vacation, she wasn't entirely sure, and it didn't matter as, thank you, Daddy, and every other angel up there, she felt the bump of the wheels touching down and felt the brakes engage. "We're down?"

"Yeah."

"Really?" Okay, now she could freak. Have a meltdown, cry, bawl, or swoon into a dead faint. "We're on the ground?"

"I swear." Cormack leaned across her and flipped up the window covering, showing them taxiing down a runway in what appeared to be the middle of nowhere. "We're on the ground."

"Holy Mary and all the lambs, thank frick-frack." She ripped off the parachute. Not that she knew what she was doing, but somehow her fingers found the right way to do it. While she wanted to throw the symbol of their scary trip somewhere hard, she didn't dare as the next people to use this plane were going to need it. Those next people were not going to include her. She was never getting on this plane again. She didn't care, she'd freaking hitchhike back to Virginia Beach first or ride the Greyhound. Getting in this tin can? There wasn't enough money on the planet to make her do it. She swatted at Cormack's chest. "Next time, pick a better plane."

"Yes, dear." The ass was smirking at her. "But it's your uncle D's plane, blame him, not me, I just work for him."

"Did you even see me when you reversed that damn bus over me, fucker?"

She couldn't help herself and smiled when Cormack ducked, just as Dalton's hand swept over the back of the seat where Cormack's head had been a second before. It was both weird and comforting to see echoes of her father in these men. Her heart ached with the loss. The gaping hole he'd left in so many lives was impossible to fill. It was always there. Not only in the places she'd shared with him, but here on this plane where she'd never before set foot. If she closed her eyes, it was a place she could see him fitting in, like he'd been born to be here.

She shook off the melancholy, she knew better than to allow it to tighten its grip on her heart. If it did, she'd struggle to breathe for days on end. The pain of losing him, it didn't ease, it didn't fade. It was still as raw as it had been when she'd received word that his helo had been shot out of the sky over some contested valley in Afghanistan. No, pain of that magnitude never left you... you just figured out a way to live with it.

"You okay, Sunshine?"

"Yes, I was just thinking of Daddy."

Cormack didn't say anything, he just smiled at her in that soft way of his that told her she was okay to keep doing what she needed. This right here was one of the reasons she'd fallen in love with the big lug. Even in his emails and letters, he'd been like this, allowing her to have her moments of grief without trying to shake her out of them. He understood that she didn't want to forget and that there were times she just wanted to hurt. Hurting meant she'd loved her dad, hurting meant he'd existed. Pushing it aside somehow felt wrong. Cormack understood that and encouraged her to own her feelings when everyone else had told her it was time to move on.

She'd never been able to figure out why she'd answered his email, he'd been one of hundreds of SEAL members who'd sent condolences. Who'd checked in multiple times, asking her if she needed anything. But Cormack, his emails had been different. He'd chatted about his days in the field. Told her about the baby goats he'd seen and the stray puppy he'd been feeding. As if he'd expected her to reply to every single message, he'd kept sending them, and eventually she'd answered.

"Time to go, Sunshine." Cormack stood out of his seat and helped her to her feet. "Let's get you to the house so you can shower and get some food in you."

"Are you telling me I stink?" She had to dig down deep for the snark she knew would make him worry just a little less.

"Nope." He held both hands up in an I surrender gesture. "I'd never, ever tell you that." He gestured to her feet. "Don't forget your flops."

"Crap." She leaned back in, giving him an eyeful of her butt as she fished her borrowed flip-flops out of the pocket where she'd stashed them and slipped them on her feet.

"You're saying I smell." She straightened and propped her hands on her hips and glared at him.

"Nope, I swear I wasn't."

"Smart man," she huffed at him as she squeezed past him and followed Uncle Dalton to the door. She couldn't wait to see where they called home.

CHAPTER SEVEN

CORMACK SLOWED the truck as they took the turn out of the private runway and toward the ranch house. The mares and foals running along beside the truck on the inside of the split rail fence had captured his girl's attention and he wanted to keep that awestruck expression on her face a little while longer.

He drove into the main yard and past the long low house which sprawled out across the wide-open space.

"Oh my, that's a pretty porch."

"Right?" He knew Willow loved a good wraparound porch, and to be fair, with its two huge rocking chairs, Dalton's porch was a freaking awesome place to watch the sunrise. He drove past the corrals and pens, around the side of Dalton's house, and down the dirt road toward the team house. "Dalton and Lina live there."

"Lina?"

"Dalton's wife?" Shit, had he forgotten to mention Lina? He shook his head, trying to recall every word he'd said to Willow over their last few conversations. But because they hadn't seen each other in person since he'd been called back to Kabul, he was going to assume he hadn't. Private shit, like his boss having a wife, wasn't something he'd normally discuss over the phone. OPESC and all was important, and he knew better than most how important it was to keep stuff like that private.

"Wasn't his wife before called Lina?"

"You knew her?"

"I met her a couple of times I think." She cocked her head to one side as if she were trying to remember. "At least I think I did. It was five or six years ago." She frowned at Cormack. "I thought they divorced?"

"Nope." He didn't know how he was going to explain it, his boss and his wife, their story was straight out of a book or a movie or some shit. "At least I don't think they ever signed the papers." That would do... right?

"She's back."

Oh, oh, he knew that tone. Willow was going to get her mad on. He pulled to a stop in front of the team house. "We're here." He hoped to divert her attention away from Dalton and Lina with the massive two-story hotel like building which had been converted into suites for them all. There were two other buildings, both of which housed Bravo and Charlie teams. But this one was for Alpha team. His team.

He watched Willow as she stepped out of the truck and felt his lips curve into a smile when she spun slowly in a circle, taking in the stunningly awesome views which was the Crazy Mountains in the distance.

"It's wow."

"Yeah." He moved around the truck to stand behind her and wrapped his arms around her shoulders, drawing her back against his chest. "Isn't it?"

"It's so quiet." She leaned into him. God, he could stay

like this forever. "I can't hear traffic or anything but cows."

"The cows are always here; you get used to them."

"Is that what the smell is?"

He inhaled deep, trying to catch what she was talking about, but all he got was the faint whiff of her. "What smell?"

"I don't know, kinda like pine trees and earthy, almost like you, but not."

"I think what you're smelling is Big Sky Country."

"Places don't have smells."

"Yeah, they do." He only had to smell a certain blend of spices and he was right back in a market in Iraq, or the smell of camel dung sent his brain to Morocco. "Remember the fish market?" He grinned against her hair when she wrinkled her nose.

"Yes, it was horrid." She tilted her head back so she could peer up at him. "You win."

"It's not about winning, Sunshine." He never wanted her to think he was lording it over her, ever. He didn't want to be the one who stole her joy in life. "My mouth sometimes can't help itself and it gets into teaching mode."

"Mmh." She made a non-committal sound and turned back to look at the view. All around them the other guys pulled their trucks into their parking spots and went into the house without interrupting or paying any attention to them. Even though he knew they were all curious as hell about Willow and what she meant to him. He was buying a case of beer for the fire pit to say thank you this weekend.

There was something about this place which soothed the soul, for every minute they stood here just watching the breeze moving the grass on the rolling foothills, he felt Willow relax just a little bit more. He rubbed his hands up and down her arms and swayed gently in place as they kept watching the view.

When she finally sighed, he knew the happy bubble shit he'd had going on was over.

"I need to pee."

"Okay, that you can do in the house."

"God, I hope so, because I'm not using a bucket."

"City slicker."

"Why, yes, yes I am."

"Come on, Sunshine." He turned her toward the house and frowned when he saw her wince. Shit, he'd forgotten all about checking her feet on the plane. He swept her into his arms and carried her up the steps to the door. "Open it, will ya?"

"Does this count as you carrying me across the threshold?" She wrapped one arm around his neck and pressed the handle with the other.

"Umm." He choked on the word. He hadn't thought of it that way, but now that he had... the possibility had legs, could possibilities have legs? He'd have to think about it.

"I'm funnin' you." She giggled close to his ear.

He had to work hard at convincing his dick to not take notice. Ah, who was he kidding, there was no way in hell his dick wasn't taking notice of that sexy as fuck husky sound. He winced when his dick rubbed off the rough material of his camo pants. That would teach him to go commando and he swallowed down a groan when her fingers stroked through the short hairs at the back of his head.

Somehow, he made it up the stairs without falling or dropping her. But if she didn't stop what she was doing to his self-control, then her need to pee would have to wait a few moments longer. "Hold on with both hands." He shifted his hold on her, as she did as he asked and wrapped her second arm around his neck. He kept one arm banded under her ass and pressed the palm of the other against the scanner next to his door. As soon as the tiny light flashed green, he heard the lock disengage and he kicked the door open with his boot.

"Fancy." Willow quirked an eyebrow.

"Your uncle Dalton is kinda anal about security." He walked down the hall and into his bedroom, taking her toward the bathroom attached to his room. He could have stopped at the guest bathroom, but he wasn't ignoring the urge to have her in his most private spaces. His room. Nobody came in here, not even Dalton.

"Pot meet the kettle," she told him. "Or do you not remember insisting that I overhaul the security on my house?"

"Not that it was much use when you answer the door without checking the freaking peephole first..." Shit, he hadn't meant to say that. He mentally slapped himself upside the head when her face fell at the reminder of what had happened. God, he was an idiot. "Uh..." He stumbled over his words trying to recover the moment, but it was gone. "Restroom is right here."

"Thank you." She held onto him until her feet were firmly on the floor then stepped back and waited.

He stared at her for a couple of heartbeats, trying to figure out what she was waiting for, she said she needed to pee. He'd assumed it was urgent.

She twirled her finger. "Out. I'm not peeing with you watching."

"Oh, oops, sorry." He'd forgotten that she wasn't a member of his team, which was ridiculous really as there wasn't a damn thing about her which screamed military. "I'll um, I'll go grab your stuff from the back of the truck."

"Thank you, Cormack."

Idiot! He bolted from the room as if someone had lit his dick on fire and he was looking for the nearest cattle trough to quench it. He disengaged the lock and paused for a second to consider if he should reengage it or not. But decided it was better not to as he hadn't programed it for her handprint or given her the master code yet.

He let himself out into the main hallway and pounded down the stairs to the front door. It took him all of five minutes to be back up the stairs with the bag Rexar's mother had packed for her and to shut his suite door behind him. He blew out a breath of relief that he'd managed to make it without encountering anyone else. He was so not in the mood for a lecture or for giving explanations right now.

"Sunshine?"

"In here," she called from the direction of his room. She couldn't still be peeing, could she? Did she need to see a doctor?

"Are you okay, Sunshine?" He dropped the bag on the bed and strode to the door of the bathroom and knocked but didn't open it.

"Yes, I just have some stuff in my foot. Do you have tweezers?"

"Sure." He crossed the room to the dresser next to the bed and searched through the drawer, looking for the small kit she'd given him for Christmas last year. "There you are." He grabbed the small leather case and returned to the bathroom door, leaving the drawer open behind him. "Can I come in?"

"Yes."

He opened the door and scowled when he got his first look at the soles of her feet. "Why didn't you say something?" He dropped to his knees next to the toilet where she sat on the closed lid and took one of her tiny feet in his hand. Fuck, something so damn tiny shouldn't have this many slices and minuscule cuts. He'd seen new recruits with less damage to their feet after their first day in basic training.

"It's okay, Cormack, I promise, I'll be fine."

He growled low in his throat; she was the one with hurt feet and here she was reassuring him that she was fine. Un-fucking-believable. The woman, his woman, had no sense of letting people know when she was hurting. He was going to make it his mission to get her to see leaning on him didn't make her weak.

He gently placed her foot on the floor and turned to the cabinet under the sink. He rummaged around in it until he found the first aid kit. Then sat with his back against the bath and took her foot in his hand again. "I never thought I'd be grateful this bathroom is so small."

"Why?" She winced when his thumb skimmed over what had to be a sensitive spot on the side of her foot.

He gentled his touch and turned her foot to peer at the spot. "Because I can sit here and still reach your feet without stretching."

"Aww."

He smiled at the teasing in her tone.

"You should take up yoga, that's good for teaching your muscles how to stretch."

"Cheeky." He glanced up at her. "This might sting." She nodded in response, and he picked up the tweezers. "Ready?"

"No, but do it anyway."

"Okay." He pressed the metal against her skin, pushing in gently until the head of the embedded thorn was visible. Her foot jerked in his hand, and he knew he was hurting her as he managed to grip the thorn with the tweezers. "Big breath, I'm gonna pull it out."

"This is not how I thought I'd ever hear you say that," she grumbled but did as he asked and inhaled deep then let it out slowly, wincing as he pulled the black thorn out of her sensitive flesh. "Ow."

"I'm sorry, baby, they have to come out." He hated hurting her. Maybe he should go get the medic, but he nixed that idea even before it had finished forming in his head. Seeing any other man's hands on her might make him kinda murdery. Scratch that, it would make him a hell of a lot more murderous than kinda. He ran his thumb over more of her foot, watching for places where she flinched, and paid close attention to those spots. God damn it, he'd faced way too many unimaginable horrors on the battlefield and done so many shit and awful things in the name of his flag and country than he wanted to remember. But none of those things came even halfway close to making him sweat as much as hurting his sunshine did. He could tell he was hurting her by the low whine she made each time he pulled out a thorn or a sliver of wood. Finally, he decided they were finished with that foot. "How does that feel?"

"Sore but better."

"Thank fuck."

"Language."

"Sorry." He picked up the other foot and went through the same process. Each time she winced was a stab to his heart, and he wanted to kick his own ass for hurting her, even though he knew it was necessary. To distract them both, he figured it was better to take both their minds off it. "What do you want for dinner?"

"There's a choice?"

"You can have anything you please, Sunshine." If Kayce didn't have it in the kitchen, then he'd drive the forty miles into town to find it. He'd go to the fucking city if he had to.

"Cake."

"You can't have cake for dinner."

"I want cake."

Did she know what that pout did to him?

"You said I can have anything I want, and I want the biggest dirtiest slice of chocolate cake you can find."

"Baby, you have to eat something nutritious first." He dropped another thorn onto the floor next to him. "Then you can have cake."

"That wasn't what you offered."

She was winding him up, she had to be.

"Cake. For dinner please, with ice cream."

"Minx."

"You asked what I wanted for dinner," she reminded him. "I told you. Cake."

Her foot jerked in his hand as he tugged at a stubborn sliver of wood, and he paused to press a kiss to her ankle, making her shiver. "Sorry, I hate hurting you."

"Well, I've had a crappy day," she huffed at him. "I deserve cake."

"I don't know that we have chocolate."

"Make it sweet and give me lashings of ice cream and I can forgive the no chocolate."

Sucker.

"Okay, we'll see what they have in the kitchen," he promised. He wasn't going to win this one and he knew it.

"Yay, cake for the win."

Christ, she looked so young when she smiled wide and clapped her hands together like that. It almost made him feel old. Not old enough to know better than to think he had a chance of keeping her for himself, mind you, but almost. Maybe he could ask Kayce, the cook, to stall on bringing it out and she'd have some of his food before it got there. His plan in place, he went back to working on her feet until finally he could find no more ouches. "I think you're done." He scrambled to his feet and switched on the shower. "Want me to bring your bag in here?"

"Yes, please."

Still sitting on the closed bowl, she wriggled out of her t-shirt, and he bit back a groan. It was official, he was a complete and utter hound dog, wanting her while she was hurt. He left the bathroom as fast as he possibly could, because staying meant he'd be tempted to do something with all that sweet, sweet skin she was exposing while she stripped. "I'll…" That croak couldn't be coming from his mouth. He cleared his throat and tried again. "I'll grab you a clean towel and your bag, you jump in the shower."

"Thank you."

In the mirror he caught a glimpse of her naked body leaning into the shower, testing the water with one hand. Fuck, he was going to hell for sure. He stepped into his bedroom and thumped his dick hard with his fist in a vain attempt to remind the asshole to behave. But he also knew there was little chance of that happening. There was no one who'd ever made him granite hard in two seconds flat like Willow did.

He took more time than was necessary locating a new bath towel. He knew Willow wouldn't care if the damn towel was new or not. But he needed a minute or two to recatch the reins of his control. Somewhere between seeing her in the mirror and the hall closet, his body had decided it had waited long enough and that he should touch her everywhere, check every inch of her beautiful body, and make sure she wasn't hurt anywhere else. "You're an asshole, Ford."

He rushed back to the bathroom like a man who was going to have shower sex for the first time since coming home from a six-month deployment. Except he reminded himself that he wasn't allowed to kick off his boots and his camo. And he definitely wasn't allowed to jump under the warm water with her. Nope, he wasn't even meant to be thinking about licking the droplets of water which ran down her throat. He adjusted his dick behind his zipper. But it did absolutely zero to relieve the ache. That was it, he was going in the guest shower in the main hallway, and he'd take care of the... um...urge there.

He grabbed her bag from the bed and blew out a pained breath before giving a fast knock on the door and walking in with his eyes squeezed shut. If he so much as caught a glimpse of her, he was fucked or rather she would be, and he was not that dick with her. He refused to be that dick with her.

Having his eyes shut had its advantages and its disadvantages. He couldn't actually see her under the shower, but he had one hell of a fantastic imagination and his mind provided the information right behind his eyelids. *Fuck my life.* He banged into something, and the towel slipped out of his grip and probably landed on the floor. His eyes popped open.

Close your eyes, you fool.

Oh, man, he was right, his imagination was on point. She was fucking gorgeous with her head back as she soaked her long hair under the water. The pose made her back arch and her breasts jut out making his mouth water.

"Cormack?"

He jerked his eyes back to her face, fuck, she'd caught him ogling her like some kind of dirty old man, all that was missing was the trench coat. He dropped her bag on the closed lid of the toilet. "I'll go shower in the other bathroom."

He didn't wait for her to reply. He already felt the heat climbing up his neck and swirling around to his ears. Her soft laughter followed after him. Damn it, he was fucked, totally and utterly F.U.C.K.E.D. He punched his fist silently off the door frame on the way into the living room. Maybe a little pain would fix him.

CHAPTER EIGHT

FIFTEEN MINUTES later he paused at the door to his suite and hesitated on pressing his palm to the scanner. The cold as ice shower had done little to quelch the desire inside him. That bitch was still riding him so hard he could feel the spikes on her spurs digging into his back.

"You alright, bro?"

He spun around at Mokaccino's voice. Shit, when was the last time he hadn't heard someone coming up the stairs? He didn't remember, that's when. "Yeah."

"Are you blushing?" Rory peered closer at him.

"What? Fuck no." He slapped his hand over the scanner. He was not staying here for Rory to start throwing him shit. He had way better things to do. "I was just going to grab Willow." *Crap, that sounds all kinds of wrong, add on the rest.* "For dinner, I was going to grab Willow for dinner."

"Huh, sure, buddy." Rory smirked at him and smacked him on the shoulder as he passed. "You may want to use the other hand on that scanner."

He squeezed his eyes shut and bit back the curse which threatened to explode from his mouth. Of course, he had to make an epic fuck-up like this while there were witnesses. There was no way on this earth he could have put the wrong hand on the lock when there was nobody around. No, that would be way too simple. He placed the correct hand on the scanner and heard the lock disengage. He filed away the memory of Rory's mocking laughter following him until he slammed the door shut, cutting it off.

"What's wrong?"

"Shit." For the second time in as many minutes he jumped two feet into the air. Some freaking operator he was. Hell, not only had he not seen or heard Rory, the dick, coming, he also hadn't noticed Willow standing right there. And considering she was the reason his brain was working out of his pants; it was ridiculous that he hadn't clocked her the second he walked in the door. "I didn't see you there."

"Um, sorry." She frowned at him and padded across the floor to stand in front of him.

Yoga pants and slim fitting t-shirts should be illegal. Throw in wet hair, which was braided over one shoulder and everything about his sunshine was any man's wet dream. He growled low in his throat at just the suggestion of his mind of another man touching her and struggled to rein in his rioting emotions. What the fuck was wrong with him? He'd never acted like this around her before.

"Cormack?"

"Hmm?"

"Cormack?"

"Hmm?"

"Jeep."

He jerked when she used his call sign. Willow rarely did unless she was being serious about something and needed him to listen right now. "Sorry, baby, are you okay?"

"That's what I was trying to ask you."

"I'm good, I swear." He would be freaking good if it killed him. Was this what it was like for her, all those times he'd been in her house, in her space? Did it make her all possessive over him as it seemed to do to him regarding her?

"Okay." She sounded doubtful, but as her belly picked that moment to grumble loud enough that he could hear it, he took the save it offered and held out his hand to her. The beast which raged inside him gentled the second she put her hand in his.

"You're hungry, Sunshine." He kissed the top of her head once she was close enough and tugged her until she fit under his arm. "Let's get you some dinner."

"Cake." She grinned up at him. "You promised me cake."

"Yes, I did." He paused at the door and tapped a code into the scanner. "Put your right hand here." He nodded to the device. "It will scan your palm, so you can open and close the door as you want to."

"You trust me with your room?"

"Suite," he corrected. "I'll show you the rest of it after dinner. And yes, I trust you in my space."

"Oh." She did as he asked and placed her hand facedown on the scanner. A red laser light ran all the way down and back up again, similar to a photocopier. When the light flashed green twice and beeped, he knew her print was now stored in their system. He made a mental note to shoot an email to Trev telling him he'd done it, or he'd have questions to answer in the morning.

He tapped the code in again to clear the system and nodded to the scanner. "Put it back there again, so we can make sure it works."

She did as he asked and within two seconds the locks disengaged, and the light flashed green. "There ya go." He tugged the door open and waved her on ahead of him.

Her fingers tightened on his when they approached the dining room, and the sounds of voices filtered through into the hallway. While Bravo and Charlie team's houses had kitchens in their suites, most of the cooking for all teams was done in this house. It made it easier for him, as second in command, to touch base with each member of the team daily. "Ready?"

"There's cake in there?"

"There sure is." There better be cake, if there wasn't then he and Kayce were going to have one hell of a come to Jesus meeting. He totally disregarded the fact he hadn't called the kitchen, and that he hadn't given him a heads up. There was always cake of some sort. Today had better not be the day that Kayce changed up his MO.

"Then I'm more than ready." She tugged lightly on his hand. "Lead on, kind sir."

"You got it." He pushed open the door to the dining room and completely ignored the silence that fell over the other men when it sank into their brains that it was him and a woman. He felt the hesitation in Willow's step and scowled darkly. "What's the matter? Y'all lose your tongues?"

"Nope."

"Not me."

"No, sir."

"Jeep, Willow!" Sensei yelled from the table they normally sat at for meals. Calling him as if he didn't know where he was going. When he felt the hesitation leave Willow, Jeep decided he wouldn't kill him for telling everyone her name.

The conversation around them was in hushed whispers, but he caught a couple of 'who's she' and a few 'I didn't know 2IC had a woman' he was going to ignore them for now. His focus was on weaving their way through the tables to where Sensei waited for them. As they approached, Logan stood and pulled out a chair between him and where he normally sat. It was then that Jeep realized Logan had moved one seat over to make room for Willow. That his friend had considered his woman important enough to do that for... it meant more than he would ever say. The people at this table were his family, it was important to him that they accepted Willow as his. However, he didn't want to have to choose between them. If they forced his hand, they wouldn't like the outcome. "Where's Rex?"

"Big house." Logan placed his mug back on the table. "He wanted to see Lina."

"Ah." He helped Willow into her seat. It made sense that Rexar would go to see Lina. It had been in his bar, The Corner Pyrate, that Lina and Dalton had met years before. "Sunshine, this is Logan, or Sensei as we call him." He reached across the table and grabbed the jug of water, filling her glass. "Sensei, this is my Willow."

Willow smiled at Logan. "Hi."

"Should have known it would take a brother's daughter to put a rope on this asshole and tame him."

"Language." Jeep swatted at Sensei's head. "Willow doesn't like when people swear."

"And she's not only a SEAL's kid, but the other half of your heart?"

He was going to ignore the incredulous tone in Sensei's voice as he asked the question. "Yup, she is," Jeep confirmed. "There's no law that says those things have to come with being okay with the amount of swearing y'all do."

"It's okay, Cormack." Willow sipped her water and arched an eyebrow at him. "Now, I remember there being a promise of cake used as a bribe to get me to brave the masses."

"Right, cake, you got it." He stroked his hand across her shoulder, hoping to reassure her she'd be okay, and pointed one finger at Sensei. "Don't be a dick."

Logan held up his hand in a possible imitation of a scout's salute. "Scout's honor," he promised.

"Wrong hand," Willow told him.

"Shi—Crap." He swapped hands while the sound of Willow's laughter reassured Cormack that she could handle the dumbass.

"I'll be back in a sec."

"I'll be here."

He wove through the tables to the hot counter, which was set up in canteen style and grabbed a tray. As he moved along the line, he filled two plates with ribs and a massive pork chop before adding a double side of mash. He tried to peer over the shoulder of the Bravo team member in front of him, trying to see the dessert section, but the man's wide ass shoulders kept the cold section from his view. By the time the line had moved along to see, he cursed silently in his head. There was cake, lemon and blueberry, and some kinda pink cheesecake. What there wasn't was chocolate cake. "Fuck."

He left his tray on the end of the counter and headed to the kitchen to look for Kayce. "Hey, Kayce?"

"Yup?" The former Green Beret turned chef kept the spoon of butter moving in the pan while he basted a steak which was probably for Dalton in the big house.

"You got any chocolate cake?"

"I don't take food orders," Kayce reminded him. "What's out there…" He lifted the spoon and pointed it toward the dining room. "Is what's on offer for the day."

"I know, my man." If it was for himself or for any of the men, he'd have told them to fuck off and make it in their own mini kitchen. But this was for Willow. "But my woman's had a rough few days and I promised her chocolate cake."

"You didn't think to call and check if I had any first?"

"No." Yeah, he knew he was an idiot. Kayce had every right to be pissed with him. "I should have. I'm sorry."

"Gimme a couple of minutes, and I'll whip together something in the microwave or make her chocolate pancakes or something," Kayce offered. "I just gotta send this up to the boss." He took the steak out of the pan and plated it before adding mash and veggies and placed the plate under the lights on the hot plate alongside two others to stay warm.

"Thanks, bro."

"You owe me, Jeep."

"Name your price."

"I think I'll hang onto this favor until there's a night I don't have a dishwasher."

Fucking fabulous. But there was no way he was going to refuse. He paid his debts, even ones for something as simple as a chocolate cake. "Deal." He headed back to the dining room and grabbed his tray. He glanced at the table and grabbed two beers for him and Sensei and a cherry cola and a sparkling water for his girl before heading back to the table where Willow and Sensei sat.

He studied his girl, her fingers drummed on the table next to her, warning him that she was either pissed as fuck or Logan was going to get one hell of a verbal beatdown. She spotted him approaching and her smile lit up the whole damn room. When she turned her sunshine on him, it warmed him right down to his bones.

"No cake?" Her eyes narrowed at the lack of dessert on his tray when he placed it in front of his seat. As if she believed he hadn't brought it on purpose. They were going to have a discussion about how he kept his promises. If he had to make the damn cake himself, she'd have had chocolate cake. Might not be a good one, and it might give her food poisoning, but she'd have cake.

"Cook's gonna make it fresh."

"Oh?"

He pulled out his chair and took his place beside her. "Sorry, Sunshine, I should have called down to check what was on offer before I promised you chocolate cake." He divided up the ribs and put one onto the side plate between him and Willow, then sliced off a decent chunk of pork chop and added a dollop of mash. He didn't bother putting veggies on that plate, as he knew he was pushing his luck already with the meat and potatoes. "Want some while you wait?"

Her stomach growled loud, telling him she was hungry, but he didn't dare push. When it came to food, his girl had some funny ideas. She ate when she was hungry, she didn't think twice about having breakfast or dessert for dinner. If she didn't have what called to her, she didn't eat. But sometimes, sometimes she would pick at the healthy stuff on his plate.

"If he's busy, I can go make some."

"Nah, Kayce will be done in a minute and he'll whip something together," Jeep promised. "I can't swear it will be fancy, but it will be cake... or pancakes."

"Sorry..."

He pressed one finger, cutting off the apology. He refused to allow her to be weird about food. He got it, she'd never been the skinny kid, she'd been bullied in school to the point where eating was an issue for her. But did his girl let that stop her from following her dreams of being a chef? Hell no, she worked her butt off as a line cook and worked her way up to designing bespoke cakes and stuff. He'd have been concerned about the impact not being at home would have on her business, except he already knew she'd wound it down with the plan to return to college later in the year. He handed her a fork. "Nibble on some if you want, Sunshine." There was no way in hell he'd pressure her into eating what she didn't feel like. He'd nudge, then let her do as she wished.

She twirled the fork in place on the tablecloth as he handed a beer to Sensei. He knew the other operator was watching every interaction and filing away information about Willow, just as he would have if it was someone else at the table. He pulled the tab on the can and placed the cherry cola next to her plate before loosening the top on the water and placing it next to it. Those were her go-to drinks; she could pick which she preferred. It was his job to make her life just a little bit simpler. Oh, he knew she could open a can or a damn bottle herself, but he liked doing it.

"Thank you." She smiled up at him and reached for the water, filling her glass before adding a splash of cola. From past experience, he knew not to watch her like a hawk when there was food on the table but had to bite back a smile of satisfaction when she picked up the fork to taste the potatoes.

"It's good."

"Eat what you want, baby." Now that she'd spoken about the food, he was good to do the same. This food thing was a delicate dance, but one they'd figured out together. He'd have to remember to thank Sensei for not commenting or remarking on it.

By the time one of Kayce's kitchen minions, as he called the two men who worked with him, arrived with a massive round mug topped with cream, she'd eaten most of the rib, all of the chop, and half the potatoes he'd put on the small plate for her.

"Here's your chocolate cake, sir."

"Thanks, Tommy." He took the offered treat and nodded to Willow's plate. "Ready for cake, Sunshine?"

"Yes." She pushed the plate to the middle of the table, making room for the mug and twisted in her chair. "Thank you. I appreciate that you took the time to make it."

"Oh, I didn't make it, ma'am, but I'll let Chef know you said so."

"Thank you." She shifted further back into her seat and under the table he could feel her leg brushing against his, telling him she was probably swinging her legs back and forth as she did when she was happy.

Cormack couldn't stop the jolt of satisfaction which swamped him when she dug her spoon into the middle of the cake and caramel erupted from the middle. The moan of appreciation she made when she popped the first bite into her mouth went straight to his dick. He scowled at Sensei when he saw the other man's eyes widen. Yeah, he got it, that noise was sexy as fuck, but… he shook off the jealousy. He was acting like an idiot. Willow was his and his alone. While he wanted those sounds to happen only in private where he could hoard them all for himself, there was no way in hell he was depriving her of the happiness a mug of microwave cake brought her.

"It's so good, Imma going to need the recipe."

"We can ask Kayce for it later." He pulled out his phone, with the mental list he had going on in his head for shit he had to remind himself of, there was no way he'd remember them all if he didn't start writing shit down. He popped the last bite of his chop into his mouth and chased it with a mouthful of beer.

By the time she finished the cake, his his sunshine was almost asleep in her chair. "Will you dump the dishes?" He knew it was shitty to ask Logan to clear up after them, but he wanted to get Willow back to his room and into bed before she face-planted into the mug.

"Of course, go."

"Thanks, man." Sensei waved him off and Jeep helped Willow to her feet and led her out of the dining room.

"What's next?" Willow asked as they climbed the stairs to their suite.

He'd think about when it had become theirs and not his later, right now, he was in look after my girl mode. "Nothing, now we sleep."

"Thank you, sweet baby Jesus."

He knew she'd slept on the plane; he'd watched her like a hawk every second her eyes were closed, but with adrenaline of the crazy wild flight and the shit of the last few days finally leaving his body, he needed to crash. If he, who was used to the dump of adrenaline, was feeling it, he could only imagine how she was feeling.

It didn't take more than five minutes to get into the suite and lead her down the hallway to the bedroom. "You need to use the bathroom?"

"No." She shook her head and flopped onto the bed. "I need to sleep."

"Me, too." He worked his belt open and stripped off his pants before reaching for a pair of shorts. While he normally slept in the raw, tired or not, there was no way he'd be able to keep his hands off her if he was naked. "Are you taking off your bra?"

"Mmh, yeah." She reached her hands back, unclasped it, and pulled the arms out through her sleeves. "Oh, that's so awesome. I've been wearing that torture device for what feels like days. Well, maybe not that one as I changed it after I showered."

"Shh, don't worry about details." He pressed a kiss to the side of her mouth. "Let me grab you a t-shirt, you ditch the yogas and the top, okay?"

Half asleep, she nodded, but he proved to himself that his self-control was still functioning when he managed to undress her and put her into his big t-shirt without taking many inappropriate touches. As tempted as he was, the need to look after her won out. Finally, they were ready to sleep, and he moved her to the middle of the bed and placed his handgun on the dresser next to where he'd be lying before climbing in on the side nearest the door. He would always be between her and any access point. If that made him overprotective, he didn't give a shit. He lay on his side and pushed one arm under her head. He fucking loved that she immediately scooted her butt back into his groin. His dick immediately took notice, but what the hell, he was a man whose woman had her butt against his dick, of course he was going to take notice.

He wrapped his other arm around her side, his palm splaying across her soft belly, and blew out a contented sigh. Finally, he was home. "Night, Sunshine."

"Night, grumpy."

"Still going with that, huh?" When he'd started calling her Sunshine in his emails, she'd replied by calling him grumpy. He chose to believe it was with affection. His eyes closed as he allowed having her in his arms to convince him she was here. She was safe. And she was his, and finally sleep claimed him.

CHAPTER NINE

STARING into the dark behind her eyelids was horrid, just horrid, but it beat the red numbers on the clock mocking her, so she squeezed her eyes shut and tried to sleep. Logically, she knew there were so many people who had it worse than her and that she was being a complete and utter ninny, but she just couldn't stop her mind from racing. Sure, she'd been manhandled, and lord knows what they'd planned for her if she hadn't escaped or if they hadn't been stupid enough to leave her alone in the van. But every time she got just to that point of where sleep *might* be possible, she heard the bang of the Glock and saw the man who'd been reaching for her fall.

Behind her she felt Cormack's soft breath against her skin, and his arm banded tight around her waist. It should have been comforting, instead she just wanted to run. This was ridiculous, she'd be better off doing something, anything to make her mind let go of the 'drive her crazy' train it was on.

Go cook something. All these people like food. Right?

Once the idea had popped into her head, she knew it was the right one. She needed to do something and getting lost in the rhythms of mixing and baking… *that* might actually help. Carefully, she shifted on the bed, easing Cormack's arm from her.

"Huh?"

"Shh, go back to sleep." She stroked his side, petting him like a huge hound dog, until his breathing evened out again and his soft snores filled the room. She slid off the bed, hopefully, if he felt her leaving, he'd think she was going to use the bathroom, and grabbed her discarded bra off the chair and her yoga pants off the floor. Then snuck out of the room, leaving the door ajar. If she attempted to shut it, Mr. ears like a hawk would wake for sure.

Outside the bedroom door, she pulled on the yoga pants and drew the t-shirt over her head to put on the bra before putting the shirt back on again. Cormack's scent engulfed her. Wrapping her up in a warm blanket of comfort, almost as good as one of those massive bear hugs he liked to give her. She padded to the suite door and paused with her hand on the handle.

Crap, the alarm. She placed her hand on the scanner and waited for the light to flash green. God, she hoped that click meant the locks had disengaged.

She couldn't see any blinking lights like her alarm system had in Virginia to tell her it was still armed, so she was going to assume that her palm print had worked. If it hadn't, she'd find out in about two point five seconds. Turning the handle, she waited for the screaming of the alarm to start. When it didn't, she huffed out a breath of relief and left the suite, pulling the door shut softly behind her.

"Where's the kitchen?" They'd come up the stairs, which meant she needed to go down to the bottom floor. Why in the name of all the stars did her feet sound so freaking loud when she wanted to be quiet? She winced when the top step

creaked, but after pausing for a couple of heartbeats, she
didn't hear anything, so she kept going. At the bottom of the
stairs, she took another right, and then a left into the room
where they'd eaten dinner earlier.

"Yes." The moon through the large windows provided
enough light that she didn't stub her toe on the way across the
room to the door the cook had brought food in through. The
kitchen should be there... right? She reached her hand around
the frame of the door, feeling for the light switch, then
blinked rapidly as the florescent row of bulbs down the center
of the kitchen over a work bench flooded the room with light.

The woman who loved to cook inside her did a little
happy dance as she looked around the massive restaurant
style kitchen. "Wow, now this is what I call a kitchen." She
walked through the kitchen, her fingers skimming over stain-
less-steel countertops. She paused to admire the massive
mixer and the ovens. "Oh, aren't you just gorgeous?" she
crooned to the combi-oven. Thankfully, there was nobody
awake to see her get a lady boner over ovens and a top of the
range kitchen. Actually, she didn't even care if someone did
see it, she loved kitchens. And she wasn't going to apologize
for it. She'd worked in many kitchens and restaurants over
the years, but Holy Moly, she'd never had access to this level
of equipment. "Gordon Ramsay, eat your heart out."

She did a little happy jig as she crossed the floor to the
opposite wall. She was guessing one of those doors was the
pantry and the other she hoped would be a walk-in fridge.
Snagging an apron from a hook near one oven, she folded it
around her waist, and after wrapping the straps around her
waist three times, she knotted them in front. She paused at the
sink next to the pantry and scrubbed her hands. There was no
freaking way she was invading another chef's kitchen without
cleaning her grubby fingers.

She walked into the pantry and thankfully her eyes were attached to her head, or she'd be picking them up from the floor when they popped out of her head. Wouldn't that be gross? But wow, the pantry was like a store. Shelves filled with produce, bins filled with flours and grains, even a refrigerated section with every kind of meat that her heart could wish for.

"What will I make?" She went to the cold section first and glanced at the row of meats, picking up package after package, checking the labels and best by dates. She bypassed the covered bowls and trays, as if they had been hers, she'd have been pissed that her prep work was stolen by another chef who snuck in for a midnight cookout. Pissing off the person who provided the food was never a good thing.

The next package she picked up contained minced pork and an idea sparked to life. "Sfincione di San Vito." In her head she remembered how many tables had been in the room as they'd had dinner last night and added up the number of people in her head before she calculated the recipe she usually used and multiplied it by half a dozen. If she was making something, then it may as well be something the chef could use for lunch or even for a snack for the guys. Her normal recipe made two nine-inch pies. Normally she had to scale the recipe down, but not this time though. The larger number would work in her favor though as the dough was much easier to make in a larger batch. "They can freeze what they don't use."

She searched through the pantry gathering all the things she needed. All-purpose flour, plus extra for dusting, dry yeast, sugar, salt, and lard. Water she could get at the sink. Her arms full, she headed back to the kitchen and almost dropped her goodies.

"What are you doing?"

"I, umm." Crap. She'd been caught. She stared at the man who scowled at her from the kitchen door. "Cooking?"

"Are you asking or telling?"

She shrugged and moved to the center work bench and placed all the items there, laying them out as she would at home. He could figure out the answer to that question all by himself, and if he couldn't then he had no business asking it in the first place. That he stayed at the door with his shoulder leaning against it and didn't approach told her he probably knew who she was. "I'm Willow."

"I know who you are." The man shifted his feet. "I just want to know what you're doing in my kitchen at zero four hundred."

"I'm sorry, I couldn't sleep, and cooking lets me do something that doesn't involve thinking too hard." She itched to move, to run from his stern gaze, but she held her ground. She was a SEAL's daughter, dang it, and it was time she remembered that backbone she had.

"Why do I ask?" The man scrubbed one hand over his chin. He pointed at her. "Don't burn shit." He barely waited for her nod before he turned and left, the kitchen door swinging behind him.

That meant she had permission from the chef... right? She was taking it as a yes, which made her ridiculously happy. She hummed to herself as she headed back to the pantry to grab the rest of the ingredients she needed.

Searching through the shelves, she found the largest mixing bowl she could. She could use the mixer to make the dough, but she'd learned from an old school Italian chef and liked to make it by hand. It always tasted better that way. But one bowl wasn't going to be big enough when the dough started rising, so she grabbed another couple and lined them up in front of her before measuring out the correct amount of dry ingredients for three pies in each bowl.

She combined the flour, yeast, and sugar and swished it with her fingers to mix thoroughly, then made a well in the center before gradually adding room temperature water while mixing by hand. She eyeballed the amount of water, adjusting it according to how soft the dough felt under her fingers. She wanted very soft but not sticky. Once the first batch was ready, she added salt and lard. After mixing thoroughly, she turned the dough out onto a floured surface and now the fun could start. Pushing and kneading the dough was good for taking all your frustrations out on something.

"Buttheads," she muttered and bitched to herself as she imagined the dough was the men who'd tried to take her. Smushing their faces into the board... awesome... it made her feel better. "Stupid fudgebucketing annoying turds." Sometimes it may be more colorful if she swore, but she could still hear her gram's voice telling her ladies don't swear. She huffed and rolled the dough into a ball before placing it in the mixing bowls and covering it with plastic wrap.

That could rise in one of the ovens with the pilot light on while she got the ingredients for the sauce cooking. She washed her hands under the sink and dried them off.

"If you were a saucepan..." She glanced around the kitchen. Skillets, bowls, ladles, and enough plates for a restaurant, those she could see. "...Where would you be hiding?"

"On the other side of the bench, under the salad bar."

"Frick-fracking Nora!" she screeched when a voice spoke, and she whirled around with her hand pressed against her chest. Not that it would stop her heart from leaping right out and going for a dance across the floor mind you, but it was worth a shot. "Why didn't you say something and let me know you were there?"

"I just did." The man disappeared back through the kitchen door and reappeared a couple of seconds later with two glasses. "You want a drink?"

She studied him for a second, trying to figure out why he was offering her a drink, but she figured it couldn't hurt to be nice. She could totally do nice if she had to. "Yes, please." She took the offered glass, sniffed it, and peered over the rim at the chef who'd come in while she was gathering ingredients. "You know I'm Willow, do you have a name?"

"Yeah." He grinned at her and pulled a bar stool from a corner, bringing it over to the work bench. "Kayce, nice to meet you. You're Jeep's woman?" He sipped from his own glass and nodded to hers. "Sweet tea and JD Tennessee honey."

""Um… yes, I suppose you could call me that." She raised the glass to her lips and took a tentative sip, and flavor and yumminess exploded on her taste buds. "Wow, I can't even taste the whiskey."

"My sister likes it for that reason." He tipped his glass toward her, and she clinked hers against it before they both took another sip.

"It's wow, your sister has awesome ideas." She placed the glass down and turned around to look for the saucepan. "You said pans are here?" Opening one door and only seeing baking trays, she shut it again.

"Yeah, next one to the right."

"Thanks."

"Whatcha making?"

"Sfincione di San Vito." She chopped the onion and threw it in the pan that could start sautéing while she got the rest of the ingredients ready. She glanced at Kayce, and seeing his confused look added on, "You know what it is?"

"Something Italian?" He raised an eyebrow in query.

"Yes, Sfincione is a type of Italian torta salata, or savory pie. This version is similar to a Chicago deep dish pizza, and it may have inspired the American classic. While no Italian would consider this to be a pizza, if you like deep dish pizza, you'll like this." She added the mince to the saucepan and stabbed at it with a wooden spoon to break it up. "It's a Sicilian dish I learned how to make when my dad was stationed at Sigonella." When the pork was browned, she added salt and pepper. "Do you have red wine?"

"You need good stuff or will cooking wine do?"

"If I put a shit wine in my Sfincione, the chef who taught me how to make it would throw his wooden spoon across the Atlantic to wallop me on the back of the knuckles." She took another sip of her drink and went back to babying the mince in the pan.

"Good stuff it is then." Kayce slipped off the stool and disappeared into the other room before returning with a bottle of red. "This is the only Italian red we have; we aren't big wine drinkers."

"Thank you." She glanced at the label and added the red wine to the pan.

"Kayce?"

"In here."

"Have you seen…" Cormack pushed in the door and glanced around the room. His eyes narrowed as if he was confused what was happening, but then he sniffed and the dark which had been clouding his face cleared. "I should have known to check the kitchen first." He walked around the counter and waited for her to sniff the pan to check the smell of alcohol had dissipated before he wrapped an arm around her and pressed a kiss to the side of her head. "You okay, Sunshine?"

"Yes, I…" She didn't know how to explain it, the need to do something, but she figured if anyone would get it, it would be Cormack, so she allowed her words to trail off.

"I'll…uh…" Kayce drained his glass and slipped off the stool. "I'll leave you to it."

"Nah, man." Cormack ran his thumb over her cheek and stepped back. "She needs to cook; I get to sit here and be the taste tester." He peered into the pan and glanced at the dirty bowls in the sink. "Torta Salata?"

"Sfincione."

"Awesome." He nodded to the empty glass. "Want another one?"

"Sure." Kayce sat back down. "Tennessee Honey."

"You got it." Cormack smiled at her. "You want something to drink, Sunshine?"

She paused with the lid of the tomato tin half open and picked up her spiked sweet tea and showed him the glass was still almost half full. "I'm good. Thank you."

"Okay, be right back."

"I'll be here."

"Me, too," Kayce chimed in.

"I wasn't telling your ugly ass that I was coming back," Cormack grumbled on the way out of the room.

She bit down on her lip and hid her face in the saucepan, adding tomato paste and the can of tomatoes so he wouldn't see her grin at the teasing between him and Cormack. She'd never seen Cormack with his team. Coming here had been an eye opener. How these men interacted together reminded her of her dad and his team guys. It brought back a bunch of warm fuzzy feelings of happier days, even if the memories were tinged with a touch of bittersweet, they were happy memories which soothed her soul.

She filled the can halfway up with water and added it to the saucepan. "Do you have fennel seeds?"

"Yup, want me to grab them?"

"Please."

"Here."

She took the offered seeds and stirred them into the sauce and half covered it with the wooden spoon between the lid and the pan to allow the steam to escape. "It needs about an hour and a half to thicken."

"It's like Bolognese?"

"Shut your mouth." Cormack placed the bottle of whiskey on the counter between them. "Last time I asked that, I had a lecture on how real Bolognaise was made with Italian sausage and the best minced beef you can find and not minced pork."

"No lectures tonight," she promised him. Much like her eyes glazed over when he talked tactics and prepping, his did when she talked the nuances between recipes. She busied herself at cleaning up the mess she'd made while Cormack and Kayce spoke softly behind her. This was a normal she could get used to really freaking fast.

You shouldn't get used to it.

But despite the internal warning, she knew she wasn't going to listen. She hadn't realized how lonely her life had been until she'd come here yesterday. She went to work, she came home, she watched TV, went to bed, and did it all again the next day. The only excitement in her life was when Cormack came to stay. Which was why she'd decided to go back to college to try something different. She finished rinsing dishes and dried her hands off before turning back to the guys.

"You said that needs about an hour?" Kayce nodded to the saucepan.

She glanced at the clock, calculating how much time had passed since she'd left it at a simmer. "Yes, about that. I might need to add some more water, so it doesn't get too thick."

"But I can use my kitchen to get a start on breakfast?"

Oh, lord, she had totally been hogging the kitchen, hadn't she? "Of course." She glanced at Cormack, willing him to read her mind and gave him a soft smile when he nodded. She turned back to Kayce. "Can I help?"

"As long as Jeep doesn't mind me stealing your time."

"Nope," Cormack reassured them. He glanced at the clock on the wall. "I'm gonna go up to the main house and see what's happening." He pointed a finger at Kayce. "Protect her as if she was your sister."

"Always, man."

"Go," she reassured Cormack. "I'll be fine."

"M'kay." He gave her a smile which warmed her from head to toe before draining his glass and leaving the kitchen.

CHAPTER TEN

CORMACK OPENED the door to his suite and stepped inside. It would have been smarter to have grabbed his boots before he went looking for Willow. But he'd known she wouldn't go far. Also, as her palm print wasn't yet set for the main door and the alarm hadn't jolted him out of bed with his weapons at ready position, he'd been pretty sure she hadn't left the building.

As he walked down the hall to his bedroom, he picked up a discarded sock and her hairbrush from the table next to the living space door. He snagged a hair tie from the floor as he walked. Rather than being pissed at having all her bits and pieces scattered in his space, having her stuff laying around somehow felt totally right.

Having spent most of his down time at her house, he should be used to having her stuff mixed with his. But having it happen here, in the place he called his own, it was different, stronger somehow, and he fucking loved it.

He grabbed his boots, tugged the bed covers into place, and sat on the bed to put them on. He shoved his hand into first one boot and then the other to adjust the Superfeet insoles. Those things were life savers, or rather feet savers when his feet were in boots almost twenty-four-seven. Now if only they made something which stopped rubbing the hairs off around his ankles, that'd be awesome.

Once he was fully dressed, he headed into the small kitchen area and opened the cupboard next to the sink. Moving some stuff around, he found the box he'd bought a few months ago. He'd meant to take it to Willow's house with him. But he hadn't come back to Montana from Kabul, and instead went directly to see his sunshine. The full day required to come pick up the single serve coffee maker would have taken a big chunk of time, which he could have spent with her.

He replaced all the stuff on the shelves and straightened with the coffee machine before using his knife to cut the security tape and he went about setting up the machine. He much preferred drip coffee, but Willow liked this stuff, so right now he was thankful he hadn't had time to come get it. Once he'd filled the reservoir with water, he went looking for the two boxes of pods which had come with the machine. Girls liked Starbucks… right? It took a couple of minutes of opening and closing presses but eventually he found the tabs in the cupboard over the fridge. "Vanilla and caramel should work… right?" he talked to himself as he popped both boxes open and placed them next to the machine. If he didn't open them, he knew Willow wouldn't. She hated to be the first or last to use anything, like coffee or food. What he wouldn't give to have five minutes alone with the dicks who'd convinced her of all the shitty thoughts she had around food. But he pushed away the rage. The quirks made her her. She wouldn't be the woman who made him lose his damn mind if she didn't have each and every one of them. He found an insulated mug and put it next to the coffee. There, that would do it.

Finally satisfied that he'd done his best to make her comfy, he grabbed a notepad from the table and scribbled some words.

Make yourself at home, Sunshine.
IKYAS.

HE CHEWED on the top of the pen. He wasn't sure what protocol was here, now that they'd told each other how they felt. Was he meant to write I love you or not? He shrugged, I love you wasn't really their thing, IKYAS… was their way of saying I love you.

He double checked he had everything and left the suite. He'd go to the war-room and see what jobs they had on that he could help with. With his experience in the field there was always some shit going down that he could either advise on or get involved with.

Leaving the building, he followed the path deeper into the ranch from the back of the building, but rather than staying on the path, he decided to take his normal shortcut and jumped the fence into the pasture. It would cut a couple of minutes off the walk to the building which housed their comms and intel offices.

He was halfway across the pasture when a noise behind him had him glancing over his shoulder. His eyes widened when he spotted the massive Texas Longhorn bull, which normally ran with the heifers on the range, eating ground as he pounded toward him.

"Fuck." Cormack had a split second to make a decision, if he bolted for the fence on the opposite side nearest HQ or if he went for the fence which ran along the side of the path. He turned and fled toward HQ. By the time he hit three strides he was running flat out. Not that he thought there was any way he could beat the damn bull, but he had to try. He had too much to live for to be gored by two thousand pounds of pissed red and white bovine.

"Fuck." He could almost feel the bull's hot breath on his back as he ran. He gripped his handgun and pulled it out of its holster and flipped off the safety. If that fucker looked like he was winning, he didn't give a fuck what Jack said about it, he was shooting him. About thirty feet from the fence line, he heard yelling, telling him someone had seen his fuckup. He kept his eyes on the prize, the fence line right in front of him. He could feel how much closer the bull was each time his hooves pounded into the ground behind him. Fuck, he wasn't going to make it.

Movement out of the corner of his eye made him lose his stride and he stumbled. Shit, he was fucked.

"Get up and run, ya fat bastard."

He didn't have time to figure out who the voice belonged to, but as soon as his hands hit the dirt in front of his nose, he bounced back up again and put on a burst of speed hoping to make up for any ground he may have lost.

Ten feet from the fence, he heard cursing behind him and risked a glance over his shoulder. One of the hands was on horseback and running interference with the bull. He wasn't about to make that effort be in vain and as soon as his hand hit the top post of the fence, he launched himself over it, landing on his ass and facing the pasture. The hand barely had his horse out of the way before the bull bellowed and hit the fence with his forehead so hard the whole thing rattled and shook. Cormack scooted backward on his ass and hands.

The bull, clearly pissed off that he'd been unable to reach the idiot human who'd invaded his space, turned his attention to the man who Cormack could now see was Sensei riding bareback on the horse nobody was supposed to be able to ride.

He knew the second both horse and rider realized the danger as the stallion spun on his hocks and took off across the field at a hard gallop. How the hell was Sensei staying on? About a quarter of the way across the field, the horse changed direction and even from where he still sat on the dirt, Cormack could see the big beast's haunches bunch as he prepared to jump. "Shiiit."

He scrambled to his feet and took off down the track as fast as his sore muscles would let him. Sensei had no tack, no saddle, no gear. If the horse jumped, he had no way to hang on. The stallion rose onto its rear legs with Sensei leaning almost flat against his neck and made the jump, momentum keeping them moving forward until finally he slowed and turned in a circle. The bull once again slammed off the fence and pawed the ground in rage when his second target of the day had managed to escape his wrath.

"You okay, bro?" Logan slid down from the horse and landed on his feet next to him.

"Me?" Was he for fucking real? "You're the one who jumped a fucking horse and ran interference with no fucking gear."

"I grew up on a ranch, you know that." Logan shrugged as if it was nothing. "I've been riding since before I could walk." He patted his hand against the horse's neck, his fingers scratching into the spot along the line of his mane. "Cobalt is just a big ole softy," he crooned to the horse. "Aren't you, buddy?"

"What the fuck did you go in the pasture with the bull for?"

"The flag's not on the fence."

"The fuck?" Logan frowned and walked back toward the point where Jeep had jumped the fence. "The flag is always on the fence when the bull is in that pasture."

"I know it should be." Jeep walked next to Logan while Cobalt walked behind them, his chin almost bopping Sensei's shoulder with every step. They paused and scanned all along the fence line, but neither of them saw the signs which should be hung over the posts when the bull was in the field. "But it's not."

"Nope," Logan agreed. "I thought you'd just missed it or something." He scowled at the bull. "Shit like this right here is why I don't like living on ranches no more. Give me the fucking sandbox any day of the week."

"You could have just shot the damn bull," he grumbled. If he'd been in his teammate's boots, the bull would be dead, the damn beast was dangerous as fuck and shouldn't be anywhere near people.

"And have Jack after my ass? Fuck no." He pointed toward the corral where Cobalt normally stayed. "Tell the boss I'll be along in a minute. I'm just gonna look after him."

"Roger that." He watched Logan and the horse walk away. "Sensei?"

"Yup?"

"Thanks, bro."

Logan didn't answer, just raised one hand in the air and kept going toward the corral.

Cormack watched him leave for a couple of minutes. Or at least that was what he hoped it would look like. In reality, he was trying to get his racing heart to stop attempting to exit his chest through his rib cage, and it was a goddamned miracle he'd been able to carry on a conversation with the way his breath was sawing in and out of his lungs.

When he turned toward the HQ building, he took the fucking path. He didn't need a second go round with the bull who'd now disappeared from view. He pulled out his cell and shot off a text.

Text: Jack, there's no flag to say the damn bull's in the pasture.

Text: Bull's on the range.

Text: Tell that to my ass. That fucker just made me sprint across the damn field.

Text: Shit.

Almost immediately Jack's swearing was followed by a second text.

Text: On it.

Cormack didn't bother to reply, Jack ran the ranch side of the business. If someone was fucking up over there, then he'd take care of it. He walked up the steps to the locked door and slapped his palm against the scanner.

"Dude, I didn't think you had it in you to run that fast."

"Shut the fuck up, Trev." The asshole barely let him get the door shut behind him before he was spitting that shit out all over the intercom. Of course, Trev had seen the whole thing happen on the security cameras. Damn it. One couldn't even fuck up in peace. Logan was right, Kabul was looking more and more peaceful by the second.

He made his way through the sequence of locked doors to the elevators and hit the button for the bottom floor which would take him down into the belly of Nemesis Inc. Thank fuck, by the time he was putting his cell in the box outside the door of the main war-room, his breathing was almost back to normal. The last thing he needed was Dalton deciding he needed to do more PT or some shit. "What we got on?" The door slammed shut behind him and everything else faded from his mind, his brain automatically clicking to work mode as soon as he stepped into the room.

"We have a request to run security for a politician who thinks it's an awesome idea to do a hearts and minds trip into the back ass of the AfPak border region of Afghanistan." Trev didn't take his eyes off the screen, where Cormack could see he was running a drone over what was probably going to be their target location.

"Is he fucking insane?" The border region between Afghanistan and Pakistan wasn't the place to go for a fucking day trip. "Where's the paperwork?"

"On your desk."

"Has Dalton seen it yet?" He walked across the room to the far corner and frowned at his desk. "Who was sitting here?"

"How do you know someone was sitting there?" Trev asked.

"Because some dumbfuck moved my mug."

"Your mug was growing stuff," Trev said dryly. "Virus and green shit, I took it to the kitchen and bleached it."

"You bleached my Black Rifle Coffee Company Yeti?" He picked up the mug and sniffed it, wrinkling his nose. "What the hell, Trev?"

"Man, I'm closed in here almost twenty-four hours a day, seven days a week," Trev muttered. "If you think I'm living with the wildlife you're cultivating in your fucking mug, you've lost your damn mind."

"I thought we were friends, bro."

"Not when your damn coffee mug is alive, we're not."

"That's harsh, dude." He picked up the file sitting on his

keyboard and flipped it open, scanning the contents. "I'll call Nem and see how he wants to handle this."

"Yeah." Trev huffed out a breath. "If you want my opinion, that one should be a big fat no."

"It looks good on the surface." Cormack didn't see what Trev's hang-up was on this one. "Talk to me, dude. What's got your panties in a bunch?"

"Call the boss, and I'll show you what I found."

"Sure." He tapped out a message to Nemesis on his cell and hit send, then sat at his desk and pulled up the website for the coffee company. He wanted a new damn mug, and the vets who ran the company would sort him out stat.

"You owe me a new mug."

"Nope, next time clean the damn mug yourself before it mutates."

"Asshole."

"Dick."

Bitching and bickering with Trev, his sunshine safe and in the kitchen with Kayce, yes, everything was finally right in his world.

CHAPTER ELEVEN

"Can you check how thick the sauce is?" She paused in slicing the salami and glanced over her shoulder at Kayce.

He stopped what he was doing at the stove and raised an eyebrow in query. "How thick do you want it?" He lifted the lid of the saucepan and peered into it.

"It should end up like a thick Bolognese."

"I think it's about ready." Kayce stirred the sauce with a wooden spoon. "Want me to season it?"

"Yes, please, just some salt, then pull it off to cool until it's just warm." She dumped the salami onto a plate and grabbed some cheese, squeezing out the water and slicing with the knife at speed to a similar size to the salami, the repetitiveness of the motion soothed her like nothing on earth.

"You got it."

They went back to working in comfortable silence, prepping for both breakfast and dinner. From what she could see, Uncle Dalton looked after his people. "How many do you feed every day?"

"Depends." Kayce broke up the minced sausage in the pan as he browned it. "There's six to a team on this side of the ranch, with three teams. Another six in intel, then the hands and anyone else we have here doing work. So maybe forty max," he told her. "But usually it's more like half that."

"You do it all yourself?"

"Nah, I have two cooks who help out, but I like to do the prep myself." He lifted one shoulder. "It's kinda my jam."

Oh, no, she was imposing, shit. She should have thought of that.

As if he heard the thoughts whirling around in her brain, Kayce snorted. "Don't go thinkin' that means I don't want you here. You know your way around a kitchen, and you aren't getting in my way."

"Umm."

Kayce laughed softly. "It's written all over your face, doll."

"Don't let Cormack hear you call me that, he may chop off important parts," she advised. "Ones you're rather attached to."

"How did you meet him?"

She could hear the curiosity in his voice. Wasn't it typical? Men were bigger gossips than a bunch of hens, but she figured it didn't matter if she told him. "My dad served with Dalton and Cormack on Teams. His Humvee went over an IED in Afghanistan two weeks before he was meant to come home from his last tour, the helo he was taking out of there went down before it reached base."

"That's rough, I'm sorry."

"Thank you." Even after all these years, she still didn't know how best to respond when someone expressed their sympathy. "Anyway, Cormack kept sending me emails and letters, checking on me. Actually, they all did." There was no way she was going to let Kayce think Dalton and the others on her father's team hadn't looked out for her or kept in touch. "But Cormack's were different, and eventually I answered." She grinned as she knew the next words out of her mouth were going to be cliched as heck. "The rest as they say is history."

"What did the other guys on the team say when they found out?"

"Um…" She could feel the heat climbing up her face. "Uncle Dalton only recently found out. Just before I came here, and umm… I haven't been alone with him since."

"Ouch." Kayce's voice was filled with sympathy. He cocked his head to one side as if he was thinking. "Do you know how to make cinnamon rolls?"

"I do." Cormack always told her that she made the best cinnamon rolls. "Why?"

"Make Dalton a bunch of them to sweeten him up."

"I don't know if that's going to cut it."

"But it can't hurt any." Kayce added chopped bacon to the pan with the sausage, the sizzle ramped up as he shook it to make sure the meat didn't stick to the bottom of the pan. "The hands would love you for them, too."

"Right." She tried to figure out if he was joking or serious. "You want me to make some?"

"If you want to." Kayce screwed up his face. "The guys keep asking for them. Every time I make them they either turn out flat or they're rock hard like hockey pucks. I usually just buy a bunch when I go to town for supplies."

"Okay." This was the least she could do. "I'll make the cinnamon rolls; you finish the pies for me."

"Deal, as long as you tell me what to do."

"Preheat an oven to four hundred degrees." She went into the pantry to gather the supplies to make the dough.

"Combi will work?"

"Yes, don't put it on steamer though."

"Sure, standard bake it is."

She dumped the ingredients for buns into the bowl and started mixing a batch of sweet dough for the rolls. "Take a lump of dough about the size of your fist and spread it by hand on a floured surface until it is large enough to completely line a nine-inch diameter metal pie pan."

"This one will work?" Kayce held up a pan about two inches deep.

"Yes, perfect." She added yeast to her bowl. "Oil the pan well and drape the dough into it, allowing the edges to over-hang slightly." She dusted the flour off her hands. "Yes, just like that. Add a thick layer of sauce to the bottom, then top with the chopped salami and cheese on this plate. Then spread out a piece of dough with your hands, same way as before, and use it to close the top."

Kayce followed her instructions. "I'm not seeing how this is like a deep pan pizza."

"You will," she promised. "Seal the pie by rolling the bottom edges over the top and pressing with a fork. Then do the stabby thing with a fork a couple of times and put in the oven."

"Yes, ma'am."

She finished making the dough for the rolls and set it aside to rise. "Now we repeat the process until we've finished all the dough and the sauce."

"Can we use this for breakfast?" Kayce eyed the pans she placed on the counter. "Pizza for breakfast was a staple for most of these guys at one point or other."

"You want to use my Sfincione on your menu?"

"Well, there isn't really a menu, there's just whatever I make, but it smells awesome." Kayce floured both hands and used the heel to shape the next round of dough. "I think it will be a hit."

"Then I'd be thrilled to have it on your non-menu." It made her heart happy to be able to do something to pay back the kindness of being allowed to work in the kitchen. Her brain settled into default mode, and she lost herself in the rhythms of cooking.

When the last pie was covered and they'd used two thirds of the sauce, she went to check the dough for the rolls. Perfect, she could work with this. "Put those in the oven for about twenty minutes or until the top is beginning to turn golden."

"You got it." Kayce grabbed two pies and took them to the oven while she got busy rolling until she had a rectangle.

"Can you melt me a couple of sticks of butter?"

"Somehow it kinda feels like you're running the kitchen this morning."

Shit, was she overstepping? Her hands paused with the rolling pin in midair. "I'm sorry, I forgot it wasn't my kitchen."

"Girl, don't you worry." Kayce handed over the butter. "I'm just teasing you."

"Phew, because I often don't see if I'm doing it, so tell me if I annoy you." She poured the butter all over the rolled-out pastry then sprinkled generously with brown sugar and cinnamon.

"Deal." He went back to the stovetop to finish putting together what looked like a cowboy breakfast casserole. "Do you frost the rolls?"

"When they're cooked, yes." Starting at one end, she moved her fingers along the longest edge of the pastry, turning the edge toward her as she went. "Do you have any flavored moonshine?"

"Moonshine? For the rolls?"

"For the frosting." Back and forth she moved, rolling the

gooey goodness into a log. "If not, I can doctor a plain version of vodka if you don't have moonshine."

"You might have to ask Jeep about moonshine, he normally brings some from back east."

"You think he still has some?" She cut the log into rounds and placed into the buttered pan. Those could rise for another bit before she put them in the oven.

"Call him and ask." Kayce pointed to the wall next to the door. "Use the phone there, hit number three, seven, four. If he's at his desk, he'll answer, if not, then you can call his cell."

"I can do that?"

"Sure, don't see why not."

"If he's busy, I don't want to disturb him."

"Don't make me call him and tell him that you were afraid to."

"I'm not afraid of..." She cut herself off. She'd missed that Kayce was teasing her again. She did a quick wash and dry of her hands before picking up the phone and dialing the number.

"Kayce? Is Willow okay?"

"It's me."

"Sunshine."

Lord, she loved how he said her name, if she'd been on her own, she'd have squeezed her thighs together. But there was no way she was doing that where eagle-eyed Kayce might see. That growl in Cormack's voice... WOW, momma, was she tempted. "Hi."

"You okay, Sunshine?"

"Yes, I'm looking for moonshine."

"Umm, it's not even six thirty in the morning."

"Not for me, silly, for the frosting. I'm making cinnamon

rolls and need some butter pecan moonshine for the cream cheese. Do you have any left from last time you were home?"

"There's a jar of Old Smokey in the cupboard over the fridge in our suite."

"Yes! Thank you."

"You're welcome." He sounded ridiculously pleased with something. She wasn't entirely sure what, but she'd figure it out eventually.

"I gotta go, I have cream frosting to make."

"Sunshine?"

"Yes?"

"Save some frosting for me."

"Um, okay."

Oh, man, didn't that just make her heart beat a little faster.

"I have a plan for that later."

It beat a little harder, too, because she loved when his voice got low and rough like that.

"I...um..."

"Willow, are these ready?"

She'd almost jumped out of her skin at the sound of Kayce's call. "Igottagobye." All her words ran together, and she slammed down the phone on Cormack. Could it still be called slamming down when you were hanging the phone on the wall? She didn't know, didn't care either. How could he make her so frick-fracking flustered just by telling her to hold back some frosting for him? She might hate to admit it, but she was a little relieved at the interruption, or she would probably have embarrassed herself. Correction... would have embarrassed herself for sure... damn, the man. "Yes. Put them on the counter please and put a thin layer of sauce over the top, add grated cheese, and some of those breadcrumbs.

I'll be right back." She saw the confused look on Kayce's face. "I'm just grabbing moonshine."

"Okay, do I put them back in again when the sauce is on?"

"Yes, for about twenty minutes, but I'll be back before then," she promised. She would go grab the moonshine and whip some into her cream cheese frosting.

CHAPTER TWELVE

CORMACK STRETCHED his neck to one side and then the other, trying to release the tightness. Almost thirty years of jumping out of planes, getting shot and injured was hard on a man's body. He pushed in the door to the dining room and sniffed.

"Man, something smells fucking awesome."

"Right?" He glanced over his shoulder at Lucifer *Devil-Man* Brady. "My girl's cooking."

"Did Nem have a come to Jesus meeting with you yet?"

"Nope." He winced internally. He knew Dalton wouldn't leave it much longer. While they'd been going over the mission specs at HQ earlier, he'd seen his boss open and close his mouth a couple of times. Every time Nemesis looked at him, his eyes narrowed and his face darkened. Jeep was fully aware how pissed off Nemesis was, but he could go fuck himself sideways with a cactus plant if he thought anything he had to say was going to make him stay away from Willow. She was his, he was hers. End of the fucking discussion. "That joy is yet to come."

They crossed to the counter and grabbed mugs, filling them with coffee. Cormack took a sip then handed it to

Lucifer. "Bring that to the table for me, will ya? I'm just going to grab Willow from the kitchen."

"Sure."

He was already at the kitchen door before Lucifer had finished speaking. He pushed open the swinging doors and leaned his shoulder against the frame just to watch her. Fuck, she made his heart race like he was a fucking teenager. She hadn't seen him yet as her back was to him as she ladled something over some huge fluffy rolls on a pan. Sometime since he'd left here earlier, she'd knotted her hair on top of her head and stuck a pen through it. Which told him she'd been working out how to fiddle with a recipe. He nodded at Kayce and waited for Willow to put the bowl on the counter. "Is that moonshine frosting, Sunshine?"

"Sugar." She jumped at the sound of his voice and whirled around, telling him she'd been lost in her own world again. Good, she needed to be, and wasn't it freaking adorable that she still used sugar to replace the word shit? Others may think it was ridiculous for a grown woman to not want to swear, but he thought it was cute as fuck. "Don't scare me like that."

"Sorry, Sunshine." She was the shot of moonshine he craved right now. She was always going to be what he needed to settle the disquiet and rage which often warred inside him. He allowed the swinging door his body had been holding open to shut and stalked across the kitchen to her. "You finished with that?" He nodded to the ladle in her hand.

"I…um…yes."

"Good." He took the spoon from her and tossed it into the bowl of frosting. Then picked her up, placed her on the counter, and pressed his mouth to hers. Her arms wrapped around his neck, pulling him closer as she kissed him back. His dick hardened behind the zipper of his camo pants. As soon as his lips touched hers, relief and happiness flooded his soul, and the rest of the world faded into the background.

She stiffened beneath his kiss for a second before softening as he stroked his fingers through her hair at her nape. Fuck, she tasted so damn sweet. He slid his tongue into her mouth, rubbing it over hers. The flavors of pecans, cream cheese, and moonshine exploded over his tastebuds, telling him she'd tasted as she'd worked. "Mm," he groaned softly into her mouth.

Willow against him, she skinned her hands up his back. She wanted him as much as he wanted her and wasn't that a fucking awesome feeling.

"Ugh, guys, seriously, that's my damn counter, get a room already."

Kayce's grumbling in the background finally filtered into his brain and he gentled the kiss. He had to force himself to pull his lips from hers. He could kiss her for a lifetime and never need a drop of air to breathe. He leaned his forehead against hers, keeping his mouth where he could inhale every breath she exhaled. The world was a shit place to be sometimes, but right here in this kitchen, with his woman in his arms, all was right in his world. He'd take it. "You ready for breakfast?"

"Yeah." She breathed out the word on a soft breath he felt down to his toes. She tapped his sides, telling him to let her get down.

He stroked one thumb over her cheek, rubbing away a smudge of flour as pink darkened her cheeks, telling him she'd just realized they had an audience. She touched her fingers to her lips, drawing his attention to her mouth. Satisfaction filled him when he could see they were swollen from his kisses. He loved that she looked like he'd spent hours kissing her.

"Dude, get out of my kitchen," Kayce said. "The only thing meant to be on fire in here is my fucking grills."

"Oh my God," Willow whispered softly. She pressed her head into his chest briefly before wriggling against him. He knew she meant it to be to tell him that she wanted to get down from her perch on the counter. But it made his dick even harder if that was possible. "Let me down."

He pressed one last fast kiss to her mouth and reluctantly lifted her off the counter and placed her on the floor. "I'm stealing her for breakfast."

"Out." Kayce pointed to the door. "I'm gonna need to stock up on bleach if you two are putting on displays like that every damn morning."

"I get to come back?"

Over Willow's head he narrowed his eyes at Kayce and nodded. He better say yes, or he was going to shove that bleach he'd just been talking about up his ass.

"Yes." Kayce took off his ball cap, ran his fingers over his head, and replaced the cap. "Of course you can come back." He pointed a finger at Cormack. "Jeep can't."

"If my girl's here, I get to be here."

"My kitchen, my rules."

What the hell did he think he was going to do, fuck her on the counter? Didn't he know there was no way in hell that he'd ever allow anyone to see his sunshine like that?

"Cormack?" Willow nudged her elbow into his belly. "Can we figure that out later?"

"N—" He cut himself off when he caught sight of her face. Shit, he was embarrassing her, he hadn't meant to do that. "Sure, Sunshine." He scowled darkly at Kayce. He could beat the shit out of him later. Fucker. "Come on, let's get you some food."

"I've been picking all morning as we've been cooking."

"Then come sit with me while I eat."

"That I can do."

He placed a hand on her lower back and ushered her out of the kitchen and into the dining room. "You want some coffee?"

"Oh, I have some." She turned back to the kitchen. "Let me grab my mug."

As much as he wanted to follow her back into the kitchen, he let her go and instead went to grab a tray and some food. He loaded up with two plates of the Italian dish she'd made and added a side plate of strawberries and another of pancakes and bacon. As soon as the cinnamon rolls were brought out, he was gonna snag a couple of those, too.

"That's a lot of food." Willow came out of the kitchen just as he reached the end of the line with the insulated mug he'd left near the coffee machine in their suite earlier.

"I'm a growing boy." He gestured her toward the table they'd eaten at last night, where Lucifer and the rest of Alpha team were seated.

"Growing boy, my ass," Lucifer muttered. "Pain in the ass, maybe." He pulled out the chair next to him and nodded to Willow. "Have a seat. I don't bite."

"Luc, if you keep flirting with my girl," Cormack muttered. "I'm telling Rome, and I'm pretty sure he does bite."

"Yeah." Lucifer, the fucking bastard, grinned at him. "I'm pretty sure he bites, too."

Willow glanced at him, and when he nodded, she sat in the chair Lucifer had indicated. He placed the tray on the table and sat next to her.

"What's the pie thing?" Snow leaned in from her seat on the other side of him to sniff at his plate. "It smells like pizza but doesn't look like any I've seen."

"Try it," Cormack advised. He went through the process of putting some of his food on a separate plate and left it near Willow's hand. "Willow made it, it's a Sicilian dish."

"Gimme." Snow reached with her fork and Cormack smacked at her hand. "Did you not just hear me say I'm a growing boy and I need all this food?" He leaned down so he could curl his arm around his plate while he hunched over it, protecting it from scavengers like their team sniper.

"Ow."

He whipped his head around so fast at the sound of a scream from Lucifer, he almost did himself an injury. His eyes widened at the sight of the fork sticking out of his hand. The stricken look on Willow's face told him everything he needed to know. "Don't touch her food, man." He bit down on his lip hard to stop laughing out loud. That was the last thing Sunshine needed. He draped one arm across the back of her chair, offering comfort and support, telling her she wasn't in trouble without drawing attention to it. "She's possessive over her food."

"I thought it was yours." Lucifer winced as he pulled the fork out of his hand and pressed a napkin to the bleeding spots.

"What's mine is hers." He shrugged. It was better they all got used to it fucking fast.

"I'm so sorry, I didn't thin…"

"Nope, don't you dare say sorry to that jackass." Cormack stroked his fingers over her shoulder. "He should know better than to try and stick his fork in someone else's plate. It's not the first time he's been stabbed for that, and it won't be the last." He tried to reassure her, but from the stiffness in her shoulders he knew he probably wasn't having much success.

From where he sat with his back to the wall, he saw trouble coming before anyone else noticed it. Buddha, Dalton and Lina's malamute puppy, came racing into the dining room. Running as fast as his three-month-old legs could go, dragging something behind him. Just as he rounded a table, his back legs going faster than the front, Buddha tripped over his feet and skidded across the floor, coming to a stop next to Willow's chair.

"Oh, who are you, cutie?"

He lifted his arm so she could push back her chair and pick up the puppy. Buddha stared at her for a heartbeat before he spat out the bullet belt and proceeded to wash her face with exuberant puppy kisses which made his whole-body wriggle.

"I'll take that." Jeep snagged the belt before it hit the floor. His eyes widened when he saw it was mostly filled. Someone was going to be very pissed indeed.

"Where is he? The little shit." The door slammed off the wall hard enough to bounce back and hit Rexar on the chin as he stormed into the room.

Willow whipped her head around to face him. "Don't you dare call him that, Uncle Rex, he's just a baby." She pressed her nose to the puppy's and smooched him. "Aren't you just the cutest thing?" She baby talked to the puppy, completely ignoring the towering grumpy man stalking toward them.

"He fucking took my belt."

"Language," Willow snapped at him. "You shouldn't have left it lying around then, should you?"

God, she was fucking beautiful. And if he was tempted to laugh out loud at the stunned look on Rexar's face, then nobody needed to know it.

"You need to look after your things better, Uncle Rex. It's dangerous to leave ammo and gear laying all over the place. Papa taught you better." She flipped the puppy over onto his back and scratched all along his belly. When the puppy's hind leg started air scratching, she concentrated on that one spot, all the while ignoring Rexar and baby talking softly to Buddha.

Fuck, was it wrong to be jealous of a puppy? Didn't matter if it was, because right now, he was so fucking jealous of this puppy.

"Give me that." Rexar leaned over Willow's shoulder and made a grab for the belt, but he was quicker and snatched it out of his brother in arm's reach.

"Apologize to Willow."

"And to the puppy." God, he fucking loved her. Going by the gasping-for-air-goldfish impression Rexar was doing, he was about two point five seconds away from losing his shit even more than he already had. He'd known the asshole a long time, and he'd never seen him go quite that shade of purple.

"He fucking took ammo, Willow…"

"And I told you my papa taught you better than to swear in the presence of a lady."

"There's only one lady at this table, and she's holding the as...butthead who stole my ammo."

"Excuse yourself." Willow stopped scratching the puppy long enough to point at Snow. "She is also a lady."

"My fucking ass." As soon as the words were out of his mouth, Rexar pinched his fingers into the corner of his eyes and winced.

"And aren't you the male equivalent of PMS today," Snow deadpanned.

He swallowed hard, trying not to laugh, but didn't quite manage it and sent coffee spewing across the table.

"Yeah, buddy, I'd be wincing, too, if I were you because now you've done it."

It was only when Sensei spoke that Cormack realized how

quiet the whole room had gone. Every freaking member of three teams, and each and every one of the hands and a couple he didn't recognize were staring at the show his girl and Rexar was putting on.

"Apologize to the lady right now, Uncle Rexar, or I'm going to make you regret it," Willow threatened softly, just as he saw Dalton and Lina arrive.

Dalton leaned against the door and drew his wife against his chest, folding his arms across her. Jeep raised an eyebrow in query, silently asking if the boss wanted him to step in, but when Nemesis just lifted a shoulder, he winked in response and turned back to the argument.

"Go on, asshat, apologize." Snow leaned back in her chair. "I'm waiting. Do your best, or Jeep's woman will make you pay." She grinned wide at Rexar. "She looks like she could be creative."

"Go ahead, Mitchell," Dalton called from the door. "Apologize to the ladies for using foul language, just like Eli taught us."

Once again, Cormack almost spat out his coffee, and Lucifer had to pound him on the back a couple of times to ensure he didn't choke when it went down the wrong pipe. Wasn't that a hoot... Nemesis Knight telling someone to apologize for swearing.

"I should have ordered popcorn for breakfast," Lucifer whispered soft enough that he knew only he heard him, or possibly Sensei on the other side of him, considering the way he was snickering like a schoolgirl after spotting her first crush on the way to class. "This show is better than the movies."

The puppy, on hearing Dalton's voice, wriggled to get down and as soon as his paws touched the floor, he grumbled low in his throat at Rexar's boot before shooting across the room toward Dalton and Lina, woo-wooing and telling them all about his adventure.

"Apologize, Mitchell," Dalton ordered.

Lina bent down to pick up Buddha and snuggled him into her chest.

"Sorry, ma'am," Rexar spat the words at Snow through gritted teeth and snatched the bullet belt from where Cormack had left it on the table.

"Fuck you very much," Snow muttered after his retreating back, then held her hands up when Willow opened her mouth. "Sorry, Willow, I hate being called ma'am."

"Me, too." Willow's shoulders relaxed and Cormack released the breath he hadn't known he'd been holding. Her eyes widened when she glanced over her shoulder, and everyone immediately turned back to focusing on their plates. He knew she hated to cause a scene just about as much as she hated swearing. She leaned into his arm, and he pressed a kiss to the top of her head. He met Dalton's gaze and shook his head when his boss opened his mouth and shut it again when Lina slammed her elbow into his ribs, apparently telling him to shut up.

"I remember you." Lina sat in the chair Dalton pulled out for her with the puppy in her lap. "You're Eli's daughter."

"Yes." Willow nodded. "I remember you, too, although I only met you maybe twice."

"Yes, the last time at your dad's final send-off." Lina scooted her chair closer to Willow to make room for Dalton to place one he'd borrowed from the next table over. They were going to have to increase the size of the table to fit everyone at this rate. "I'm sorry you lost him. He was a good man and a great warrior."

"That he was." Willow turned in her seat so she could rest her back against his side.

He spotted one of Kayce's kitchen staff putting cinnamon rolls onto the counter. "How many trays of rolls did you make?" he asked her.

"A dozen with a dozen rolls on each."

"I'll be right back."

"Okay."

He could already see the people at the tables nearest the counter twisting in their seats to see what had been brought out. Hungry savages, the lot of them. He hurried across the room and grabbed a full tray for their table. A dozen should be enough for them all. He paused mid step… nope, a dozen would never be enough, and retraced his steps to the counter to add another six rolls to the tray.

"Cinnamon rolls?"

"Yes, Boss, cinnamon rolls." He leaned over his chair to place the rolls on the center of the table, putting one on Willow's plate and two on his own before sitting back down. "Willow made them."

"We're keeping her… right?" Sensei grabbed a roll from the tray and brought it to his nose, inhaling deep before he took a large bite and groaned. "Yum. What's the frosting?"

"Butter pecan moonshine and cream cheese." Willow grabbed a butter knife and cut her roll in quarters before picking up one and nibbling on it.

"Yup." Cormack ignored Dalton's grunt and instead winked at Willow. "I sure am keeping her. It remains to be seen if I will allow her to cook for y'all though."

"You don't allow me to do anything." Willow raised both eyebrows and dared him to argue with her.

Nope, not happening. He'd installed his brain cells this morning, thank you. There was no way he was going to be the talk of the ranch. His escapade with the damn bull would hopefully get lost in the gossip of Willow taking on Rexar and winning, even if that winning came with Nemesis backing her up. "Right, I meant as long as she wants to, she can, if she doesn't then she doesn't have to."

"How much moonshine is in them?" Dalton eyed the roll his pregnant wife had just picked up as if he were about to smack it out of her hand.

"Only a couple of tablespoons."

"I'm eating it." Lina scowled at her husband. "The baby has a craving."

"Princess."

"Don't you princess me," Lina warned. "I'm pregnant, not sick, and I'm eating the damn roll."

Cormack didn't bother to hide the smirk he sent Dalton's way. It was fucking awesome to see his big bad boss trying to figure out how he could put his foot down while knowing it just wasn't possible.

"I like how you have your man trained, Willow, mine's a pain in the butt." Lina tugged the edge of the roll free and unwound it out into a long line. "It's smart to train them early, so they don't end up like this one."

"Girl, Grumpy is a work in progress, much like your puppy."

"Grumpy, I like that."

"Well, if he's going to call me Sunshine, then he gets to be Grumpy."

Sitting here listening to his girl chatter and talk to Dalton's woman as they munched on breakfast did happy things to his heart. This shit right here was what he hadn't known was missing. Maybe, just maybe if she made friends here, then he could persuade her to stay for good.

"Grumpy…" Lina handed a tiny piece of roll with no frosting to Buddha and scratched his ears when he wooed in response from his place on her lap.

"Where did you go when you left?"

Whoa, that was out of the left field, but he should have known Willow would be protective of her uncle. She'd had seen the shit he went through after his wife disappeared. But she hadn't been around since Lina came back into their lives and hadn't seen Dalton had stopped living for war-fighting and had started breathing and living for love, fun, and laughter again. But she would see it and she'd know Lina being back was a good thing for her pseudo uncle.

Lina slowly chewed on the food in her mouth as if she was trying to think of a diplomatic way to answer. "That's a story for when they go out tomorrow."

Willow sucked in a harsh breath and turned to look at him with her eyes huge in her head. "You're going out?"

"Shit." Now he was the one wincing. Not only had he said shit, but he'd also not been the one to tell her there was a mission in the planning. "Yes, Sunshine, I was going to talk to you when we were done here."

"Crap." Lina looked stricken, for a badass she really did have a soft heart. "I didn't know you hadn't talked to her about it yet."

"It's okay." Willow lifted one shoulder. He could tell she was trying to not let the others see her worry. But under the table he could see her fingers shake. Damn it, he'd wanted to talk to her first. But he couldn't and wouldn't be pissed with Lina either. This was their world. This was what they did. Willow knew it. They all knew it. But just because she knew it didn't mean each trip or mission didn't worry the hell out of her.

"Are you finished eating?" he whispered the words against the side of her head.

"Yes."

"C'mon." He pushed back his chair and helped her out of

hers. "You should sleep some, you've been up since all the clocks."

"All the clocks?"

"Yeah, early as heck." He nodded to the others and led her from the room, catching her as she tripped over her own feet as they went through the door into the hallway.

"Fabulous, now they'll all see I'm an awkward klutz and I won't be allowed near the kitchen again."

"Sunshine, you're not awkward, you're cute and sexy and mine." Jeep tugged her under his arm as they walked side by side up the stairs. "After the food you provided this morning, there is zero chance of you being banned from the kitchen. Kayce will have a riot on his hands if he tries it."

"Oh."

"Yeah, oh." He dropped a kiss on her lips. Did it make him an asshole that he didn't want to talk? Probably. There were so many other things he wanted to do to Willow and talking was way down the end of the list.

CHAPTER THIRTEEN

Seriously, you tripped over your own feet again?

Silently, she yelled at herself for being a klutz in her head. She couldn't even walk across a frick-fracking room without making an idiot out of herself. She needed to come with a warning sign or one of those beeping alarms trucks had for reversing to warn everyone to stay out of her way in case she bumped their elbow just as they put a coffee mug to their mouth.

How freaking embarrassing. And did you see how they were all staring at you?

Heat and fire climbed up her face, inch by inch, until she was sure she'd be able to light a candle without a match.

"Hey." Cormack tugged on her hand. "Sunshine?"

"Hm?"

He pulled them to a stop and crowded her against the wall next to the suite door. "Hey, baby, stop it."

"Stop what?"

He tucked his finger under her chin and tilted her head up. It took a couple of heartbeats before she lifted her eyelids and peered up at him. "Stop reliving the five seconds before you left the dining room."

"How do you know that's what I'm doing?"

"What is it you told me once?" He pressed one arm against the wall over her head, widened his stance, and pressed his body against hers. "That your head makes you relive everything, over and over until you're convinced you made an idiot out of yourself?"

God, she loved the weight of him against her. When he did this it was like he surrounded her. But could he not remember every tiny little thing she mentioned in an email? "Um." He expected her to think when his mouth hovered over hers like that? She was meant to engage brain cells and have a conversation? Yeah, no, that would just not be possible today. She pressed a kiss to the side of his mouth, lingering a second before pulling back.

"You're trying to distract me."

"Is it working?"

"I was the one distracting you."

"Semantics." She pressed a kiss to the other side of his mouth, and that growl...WOW. She watched his mouth. Would he take over? Would he see where she was going with this? Last night had been the first night that they'd been together after a mission where he'd just curled up around her and gone to sleep. She didn't know what to make of that. Did it mean he wasn't attracted to her anymore?

"Baby," Cormack warned. "We need to talk about the mission."

"Unless you're leaving in the next hour, the mission can wait." She tugged at his shirt and slid her hands up his back, her fingers stroking and kneading along his skin.

"Fuck." Cormack lifted her off her feet, easily taking her weight. She wrapped her legs around his waist, crossing them behind his back, locking her in place. From where she sat on his waist she could feel his growing hard-on against her because every swipe of her tongue across his lips had his dick jerking against his pants, each nudge she felt pushing against her. Yum.

She wrapped her arms around his neck as he planted one hand under her bottom and slapped the other against the lock on his door. She did her best to distract him as he got them in the door and kicked it shut behind them.

Slowly, he walked them down the hallway and into the bedroom and lay her on the bed like she was the most precious cargo in his world and followed her down onto the mattress. He skimmed his hands up her sides and down again, then across her stomach, pausing as he did to press a kiss to her mouth while his hands rested on her belly. Even just that touch made her ache. It made her yearn for things she shouldn't want, but she did want it. She wasn't going to lie to herself. She wanted Cormack, wanted his babies. Wanted to build a world, a family, a life with him. But to do that she had to be able to survive his work. She couldn't and wouldn't stop him from doing the job he was born to do. Her man was a protector to the core, asking him to change that would be like telling him to stop being right-handed.

She wanted to be a better wife than her own had been to her father.

He hasn't asked you to marry him.

Shut your mouth.

A girl could dream… right?

She also wanted him to be inside her again, soon. She needed for him to settle the disquiet in her soul.

"I want to taste that sweet little pussy again."

There he was, when he was getting descriptive, then she knew his brain wasn't in charge. She smiled up at him. Him bringing her here to Montana was like driving down the road of life with their future stretched out in front of them. Deciding which direction to go at the crossroads would decide their future. She didn't want him to let her go… or to send her home. Until just this moment, with him resting between her thighs, his mouth pressing kisses to her throat, and her fingers buried into the back of his head, she hadn't known how much her own house had become a prison, keeping her trapped in the past.

He peered down at her, and she loved the soft look on his face. Did he even know how gorgeous he was to her? She trailed her fingers over his cheeks, mapping every line, and that seriously sexy dimple that appeared on the left side when he smiled.

He dipped down and pressed his mouth to hers again. His tongue pushed past her lips, licking, sucking, and devouring her mouth like a starving man. Taking them over the line where stopping would be possible.

"Don't stop," she whispered softly between kisses.

"Not planning on stopping, baby." He lifted off her to pull her yoga pants down, growling in approval at her lack of underwear a moment later. She watched him from under lowered lids as he stared at her pussy. And yes, she could call it a pussy, because from experience, the word vagina was way too prim and proper for what she hoped was the delights to come.

"Fuck." He buried his face in between her thighs, sniffing and smelling her scent.

Her whole body clenched at the groan of approval. She bunched her fingers into the covers, needing something to hold on to.

"You're wet, soaked, for me." He licked through her folds, tasting her, humming as she relished the sensations his tongue sent sparking through her, like little shots of electricity.

Her back arched off the bed and she gave a moan so garbled that even she couldn't decipher it.

"Someday I'm going to have a mirror on that ceiling." He lifted his head long enough to jerk his chin upward. "So you can see how beautiful your pussy is as I do this." He parted her folds and licked her from front to back, dipping his tongue inside her channel, swirling it around before withdrawing and pushing in again for another taste.

He wanted to talk. How was he talking? She could barely breathe, never mind find the word for a full-blown conversation on decorating the room. She lifted her hips as much as she could, pushing herself against his mouth. Wanting... no, needing more. "Please."

"Please what, baby?"

"More."

"More what? Talking?" He moved over her, his clothes rubbing over her sensitive flesh as he covered her body with his. Resting on his elbows, he brushed the hair back from her face. "I love having you here in my bed."

"Why are you talking?" She pouted at him. Not that she thought she did a very good job of it as he chuckled in response.

"More kissing?" He pressed a fast kiss to her lips.

"You're teasing me."

"Mmh, I like teasing you." He used his hands to catch the end of her t-shirt and pulled it up her body and over her head. "You blush all pretty when I do." He tangled the t-shirt in her hands and pressed them into the pillow behind her. "Keep them there?"

She nodded yes, she would do as he asked if it meant he went back to driving her crazy.

"That's my girl." He pressed a trail of kisses down her throat, across her collarbone, and down her body, pausing to lick over one nipple. "Damn, I forgot the frosting." He sucked her nipple into his mouth and rolled the other between his thumb and forefinger, making her back arch. He released the nipple in his mouth with a pop before swapping to the other.

"Cormack."

"Hm?" He glanced at her from under hooded lids.

She shifted restlessly under him. "Please…"

"Please what?"

The meanie was totally laughing at her. Teasing her. She could see it in the way the corners of his eyes crinkled. "You know what."

"Nope." He flicked his thumbnail over her nipples. "You gotta say the words, baby."

"You're mean."

"You love it."

Yes, she did love it, not that she was telling him that though. Her girly bits were totally on board with the teasing, but when he teased and didn't *do* something, anything to said girly bits, it made her crazy. "Cormack." She put as much warning into her tone as she could. If it weren't for it would deprive her of the fun to come, she'd get up off this bed right this minute.

"Willow."

"Do something. You're making me insane." If her hands were free, she'd smack them into his sides and dig her fingers into his ribs, tickling him, just where she knew it would make him jump. But she'd already promised to keep them over her head. Dang it.

"I like making you insane." He tugged and pulled on her nipples, cupping her breasts with both hands and pressing them together while he swiped his tongue across both nipples.

"It turns me on." He pressed his groin harder against her, allowing her to feel how hard he was through his pants.

She lifted her hips, pressing against him, trying to get some relief for her aching clit. But the butthead pulled back just enough that she couldn't quite get the friction she needed. Frustration bubbled up from her belly and she glared at him. "Kiss my clit, please."

"Well, why didn't you say so?" It should be freaking illegal how sexy that smirk of his was. There was no way on earth she was telling him that right now though. Because if he didn't do as she asked right this second, she was taking matters into her own hands.

As if he heard the grumbling in her head, he pressed one last kiss to each nipple and slid down to settle his shoulders between her thighs.

Finally, maybe now they could get this show on the road. If that made her needy, she no longer cared.

He leaned in and blew on her sensitive skin. She could feel the goose bumps as she shuddered at the heat of his breath. When he finally closed the distance between his lips and her clit, she moaned out loud. He circled the little bud over and over until she was writhing on the bed.

He pulled his mouth away and she cried out in protest but quieted again when he pressed his thumb to her clit. "I love seeing you like this. Spread out for me."

She didn't have the words to tell him that she thought this was her favorite place in the world to be. What he was doing to her had stolen every word she had.

"I want to be inside you." Cormack ran his thumb down her pussy and over her opening. As soon as she felt him dip inside, she clenched around him.

"But I don't want to rush this." Cormack swapped his thumb for two fingers and pressed the heel of his hand against her clit as he began a slow slide in and out of her. "I want to take my time with you, and I don't want it to be over too soon."

She tossed her head from side to side; she didn't want it to be over anytime soon either. But she needed more. His fingers grazed over a spot deep inside her. "Cormack," she moaned. "There, oh my, just there."

"So fucking beautiful." He turned his hand while keeping his fingers buried deep inside, and once again put his mouth to her clit, sucking it hard, then lapping it with his tongue.

She could feel her orgasm building and chased it, lifting her hips and rocking against his mouth and fingers. When he sucked harder and lapped faster, she knew there was no holding it back, as he was determined to bring her to climax, and she was determined to let him.

"I fucking love eating you out," Cormack muttered against her as she exploded around him. He pulled his fingers free and pushed his tongue into her pussy, licking, sucking, and tasting. "I love the taste of you in my mouth."

As her orgasm started to fade, he pulled back and swiped one hand over his mouth. She should probably be embarrassed or something that she could see her juices glistening on his chin, but it only made her ache more. He pressed one kiss to each thigh and stood to unzip his camo.

He stepped away from the bed, and she tried to capture him with her legs. "No, don't leave."

"I'm not going anywhere." He leaned down and braced himself over her with a hand on either side of her head to kiss her thoroughly on the lips. "I'm just getting a condom."

The flavor and taste of them both on his lips exploded over her tastebuds. She loved when he did this, kissed her after making her come with his mouth. It somehow made them feel more connected, more intimate. "No, I got the shot like we talked about."

"Damn." He squeezed his eyes shut. "I've never gone bare before. I've always gloved up."

"I know." She'd been bitching at him for slowing things down, and here she was throwing him a curveball.

"If we do this, do you know what it means?"

She tugged at her hands, freeing them from the t-shirt which restrained them, so she could cup his face. "Yes, it means I'm yours."

"It means, baby, that if we do this, I'm never letting you go. You're mine, and you stay here with me."

She blinked at him, had he always sounded so…possessive… so determined? Despite the protests from her girlie bits at the delay, she gave his demand the consideration it deserved before nodding.

"Words." He was so still he'd give the David statue a run for its money.

"I'm yours until you tell me to go."

"Never gonna happen." He claimed her mouth before she could answer and reached between them to pull his dick out of his pants before sliding home.

It felt so different to have him enter her without a condom. Hotter. Harder. Yummier. Closer. And a million other sensations she could never hope to describe. Her pussy clamped around him, trying to suck him deeper inside her. "Oh, god, that's so good."

"Fuck, yes." Cormack pushed deep inside her; his hips pressed to her pussy as he buried himself to the root.

"Move." She shifted her hips, widening them as much as possible to give him more room. "Please."

"Yeah," he grunted, dragging his dick out of her almost to the point where it slipped free before pushing back in hard.

He set a slow pace to start, then increased to a pounding rhythm. Each thrust shifted her up the bed, and he wrapped his hands around her waist to keep her in place with his pants around his knees as he fucked her hard and fast.

He grunted every time he bottomed out inside her, his balls slapping off her skin, the sounds mingled with her moans, adding to the symphony which was somehow wilder, hotter, and everything more than it had ever been between them before. She caught his gaze. His eyes never left hers, boring into her, ramping up the heat between them. Their connection had always been epic from the very first, but now it was undeniable. *I love him.*

It had never been like this between them. Not even their first time when he'd pinned her arms behind her back, spanked her butt, and made her come harder than she'd even known was possible. Three times. Three freaking times.

He pressed one hand against her breast, flicking and rolling the nipple. The bite of pain sending her over the edge again. He leaned over her to claim her lips, his hips kept moving as she spasmed around him.

"Mine."

His possessive growl sent a full body shudder through her as he spilled inside her. In that moment she realized that even if she wanted to walk away, she'd be leaving her heart after her because as much as she was his, he was hers. "Yes, yours. I promise."

CHAPTER FOURTEEN

"Mмн." Her kiss was so soft, so perfect. Just what his body needed to settle after the euphoria of the orgasm. He carefully pulled out of her. "One sec." He went to the bathroom for a damp cloth and hurried back to carefully clean up the mess. He pressed a kiss to each of her thighs and discarded the cloth on the floor next to the bed, his t-shirt followed behind it. He needed to lay next to her, skin on skin. "You okay, Sunshine?"

"Yes." She curled into him, and he lifted his arm so her head could rest on his chest. "I love hearing your heartbeat."

"It's a repetitive sound."

"This one I like."

"Mm, good, because stopping it may be kind of awkward." He stroked his fingers through her hair. "Might hurt, too."

"Don't even joke about it, Grumpy."

"I can assure you, grumpy is something I definitely am not right now." He freaking loved that just the slightest reminder of what they'd just done could make her whole-body blush. How could someone who made his dick stand to attention with just the barest hint of her scent or her voice be so fucking adorable?

"It's mean of you to mention it." She smacked his belly with her palm.

His dick twitched between his legs, and he squeezed his eyes shut, willing his second head to behave. He was a dick, no pun intended, for even twitching, never mind hardening as his body was attempting to do. *Stop it,* he warned himself.

"You're going out?"

He'd wondered how long it would take for her brain to come back online and for the question to be asked.

"Yeah, just a routine job."

"You remember who you're talking to, right?" She shifted, putting one leg over his and sliding half across him, resting her chin on his chest as she looked into his face. "You don't need to downplay it."

"Seriously, all the intel we have says it's a routine personal protection detail."

"Where?"

"I can't tell you that."

She chewed on the corner of her lip for a couple of heart-beats. "That's what I thought."

He ran his thumb along her mouth. "This is what I do, Sunshine, if it's something you can't handle, then you better tell me now."

"And if I can't?"

Shit, what could an old washed-up warrior like him do if he didn't go to stupid places around the globe with a team at his six, a rifle on a sling, and protection in his soul? "Then I'm gonna need to talk to Nemesis about having a role here at base instead of going in the field." He could deal without going out again... right? No, probably not, he'd been born to be a warrior, it was in his blood going back generations. He didn't know how to be anything but a warrior. For her, for his sunshine, he'd give it one hell of a shot.

Her eyes widened at his words, then she squeezed them shut and shook her head, her chin rubbing off his chest. "I can't believe you said that."

"Huh?" Okay, now he was all kinds of confused. Did she want him to stop going out or not?

"I wasn't asking you to stop doing what you love." She tapped her finger over his heart. "Being a soldier is as much a part of who you are as your dark hair is."

"Dark hair goes gray." He rubbed the corner of his right eye with his index finger. "Mine's already gray."

"Probably from spending so much time with me," she quipped, then wrapped her fingers into his. "I'm not going to lie, you going out scares me more than I can ever explain, but if you stop because of me, then how is that fair? You are you, and being a soldier is part of who you are."

"SEALs aren't soldiers, baby, we're better."

"Cockier, too."

"Damn straight." He sobered. "But war is a young man's game, maybe it's time I think of settling down and doing something else." He could do that for her. He would do that for her. After decades of jumping out of planes and scrambling up and down mountains and through jungles, his knees already told him the weather forecast with a better accuracy than the dude who you hoped didn't show up in your hometown during a hurricane.

"This is your home, your family." She lifted both their hands so she could gesture toward the window. "You are as much a part of them as they are a part of you. I couldn't live with myself if you stopped being who you are because I'm being silly."

"Baby, you know the cost of war just as much as I do.

You've spent your whole life living as a member of the family..." He tugged his hand free of her fingers to rub up and down her back. He struggled to concentrate on the conversation. There was only so much focus a man could have when a sexy as hell woman was sprawled across his chest... naked.

She placed her finger over his lips, stopping his words. "If you stop because of me, then I'm going back to Virginia."

His hand stilled on her back when the impact of her words filtered into his brain. "You didn't say home?"

"No, I didn't." Her eyes softened as much as her smile. "On purpose."

"Tell me what it means?"

Confusion crossed her face. "I don't understand."

"If Virginia's not home, where is?"

"Oh." She lowered her eyes to where her fingers played with the hair on his chest. He waited, not pushing, giving her time to get her thoughts together.

Please let it mean what I think it does.

He'd be lying to himself if he didn't think her answer wouldn't determine their future. He'd also be lying to himself if he didn't need and want to hear her tell him that she wanted her home to be here with him. Was it selfish to hope she'd walk away from everything she owned, and everything she'd ever known for him? Yes, yes it was... did it matter? Nope, he couldn't make himself think it did right now either.

"Um."

He felt her swallow against his chest, and his heart nosedived into his toes. "It's okay, Sunshine, you don't have to figure it out right now." He wasn't ready to have her tell him she'd made a mistake. Not just yet. He was an idiot for pushing.

"No, don't put words in my mouth."

He internally winced, even without hearing the words, the

rejection hurt. But he wouldn't push her for more than she was ready to give. "I didn't say anything."

"I can hear you thinking." She stroked her fingers down his cheek and scratched her nails through the scruff on his face, and he leaned into her touch. "It's written all over your face."

"Now who's putting words in whose mouth?"

"Are you seriously trying to start an argument right now?"

He could practically feel the frustration and annoyance pouring off her, seeping into his skin. "No, I swear," he promised. "I don't want to push for more than you're ready to give me."

"Virginia isn't home." She stopped him in his tracks. "Maybe I'm being an idiot for telling you this, and it's clichéd as all get out, but home for me is where you are."

"Thank fuck." He hauled her up his chest and smashed their lips together. He'd spent the last hour touching and tasting every inch of her, but he found every inch of him craved to do it all over again. He rolled until she was under him, careful not to crush her with his weight. He got his elbows under him and buried his fingers into her hair. "You'll stay with me?"

"If you want me to."

"If I want you to?"

"Yes."

"Damn, if you have to ask me that, I must be slacking…" He kissed her. Lips soft and warm with a fiery passion that made his heart feel two sizes too big. His lips on hers weren't exactly gentle. They were desperate in his need to show her how much her trust, how much her loving him enough to want to be here meant, and he wanted to revel in the joy that sang in his heart because of it.

He slowed the kiss, tilted Willow's face up a little more, shifting his legs until his thighs were on either side of hers, pulling her flush against him. He cupped her cheek in one hand and gently held her where he wanted her and kissed her again. Slower this time with open lips, needy and devastating. He tilted his head, kissing her a little deeper, and after a second, as if she was dazed, Willow kissed him back.

Her eyelids slowly closed and his followed suit. Open mouths, warm tongues, and hands exploring, stroking skin, petting each other, fingers holding on tight. He hadn't known it was possible, but he deepened the kiss and Willow let him, urging him on with those sexy little noises in the back of her throat. His heart surrendered the fight and placed itself in her small hands. No longer did it belong to him, it was official, he had fallen, hook, line, and sinker, his heart beat for her and her alone. Jeez, wasn't he just a goddamned poet? The guys would laugh their asses off at him if they could hear the thoughts running through his head right now.

He explored and teased her mouth with his tongue, sucking on her bottom lip, biting down gently before soothing it with small pecks and a swipe of his tongue.

"Please, Cormack, fuck me deep and slow," Willow murmured.

His breath caught, not at her words, but at her eyes wide and pleading as they peered up at him, honest, vulnerable, and filled with love.

He tucked his hand into her hair, bunching it in his fingers and tugging until her head tilted back, exposing her throat. "Yes?"

She swallowed deep as he pressed his lips to the delicate skin under her chin. "Yes, yes. Please."

He kissed and nipped at her throat, sucking up marks making her moan as his arousal was hot and hard against her pussy. The flame which smoldered in his belly burst from a spark into an inferno, and he wanted nothing more than to be inside her again, buried deep, until he couldn't tell where she ended and he began.

He sucked a nipple into his mouth, making her mumble incoherently and tweaking the other with his fingers.

"Please, Cormack."

He couldn't wait another second. He released her nipple and gripped himself, rubbing the head of his dick over her opening, coating it in her juices. He leaned over her and sank inside her.

Willow's eyes went wide before they rolled back in her head, her mouth dropping open on a cry as Cormack pushed all the way in to the hilt. He wanted to take this slow, he wanted to feel the connection between them, but even though he'd come deep inside her less than an hour ago, he wasn't sure how long he'd last.

She was tight and welcoming, taking every inch he gave her. When he was buried as far as he could go, he leaned forward so he could kiss her again, claiming her at both ends.

Willow groaned, low husky sounds of pleasure which were driving him crazy, urging him to move faster. He clamped down hard on the urge to drive into her and thrust slowly, rocking his hips, gliding in and out, deep and slow. His dick and his tongue buried deep inside her.

This… this between them felt so good.

His whole body tensed with determination, every fiber of his being urged him to go faster, deeper. But he would give her what she asked for, even if it killed him. She'd asked him to fuck her slow and deep and that was what he was going to do.

Her pussy clenched around him, sucking him in as he pushed forward and trying to keep him there when he slowly withdrew. Willow's small, hot hands trailed down his back, holding, kneading. She lifted her hips, trying to take him deeper.

"Easy, baby," Cormack whispered.

Her lips were wet, red, and swollen from their kisses. Her eyes locked on his. Her nails were digging into the skin on his sides. "I need... please... I need more... please." She widened her hips, digging her heels into the bed, pushing herself up to meet his thrusts.

So beautiful.

"Slow and deep, baby." He squeezed his eyes shut and tried to recite something... anything... to keep from losing it right now, but his brain refused to focus on anything but her. He captured both of her hands with his and pinned them to the mattress above their heads, allowing him to thrust a little harder, a little deeper, a little slower.

Willow moaned and whined as he managed to hook one of her legs over one arm and push it to his shoulder as he kept her hands in place with the other hand, leaning over her, opening her more for him. Her hips lifted and he drove deeper into her. Fuck, the pleasure of this angle was too much. The angle too perfect as his balls slapped off her ass each time he filled her. He was rapidly losing the ability to go slow. He moved deep inside her until he could take it no more.

Lowering her leg, he moved his fingers to her clit, pinching, rolling, and pulling. Each movement made her clench harder and him growl lower.

"I..." Her eyes widened, and every muscle in her body clenched hard, enveloping his dick. Squeezing him. Milking the orgasm from him as she exploded around him.

It was too much. It felt too damn good, and his orgasm slammed into him like a tsunami. He threw his head back, the muscles in his neck standing out as he thrust in deep, one last time. His dick swelled and pulsed—and he came.

She whimpered. "Cormack, yes." And when he collapsed over her, his dick still buried deep inside her pussy, she wrapped her arms around him, kissing his neck and chin. She rolled her hips, clenching her muscles, clearly not wanting the sensual movements to stop, and when he began to pull out, she wrapped her legs around him, holding him in place. "Stay inside me."

He was home. She was his home. He never wanted to leave. As if his dick agreed, it pulsed once more, making them both groan.

"Please stay."

"I'm not going anywhere." They'd have to drag him out of here with her wrapped around him like a monkey. Then he'd have to kill them all for seeing her sexy as hell naked body. His growl turned into a moan as his brain finally switched back on. He softly kissed her neck, her cheek, her lips. They kissed, soft and slow. There was no denying the tenderness and deep emotions swirling around them. This right here, right now, was what his dreams were made of. He'd be an idiot to fuck it up by opening his mouth right now.

When she shifted and he slipped out of her, he rolled them onto their sides, still holding her in his arms. Willow cuddled against him, her head on his chest, burrowing into him. She wrinkled her nose as she inhaled. "God, we need a shower, we stink."

He snorted out a laugh, his hand stroking softly on her lower back. He tried to be discreet about it, but when she giggled, he knew she'd caught his sniff. She was right, they did stink. Of sex. Of happiness. Of them. He fucking loved it and didn't want it to dissipate too soon. "Can we sleep first?"

Willow hummed, a low contented sound which stroked his ego and warmed his heart. "Can we do that again?"

He tightened his arms and pressed a kiss to the top of her head. "Baby, you gotta give me a few minutes to recover."

"Mmh, not just yet." She petted his chest, her eyes drooping. "Put it on the list of things to do again."

He raised an eyebrow, not that she could see it from where she dozed against his chest. "There's a list?"

Willow sighed contentedly; her words slurred by sleep. "Mm… mm… I'm tired."

"Me, too." As much as he wanted to know what was on the list, he wouldn't push her on it just yet. But he did have one thing to add to it. "Add your buttercream frosting to the list for when I get back."

"Yes, good thinking." He could barely hear her words. "I'll do that."

"Good girl." He would just rest his eyes for a while before he had to go gather his gear for the mission. Willow was wrapped tight in his arms, her cheek resting on his heart. Her long lashes brushed off her high cheekbones, sound asleep. Ten minutes, just ten more minutes, he promised himself as he drifted off.

CHAPTER FIFTEEN

WHAT ON EARTH was that obnoxious buzzing noise? She blinked her eyes open and scooted to sit up on the bed. It took a couple of seconds to remember where she was while the buzzing kept on freaking going. If Cormack left an alarm switched on somewhere, she was going to kill him. As slowly and as painfully as she possibly could. She could let her creative side have free rein.

Willow pressed both hands over her ears. "Cormack?"

She wouldn't be able to hear him over the freaking buzzing. For heaven's sake, did he leave toast under the grill again and forget about it? Not that she'd minded having a bunch of hot firefighters come over because her neighbor reported the resulting smoke. But Cormack had growled and grumbled about it for a week.

Her head was going to fall off her head if that noise didn't stop, that and the fact she needed to check the grill got her butt out of bed. She reached for his t-shirt and pulled it over her head before leaving the bedroom. "Cormack?"

She knew the suite was empty aside from her. It had that feel to it, despite the buzzing driving her mad, the place was quiet, still, like how her house felt when Cormack left to go back to his team. She really hoped she was wrong. Had he left for the mission without telling her? He wouldn't do that, would he? She padded through the living room and into the kitchen, looking for the source of the noise.

She checked the tiny electric oven. Nope, it wasn't even plugged in. Spinning in a circle she took in the small kitchen and couldn't see any smoke, or nothing with an alarm. "Stop it already."

As if the suite was haunted and the ghost had just been waiting for her acknowledgement, the buzzing stopped. It was a good thing she didn't believe in ghosts, or she'd have been running out of there screaming her head off. Then the knocking started.

"Oh, for heaven's sake." Had that buzzing noise been a doorbell? She went to the door and peered through the peephole. She squinted and looked again then stepped back and opened the door, ducking to avoid Lina's fist as she went to knock again.

"Lina?"

"Shit, sorry." Lina winced then looked at her feet. "Crap. Buddha, get your furry tail back here, puppy."

"Woo, roo, wooo."

"Don't talk back to me, woofer, bring your skinny butt back here now." Lina walked toward the stairs, apparently following the sound of the malamute's woos. "No, bad puppy, don't pee there."

"Hello, twilight zone," Willow muttered. "Be gentle, I haven't had coffee yet." She turned back into her suite, then paused and stuck her head around the door and called after Lina, "Door's open, I'm making coffee." She headed back to the kitchen and the single pod machine Cormack had set up for her.

"I'll be there in a sec!" Lina shouted. There was a pause and a muttered curse followed by, "I'm gonna need a mop."

She braced both hands on the counter and dropped her head with a sigh, coffee would have to wait a couple of more minutes until she figured out where Cormack kept his cleaning supplies. She didn't remember seeing any over the last two days. Not that she'd spent much time in the suite unless it was in bed. She scanned the living space. "If you were a mop, where would you hide?"

"In the closet next to the guest bathroom door."

If she'd had energy or coffee, she'd have jumped two feet into the air at Lina's voice directly behind her. But instead, she settled for flinching away from her. "You are as bad as Cormack, make some noise."

"Sorry." Lina gestured to the floor. "Can I put him down?"

"Is he gonna pee?" She went down the hallway toward the bathroom and found the closet Lina had mentioned. "There you are," she muttered to the mop and bucket. She grabbed both and a bottle of disinfectant.

"Considering the size of the puddle at the top of the stairs, I hope not. I seriously don't know how that much liquid fits in a body that size."

"Then go ahead." She attempted to be polite but knew from the sound of her voice she didn't quite hit the mark. "Sorry, I was sleeping, I haven't had coffee yet."

"Ouch, no problem, I've been known to rip people's heads clean off their shoulders before I've had caffeine." Lina put the pup on the floor and followed Willow to the bathroom. "Want me to hold that?" She nodded to the bucket Willow held under the faucet in the bathtub.

"No, I got it, thanks though." She half-filled the bucket

and swirled in the disinfectant before adding the mop to the bucket. "Where's the pee?"

"I can do it." Lina held out her hand for the mop and bucket.

"No." She didn't want to insult Lina. But she also didn't want her to hurt herself. She knew absolutely nothing about pregnant women, none of her friends had gotten to that stage of their lives yet. But from how her uncle Dalton had acted at the breakfast table; Lina wasn't supposed to lift anything heavier than a fork.

"Nemy told you I wasn't to do anything, didn't he?" Lina followed her out of the suite into the hallway. "I'm going to kick his pretty butt."

"No." She squelched the water out of the mop and dabbed it on the puddle at the top of the stairs, trying to soak up as much of it as she could before washing out the mop again. "I know nothing about babies, I'm only guessing from what I heard at breakfast earlier."

"Yesterday."

"What?"

"Breakfast was yesterday." Lina's lips curved into a slight smile. "You slept almost around the clock."

"Crap." Oh my holy frick-fracking candy dance, she'd slept almost twenty-four hours. But despite having never done that before, it wasn't the long hours of sleep that sent a twinge of sadness into her heart. "They've gone already, haven't they?" She forced herself to keep her eyes on the floor and not to let Lina see her upset.

"Yes," Lina replied. "They went wheels up at four thirty this morning."

"Oh." She didn't know how to feel about that. He hadn't woken her up to say goodbye. That hurt. She swallowed down the hurt. She wouldn't let anyone see it. It was hers alone. She should be used to this. Should be used to being the one left behind. But she wasn't. She was an idiot for having hoped it would be different now she was here in Montana. But apparently not. Duty called and he went, except now she didn't even warrant so much as a goodbye.

"That spot's not going to get any cleaner." Lina's voice snapped her out of her funk.

"Sorry, it's the lack of coffee."

"Sure, it is." Lina led the way back to the suite. "I'll make you coffee while you empty that bucket," she offered.

If she was a huggy person she'd totally have considered hugging her. She side-eyed Lina, yeah, she probably wasn't much of a huggy person either, so she settled for saying, "You're a lifesaver, thank you."

"What kind of coffee do you want?"

She dumped the dirty water in the toilet. "Caramel Star-bucks, please."

She heard the machine kick in a couple of seconds later. "You got it."

"Make yourself one, too, I'll be out in a sec." She stashed the bucket and the mop, detoured into the bedroom for a pair of yoga pants, and went back to the living space. Catching a glimpse of herself in the mirror as she walked past, she scowled at her reflection. Why couldn't she be one of those girls who managed to wake up looking cute? Nope, she was one of those haystack, hair standing in weird shapes, and a blotchy face waker-uppers. "Of course, I'm a mess. Why wouldn't I be a mess?" She looked around for her bag but didn't see it. Where the heck were her clothes?

After searching under the bed, in the bathroom, and everywhere she could think of in the room, she finally opened the door to what she hoped was the closet. "There you are." She spotted her bag on the floor under a shelf which held her clothes along with her tennis shoes. She'd have to remember to boot Cormack's butt for not telling her he'd put her stuff in the closet.

"Coffee's ready," Lina called.

"Two minutes." She grabbed some clothes and hurriedly put them on. She'd have to shower later because there was no way she was keeping Lina waiting any longer. She did take the time to grab a spray bottle of Cormack's deodorant on her way back through the bedroom though. That might help to mask the B.O. As mortified as she was not to have showered, in her defense, Lina had just showed up and not given her any warning that she was coming.

She could already smell the caramel coffee on her way down the short hallway, and she sped up her steps. "Sorry, I had to search for clothes." She took the mug Lina offered and gratefully sniffed before taking a sip. "Yum."

"I'm kinda shocked Jeep had a Dolce Gusto machine." Lina followed her into the living room and took a seat on the opposite side of the couch. "He's always been kinda rough and ready, so I saw him as more a drip brew kinda guy."

"Oh, he is." Willow pointed to the trash can near the fridge. "The box is there, so my guess is he bought it for me."

"Consider my mind blown."

"It surprises you?"

Lina fished in her pockets and pulled out a chew stick for the puppy and clicked her tongue to call him to her. Buddha took the chew and settled on the floor at her feet to eat it. "I've only known him a couple of weeks, he wasn't one of the guys from before…" Her voice trailed off before she continued. "So I've never seen him with a woman before."

"He's been with me for about two years."

"How the hell did you meet?"

"He came to my dad's funeral." She scratched at the skin

on the inside of her wrist, then frowned at the spot. Was that a mosquito bite? Dang it, she'd hoped she escaped the nasties when she'd come here. "He sent me an email after he got back to Afghanistan."

"Jeep sent an email?" Lina's eyebrows almost disappeared into her hairline. "I didn't even know he could turn on a computer without needing Trev to fix it two minutes later."

She laughed at the incredulous tone in Lina's voice and grinned at her. "Right?"

"How that man manages to be the one to work all the mechanical stuff but can't make a cell phone stay alive for more than a week is beyond me."

"That's why I'm kinda stunned at the email."

"I am, too, now," she admitted. "But back then, I didn't know he was megabyte challenged." She sipped her coffee and settled back into the couch. Getting to know her uncle Dalton's wife was a good thing... right? Oh, oops, wait. "Um." She glanced at Lina. "If you're my uncle D's wife, that doesn't mean I have to call you aunt, does it?"

"Only if you want to die in horrible pain." Lina eyed her over the rim of her mug. "I'm not old enough to be anyone's aunt." She scratched the puppy's ears. "Go on."

Why was she being so insistent on hearing the story? "Dalton told you to ask me?" See if he got anymore cinnamon rolls. Butthead.

"Nope." Lina shook her head. "But he's majorly pissy with Jeep and that could be a problem."

"They better not fight over me or I'm not baking for the rest of the year."

"So, you're staying?"

"That's the plan." There was no way she was going to let anyone aside from Cormack and herself be part of the decision-making process. "Does it bother you?"

"What? No." Lina shrugged. "It could be fun to see someone shake this place up a little. Since you've been here, I've had more fun in two days than I've had in two months."

"Nuh-uh, I think that was your puppy shaking things up."

"He's fun." Lina's lips curved up at one side into a smirk. "He's keeping us on our toes, that's for sure." She waved one hand at Willow and nodded to her. "Go on, so how did you and Jeep end up together?"

"Where was I?"

"He sent you an email."

"Multiple emails." Willow snorted. "I didn't answer for months. Then one night, I watched sad movies, bawled my eyes out, and ping, another dang email, making sure I was alright." She wasn't going to apologize for having a bad day, not that she thought she'd have to, but still. "I don't know why I did it, but I answered."

"And before you knew it, you were emailing back and forth?"

"Yeah."

"So how did he end up in Virginia?"

"About a year after we started emailing, I gave him my number and the next time he was in town he called and asked me out to the Corner Pyrate…What started out as one night turned to six months just like that." She snapped her fingers. "And before I knew it, I was waiting for him to come home every night, even when I knew it was impossible because he was a half a dozen time zones away in a country I never want to hear the name of again, fighting for his life and for the honor of the flag my father died for."

"It's who they are."

"Yes, it is." And she wouldn't change him for the world. "Sooo, you and my uncle D., huh?"

"Yes, me and Nemy."

She spewed the mouthful of coffee she'd just taken as she attempted to laugh before she'd swallowed the liquid. "It's hilarious that you call him that."

"Right? He gets all huffy and shit, it's all I can do to keep from laughing in his face." Lina grinned wide. "But I think secretly he likes it."

"I don't know, but I think if anyone else called him that, he'd shoot them."

"Agree, which is why I keep doing it. And I make sure to do it in front of the guys and he can't say a damn thing, or I'll cut him off from sexy times."

Willow pressed her hands to her face. It was probably ridiculous to be blushing at the mention of sex. She couldn't help it that her grandmother had been a prude who'd insisted sex was never something to be mentioned in polite company, and she'd drilled it into her head until it was a part of her makeup. "Want another coffee?" She jumped to her feet and held out her hand for Lina's mug.

"Umm, no, thank you though." Lina scowled at the mug. "I've had one already today and this one." She ran her hand across her stomach with a soft smile on her face. "I get queasy if I have too much, but none is worse."

"Would you like some water instead?" They still hadn't gotten to the reason Lina was here, but her grandmother had also drilled Southern manners into her, and she wouldn't be the one to bring it up first. She'd just have to wait for the other woman to spit it out.

"Yes, please," Lina replied. "But that caramel stuff isn't bad if I only double up on the milk and only put one measure of the coffee pods in it. At least it tastes like coffee and not a frou-frou drink."

"You normally take it black?" She set the machine to

brew and grabbed Lina's water out of the fridge. "You want a glass?"

"Girl, I'm not fancy, the bottle is just fine." Lina gave the puppy another chew. "And yes, I normally take my coffee as black as my soul."

"And what would Dalton say if he heard you talking about yourself like that?"

"He'd swat my ass and laugh his head off." Lina slapped one hand over her mouth as soon as she saw Willow's eyebrows shoot up. "Oops, I said that out loud. Sorry."

"You're not one bit sorry." She could see the other woman's eyes twinkling.

"Sorry, I kinda like you," Lina told her. "My mouth loses the run of itself when I like people. I haven't had many friends lately."

How the heck didn't someone like Lina have friends? So far everything she'd seen, despite the fact she'd broken Dalton's heart before apparently fixing it again, she was lovely. "Me either."

"Then what do you say we be friends?" Lina asked. "You can tame me, and I'll corrupt you? It will make the boys batshit."

"I'd like that." You know what, there was probably only a handful of women across the globe who understood what it was to send the man you loved out on a mission and not know when he'd be back. Who knew the panic of a twenty-four-hour rapid deploy notice for wheels up? Who got that it was impossible to tell anyone when their man would be home? Despite the reservations she'd had at the breakfast table yesterday, that Lina understood the fear in her heart, and the uneasy feeling in her stomach, that meant a lot. "Deal." She held her mug out to Lina and tapped it off the other woman's bottle of water. "Mission drive the boys batty is a go."

"First thing I'm teaching you is how to swear," Lina promised.

"Cormack tried." Willow went back to the kitchen and rummaged through the cupboards until she found a Tupperware box full of cookies. Those would totally do for breakfast and to celebrate her newfound friend. "Swearing isn't as effective when you're blushing your way through saying the words. So, I get creative and make them up, like fudgebuckets and frick-fracking." She nodded to Lina's belly. "Are you going to stop swearing when the baby comes?"

"Hell no." Lina peered into the box and picked a cookie. "This baby is going to have a bunch of Black Ops operators for uncles, if you think swearing isn't going to happen, you need your head examined."

"Get a swear jar and fine them ten dollars a cuss word." She munched on a white Oreo cookie. "You'll have college paid for before that baby is five."

"I like your style, but I don't know that my income can keep up with my mouth enough to have a swear jar." Lina high-fived her with a cookie. "You know, maybe this having a friend thing will be fun."

"You don't have friends?"

"No."

"Why not?"

But before Lina could answer, her phone beeped. She turned it over and glanced at the screen before unlocking it and holding it out to Willow. "That's for you."

"What?"

"Jeep sent you an email," Lina explained. "He knew you have no phone and made me promise to get you one. But to get to the storage I have to pass the barn, and well..." She wrinkled her nose. "The baby wasn't too thrilled by the smell so I came here instead after I told Nemy to have Jeep CC my email address so you could read what he sends you."

"Thank you." She took the cell from Lina. Excitement bubbled in her belly. He hadn't forgotten to talk to her before being out of touch for work.

CHAPTER SIXTEEN

CORMACK PUNCHED at the pillow behind his head and shifted his ass, trying to get comfortable. Despite the fancy ass plane they were on, his stomach clenched and rolled. What the hell? Was he sick?

"Dude, if you're gonna barf, do it in this, will ya?" Sensei pulled off his headset and reached for a barf-bag from the side pocket of the reclining chair and tossed it into his lap.

"Real men don't barf on planes," Mokaccino teased from the seat on the other side of him.

If they didn't stop, he was going to throw up on them both just to spite them. "Real men wear fishnets and burlap. And I've seen plenty of dudes in ghillie suits barfing on planes."

"After they've taken care of business," Sensei said dryly.

"If you're calling me a man," Snow leaned around her seat and scowled at him, "Then I'm gonna use my damn fishnets to string you up by the balls."

"Children, children," Dalton whisper shouted. "We are in a public place." In other words, shut the hell up before I haul your asses out of the seats and make you do push-ups in the aisle until you do puke.

He dug his fingers into his scalp, just at the front of his head and scratched all the way to the back, trying to keep himself from giving snark back. Out of the corner of his eye, he could see the two bodyguards assigned to Senator Greg Ricketts watching them like they were a circus sideshow. Not that he gave a shit, these two didn't look like they'd know a wadi from a donkey.

He pulled out his cell, maybe if he looked at some photos of his sunshine, his brain and belly would finally settle. As he did, he noticed the signal icon was working. That little thing with three lines was the signal, right? "Do we have signal on the plane?" He showed Sensei the screen and tapped the icon.

"Looks like it." Sensei reached for his own cell. "Score."

While Nemesis Inc. had their own private jet and often used it, today they were flying courtesy of the US government. Which apparently had perks like working wi-fi while they were in the air. He tapped through the screens and pulled up the email app. He'd asked Lina to make sure she got a spare cell to Willow, so he could have some contact with her, and at least keep up their tradition of sending emails. He hadn't had the heart to wake her before he'd left and hadn't had time to grab a cell from storage and drop it back to the suite. The app opened to his inbox, and he frowned when he spotted an email from Lina but tapped on it to open it.

From: Lina Maxwell-Knight
To: Jeep Ford
Jeep, storage isn't happening. It stinks near the barn and the baby doesn't like it. CC this email if you send something to your girl before tomorrow and I'll make sure she gets it.

CHAPTER SEVENTEEN

DAMN IT, he didn't like the idea of Lina having access to his and Willow's private words. But he wouldn't leave his sunshine thinking he didn't remember either. What a pain in the ass, but he hit reply to the email.

From: Jeep Ford
To: Lina Maxwell-Knight
Thanks, I'll have something for her within the next half hour.
She might still be sleeping, but if you lean on the bell, she'll
hear you. Do you want me to tell Nem that you're sick?
J.

SHE MUST HAVE BEEN WAITING for him to reply as he got an immediate response.

From: Lina Maxwell-Knight
To: Jeep Ford
Don't you dare, or he'll be a bear the whole trip. I'm on my
way over there right now.

CHAPTER EIGHTEEN

LINA WAS PROBABLY RIGHT. Nemesis could be a dick at the best of times when he was worried about his wife…everyone needed to stand clear, as in about ten miles down the road clear.

From: Jeep Ford
To: Lina Maxwell-Knight
Roger that. The next email will be for Willow. Thanks for doing this, Lina.
J.

From: Lina Maxwell-Knight
To: Jeep Ford

CHAPTER NINETEEN

HE FROWNED AT THE SCREEN, how the hell did one make a smiley face like that? But he didn't have time to try and figure it out right now. He tapped the compose message and typed in Willow's email address.

From: Jeep Ford
To: Willow Black
CC. Lina Maxwell-Knight
Subject: For Willow.
Hi Sunshine.
I'm sorry I didn't wake you up before I left. I gotta admit it was purely selfish on my part. My ego likes you sleeping in my bed, and my heart refused to disturb you. So, I'm sorry for leaving without telling you, but not sorry enough because I'll probably do it again.

IT WAS BETTER to warn her that he was going to go all caveman, right? Not that he hadn't been before. But now that she was in his bed, in his home… the caveman side of him was faster to make an appearance than ever before.

I hate having to leave so soon after you got here. I wanted to show you the pond and the sunrise, but I promise we will do all that stuff when I get back. If you're looking for your clothes, I put them in the closet with mine.

AND HE'D FUCKING LOVED DOING that. Not that he'd ever admit that to anyone ever. As he typed, his insides stopped swirling and the nausea retreated. Well, look at that, all he needed was a little bit of sunshine to fix himself.

I spoke to Kayce, he said if you want to go talk to him about working in the kitchen, he'd be thrilled to have you there. (I'd be thrilled, too, if you promise me goodies). There's no rush though, so if you want to wait until I get back to do that, then that's okay, too. You decide what works for you, Sunshine, k?

SHIT, he didn't want her to think he was pressuring her to work. That wasn't the objective at all. He knew she loved to cook and bake. When she had access to a decent kitchen, her brain worked better. He fucking loved her awesome brain.

Lina said she'd fix you up with a cell phone, so you should have access to the net and stuff. Ask her about getting Trev to give you wi-fi access, too, so you can update your blog and stuff.

Okay, that was the stuff she needed to know. If he didn't have Lina CC'd on this email, he'd tell her how much last night had blown his mind. How much he fucking loved having her in his space. But he knew his girl, she'd be mortified to have even the possibility of Lina reading it.

You should see the plane we're on, Sunshine. If you thought Nem's plane was fancy, it's got nothing on this. I'm in the wrong job, this dude we're on protection detail for travels like a rockstar. I can even ignore the fact it's all done on the taxpayer's dime. If it was possible, I'd send you pictures. Sensei (Logan) is getting his zen on, but I think the dude across the way is going to need a bucket for the drool, with the way he's staring at Sensei's butt as he's pulling yoga poses. A-hole (Sensei) is doing it on purpose. But it has wi-fi so I'm not gonna complain, as it means I can send you this sooner than I thought.

HE LOVED TELLING her snippets of what was going on. He could never give her too many details but giving her an insight let her picture his world as shit was happening.

Nem is growly as all get out, and I defs see a come to Jesus meeting in our near future. Before you start freaking, we'll be fine. We've been through too much crap together for this to kill our friendship. He'll figure it out eventually that you are

*my sunshine and having you in my world is like having the
sun warm me from the inside out.
Now that I've been all sappy and stuff, I better go do some
work and figure out how to keep this dude from doing a
stupid while in theater.
India. Kilo, Yankee. Alpha. Sierra. Sunshine.
Grumpy.*

HE MIGHT GIVE her crap for calling him Grumpy, yet here he
was still signing off his emails with it. He tapped send and
watched the little swirly circle do its thing. It was time to go
to work.

———

HE STRETCHED his neck to one side and then the other until it
cracked. Driving in a truck over the rough as heck dirt tracks
which doubled as roads in this shit hole part of Afghanistan
was playing hell on his body. He glanced at Dalton in the
driver's seat before nodding to their VIP in the rear seat and
scanning ahead to see if he spotted anything of concern. But
all he could see was the back ass of the truck Sensei was
driving lead on their three-truck convoy, with Devil-Man and
one of Senator Ricketts' bodyguards riding shotgun. The
other bodyguard sat behind him, next to the senator and Rory,
and Snow followed up in the other truck on their six.

"See anything?" Nemesis asked softly.

He'd been concerned that Dalton would allow his recent
knowledge of the relationship with Willow to affect them in
the field, but he should have known better. "Nope, all clear."

"Can we stop?" the bodyguard asked.

"Hell no," Jeep replied. "We're just coming up on the AfPak border and there's no way we're stopping until we get to the village."

"That's just cruel, man, I gotta take a leak."

"I told you to take a damn leak before we left the safe house two hours ago."

"It's so hot, I've been drinking water."

Someone save him from people who had no business being in this fuckhole country. "We're not stopping." He tossed an empty water bottle over his shoulder into the rear seat. "Piss in the bottle."

"There's no reason to be crude," the senator chastised. "It's uncivilized to pee in a bottle."

Next to him, he could see Dalton's jaw clench, so he answered before Nem opened his trap and let rip. "No disrespect, sir, but you're in our world now. We say no stopping for any reason. It's not safe to do so."

"Agree," Dalton muttered. "The DOD is paying me a shitload of money to keep your asses safe. We can't get you back to your families in one piece if you want to stop and leave yourselves exposed to potential enemy fire every ten miles."

He blew out a silent breath of relief. Wow, that had been more diplomatic than he'd expected from his boss, but he did his best to reinforce it. "Our job is to keep your asses safe. You agreed to follow our directives," Jeep reminded them of the debriefing on the plane, just before landing in Kabul. "We'll be at the village in about twenty minutes. If you don't want to use the bottle, you're gonna have to hold it until then."

He glanced over his shoulder and caught the look the two in the back exchanged. Thankfully the senator shook his head, silently telling the bodyguard to not push the issue. At least one of them had brain cells and was willing to utilize them.

"He'll wait." The senator caught Jeep's gaze.

"Roger that." He pointed to the bodyguard. "Make sure you don't piss against someone's house or property when we get to the village," he warned. "The last thing you want to do is insult these people before you even start."

"Can I not ask to use one of their bathrooms?"

"Ain't no indoor plumbing in this place, kid."

"Crap."

"That's what bushes are for. Just do what ya got to do out of sight of the women." The crackling of the radio changed the subject.

"Nemesis Three, this is Two," Lucifer called. "Five klicks to the village, all clear, once you take this next turn you should have a clear view direct to our target location."

"Roger that, Two," Cormack replied. "Tell Five not to kick up dirt as he pulls in." He figured it was better to warn Logan not to do NASCAR stunts this time. The only time he forgot to give the order and Sensei had landed his truck in a goat pen, they'd had to hand over a shitload of cash to the elders for replacing it.

"Copy." He could hear the grin in Lucifer's voice as he replied and knew the asshole was probably teasing the heck out of Logan. But at least that would remind the idiot to behave. Maybe.

Two hours later, he stood with his back against the wall of the hut, watching the senator as he tried to engage the men seated around the fire in conversation. He met Dalton's gaze across the room and lifted one shoulder. Ricketts was getting nowhere fast. Why the hell did these people come here and not even know how to speak the fucking language and think they'd be able to have a meaningful conversation?

"Six to Three." Snow's voice broke in over the radio. She had set up on an outcropping which formed part of the external wall of the village and was overwatch to give them a heads up on any potential problems. "Jeep, you might wanna come out here and take a look at this."

He gestured to Dalton and barely waited for the other man's nod of approval before he left the hut. He clicked comms. "Whatcha got, Snow?"

"I'm looking at about twelve trucks, fully loaded with potential tangos, coming in from the south."

"Is this our escort to the next village?"

"No, I don't think so," Snow said. "I know we're supposed to be meeting an escort, but I don't think these are our guys."

Well shit, he made his way around the perimeter of the village and scrambled up the wall to the rock Snow had staged up on. "Three approaching on your six," he warned her just as Snow spun around with her handgun aimed straight at his heart. "Show me what you got."

"They're about five or six klicks out, but if they keep coming straight and don't turn off on one of those goat tracks then they're gonna drive straight into this village." She held out a pair of binos to him as he settled himself onto the ground next to her so he didn't skyline himself where a sniper would have an easy shot.

"How many on each truck?"

"Best estimate about twelve to fifteen males, all armed with AKs. And check out that second truck, that's an RPG."

Fuck, that didn't sound like any peaceful escort he'd encountered before. That many fighters approaching a village in this part of the world in his experience meant one thing... Taliban. He scanned the approaching vehicles, marking all the intel Snow had provided. Confirming the weapons and the numbers. "Yeah, that's an RPG." He clicked on his comms unit. "One, this is Three, we got company. Get them outta there."

"Shit! Copy," Dalton immediately answered. "Four and Five, get your asses to my location, stat."

"Roger."

"Copy."

"They're coming in fast," Snow observed. "I don't think we're gonna have time to get outta here."

He didn't think so either, but they had to be ready to run if necessary. Engaging with a force that size was suicide. Dying or losing a principle was not on the agenda for today. He had a woman waiting for him at home. He didn't have time to high tail it, dodging terrorists all across this fucking mountain, thank you.

Through binos he watched the incoming force stop about a mile from the entrance to the village. After a couple of minutes, they swapped around their positions and the second and third trucks continued toward them while the others stayed in place. Maybe this was just an envoy from another village.

"Put your fucking weapons down."

"Fuck, that's the boss." He scrambled to his knees and crawled to the edge of the outcrop so he could drop to the ground.

"Drop your weapons!"

Dalton's roar was in English and not in one Pashtun or Dari, telling Jeep that one of the senator's bodyguards was freaking the fuck out. If they shot... Just as the thought flashed through his brain, gunfire rang out.

"No! No! No! You goddamned idiot, they're friendlies!" Dalton's bellow of rage over comms was not fucking good. He rarely lost his shit, that he was doing it now meant shit was more than hitting the proverbial fan. "They're fucking friendlies! Stand down, asshole, or I'll put a bullet through your goddamned brain."

"Six to Three, the rest of those trucks started burning rubber this way as soon as that gunshot let loose."

"Copy." He'd deal with that shit just as soon as he had to. Right now, he needed to get his ass to Dalton and their principles. He sprinted straight across the village, not bothering to go around the edge of the circular clear space between the huts. His foot hit the door first, kicking it inward. He took in the scene with one glance. The senator sat with his back against the wall, Sensei in front of him, protecting him with his own body. Mokaccino knelt on the floor next to one of the elders who'd been sitting around the fireplace with the senator when Jeep had left to answer Snow. "Weapons down!"

"Get this fucker up and cuff him," Dalton snarled. "Get him outta my sight before I shoot the fucker."

"Roger that, sir." This shit right here was why you didn't allow bodyguards who weren't former military and who hadn't worked in this part of the world escort anyone into the Hindu Kush. He grabbed the flexicuffs from the hook on his vest and snapped them over the bodyguard's wrists.

"He's a terrorist."

"Shut up, don't make this worse."

"They don't speak English."

"I don't give a fuck, you shot an unarmed man in his own house," Jeep snarled. "Are you fucking stupid? This breaks every rule of engagement we have."

"This is war."

"The war is over, fuckwad. Don't you listen to the news? Didn't you see the shit show that was the withdrawal? These people are innocent of whatever you think they did." He dragged the man to his feet and pushed him across the room to the wall, pressing on his shoulders to make him sit. "Stay the fuck there until I tell you to move."

"He's sorry," the senator called from where he sat behind Sensei.

"That's your fucking escort." Dalton pointed a finger at Ricketts. "His actions are your responsibility."

"Boss, what's the solution?"

"Take action and get the mission done," Dalton muttered. "We've got a bigger problem with those incoming trucks."

"Agree, you want to stay here or be the welcoming committee?"

"I'm going out, because if I have to look at that asshole for two more minutes, I'm going to shoot him myself."

Fuck. "Roger that."

Dalton paused next to where the Rory bandaged the village elder's arm and spoke softly to them before he turned a dark scowl on the senator and his bodyguards and left the house, followed by the two uninjured elders.

"If you could just tell him that we apologize?"

"Senator, the best thing you can do now is shut the hell up," Jeep advised. He could hear the trucks pulling into the village. "Sensei, Mokaccino, you got this?"

"Yes, sir."

"Good. Keep these fuckers locked down." He walked out into the sunshine and stepped up behind where Dalton faced the driver of the first truck.

"You team leader?" the driver asked in broken English.

"Yeah, I am."

Jeep kept his hands ready on his weapons, while trying not to look like he was going to pop off a shot. He glanced at the other men in the backs of the trucks. He didn't like how they shifted and milled restlessly as if they were nervous. They outnumbered his team by more than five to one. They had no reason to be nervous unless they planned Jihad.

"You speak Dari?"

"Some," Dalton answered.

Liar, the man spoke multiple languages fluently, and Jeep knew Dari was one of them. He kept his face blank. Nemesis didn't do shit without a reason, if he was saying he didn't speak the language, then he didn't.

"How's your Uzbek?"

"His is better than mine." Dalton gestured to him.

"Thanks, buddy."

"You're welcome." Dalton's face broke into an eat shit grin before it returned to his normal resting bitch face. Asshole, he was going to make him pay for that. "His Russian is better than his Uzbek though," Dalton added on.

Well, why not put his damn resume on a fucking piece of paper and hand it the fuck over?

"My Russian is shit." The Afghan shifted from where he leaned against the hood of the truck and gestured toward the hut. "But we shall talk to my grandfather, he speaks enough Russian to speak to you."

He resisted the urge to squeeze his eyes shut in frustration and instead kept his eye on the other vehicles now pulling into the village clearing. Wonderful, fabulous, what's the betting the injured old man is this punk's grandfather? He exchanged glances with Nemesis, this could get bad, real fast.

"Let's go, grab your gear," the Afghan called to his men.

Shit. Just shit. There was no way around it, they would have to allow the man into the hut to see his grandfather. He hesitated on moving aside, even with the Afghan stepping forward until he was almost under his nose. Something was off, he couldn't put his finger on it. But something besides the shit the bodyguard had caused was very wrong. The feeling of spiders crawling all over his skin confirmed it. "Something's off, Boss."

He knew the others would be able to hear him over their comms units.

"Agree," Dalton muttered just loud enough that if he hadn't been wearing their communication devices, he wouldn't have been able to hear him.

"It's the women," Snow said in his earpiece. "There's no women in this village."

Fuck, she was right. They'd been here for more than two hours, and he hadn't seen one female. Even the refreshments provided to them when they'd arrived had been distributed by the elder. "That's worrying."

"Move." The Afghan pushed the muzzle of his AK into the plate on Jeep's flak jacket.

"Hey." He moved the muzzle to one side, away from his body. "Back up."

"No, you move, this is my home, not yours."

"Yo, yo, yo." Dalton snapped his fingers, breaking the tension between Jeep and the Afghan. "What's your name?"

"Mohammad."

"Of course, it is."

"Quiet," Dalton growled at his snarky remark. "Don't start piling shit on top of shit."

"Sorry, Boss."

"Find the women," Dalton ordered. "I'll go attempt to make peace and fix the mess in there." He barely moved his chin in the direction of the house, but Mohammad saw it anyway, and his eyes widened and nostrils flared, letting them know he was concerned at the conversation. He pushed past them with Dalton hot on his heels.

"Yes, sir." All he could do was watch them go. He'd follow orders. He didn't have to like them. He scrubbed his hand down his face and clicked his comms. "Devil-Man, keep an eye on my six."

"Copy that."

He scowled at the raised voices and clicked his comms but released it again. Nemesis could handle one hothead, especially as he had Sensei and Mokaccino with him. He turned to his right and began a systematic search of the village while a couple of the Afghani men who'd traveled with Mohammad trailed after him.

"What it is you are looking for?"

"Where are the rest of the village people? The women, the children."

"There are no children in this village anymore." The man's face darkened in pain. "Once we were many, now it is only us men who remain."

That didn't sound right. "What happened?"

"Do you know who AQI are?"

"Al Qaeda?"

"Yes." The man scowled. "They wanted to use our village to capture some of your soldiers, and when we refused, they killed all our women and children. It was on this day that we decided to join the fight."

It sounded like this village had every reason to fight on the same side he did. But he'd learned long ago not to take anything at face value. Even so it was hard to argue with the pain which filled the other man's voice. "I'm sorry for your loss."

"Thank you." The corners of the man's lips curved. "It is not often someone comes here and apologizes for the actions of either side."

"Ain't that the truth." Cormack ducked his head inside the door of a building and scanned the single room. The walls were bare, and the floor made of dirt.

"I do not understand?"

"It means this is true." He checked another building and moved to the next. This one had a closed door.

"Ah." The man walked past that building and onto the next. "Yes, we the people who have lived here for generations will always be the ones who suffer the wrath of others. No matter which side we pick, we are exposed and end up being hurt."

Jeep stopped at the door and waited for the man to turn to see why he didn't follow him. "Open it." He gestured to the door with the padlock securing it closed with the muzzle of his weapon.

"There is nothing in there, the same as the last building."

"Then it won't matter if I look, open it."

"There is nothing there."

"Open it, or I'll shoot through it," Jeep threatened.

"I was starting to think you might not be like the others," the man said. "But you, too, are a bully."

"No," Jeep said softly. "I'm a careful man, and checking the perimeter means I check all of it. Open the door or I shoot the lock off."

"Take it easy, Jeep," Lucifer muttered over comms. "Talk, don't freak."

"He opens the door, or I shoot the lock off."

"Three, this is Six," Snow interrupted. "There's a dude here pulling an RPG out of the back of the truck outside the gate."

"Fuck." Jeep fisted his hands until his knuckles turned white. "When I get back here, I expect that door to be open."

"I will go talk to Mohammad," the Afghan promised.

"Sir, he's aiming that RPG right at your head," Snow warned. "Shit... Incoming."

"Get down!" Jeep hit the ground as he yelled the warning.

Even if this man was being stubborn, he couldn't just drop himself into cover without warning him, too. The words were barely out of his mouth when the door of the building behind him exploded. He folded his arms over his head and breathed out to try and protect his lungs from the percussion blast. "Get that fucker, Snow."

"Roger that, sir."

The explosion he'd been expecting never came and he risked a glance over his shoulder. The door was gone, the gaping black hole of the building smoldered, but the building still stood. He could hear Dalton shouting through comms but didn't have time to listen to it.

"Run, run." The Afghani man he'd been with a few seconds before scrambled to his feet and took off as fast as his legs would take him.

"Well, that's not good."

"Jeep, answer me, asshole," Dalton's voice in his ear demanded.

"I'm good, Boss." He belly-crawled across the ground to the door and peered inside. The man had been so insistent there was nothing in there… yeah, he wasn't believing that for a second.

"Contact," Lucifer warned as gunfire exploded into the village from the trucks still parked outside the compound walls. "Permission to return fire, sir?"

"Shoot back, dumbass." Dalton sprinted toward Jeep with Mokaccino hot on his heels. "Sensei has our VIPs. What ya got?"

"Boss, we're gonna need backup, stat," Snow called. "We've got at least thirty males approaching."

"I got it." Jeep got to his feet and studied the house. No wonder the fucker hadn't wanted to unlock the door and show him what was inside. "I have a live, unexploded rocket-propelled grenade in a fucking shack filled with ordnance."

"What?"

Jeep double checked his weapon was secure on its sling and pushed it under his arm behind his back. He was going to need both hands for this. If he didn't clear that shit outta there, this whole village was going to be wiped off the map, taking him, his team, and their VIPs with it. That could not happen.

Already he could see the fire from the RPG was spreading. He couldn't fucking reach it where it had landed. "Move the fucking boxes." He flexed his fingers, every instinct he had screamed at him to high tail it as fast and as far as he could away from this building. But damn it, they didn't have time. "Sensei, move the VIPs, stat, I got a live RPG and a house full of ammo."

"Are you shitting me?"

"Nope. Move it." He grabbed the first box which stood in his way of getting to that damn RPG and hefted it up. Running with the box, he glanced both ways when he exited the building. Where the fuck was he going to put this so it didn't get caught in the explosion? "Outside the wall."

He raced across the open space in the center of the village, zig-zagging as he moved, hoping to avoid the bullets which were now rhythmically kicking up dirt despite the return fire from his team. Dalton was going to boot his ass for exposing himself to direct enemy fire as he raced across the space with the wall on the opposite side in his sights. He scrambled up the rubble of the broken-down wall and dumped the box over it. It landed with a solid thump, but he didn't take the time to see where it fell. Instead, he bolted back across the clearing to the house for another box.

After throwing four more boxes over the wall, he thought

he might finally be able to access the smoldering and undetonated warhead. "Don't fucking kill me, asshole," he muttered to the weapon as he grabbed it with his bare hands and raced for the exterior wall.

It took him exactly two seconds after releasing the RPG and dropping it over the compound wall to realize that the ordnance was still a fucking big problem. "Stupid fuck," he screamed at himself. "Fucking idiot." Dropping the fucking bomb on the ammo was the stupidest move he'd ever made. Okay, it was five boxes of ammo and not a full fucking hut, but still if the fire spread to the boxes, then that ammo would go up with one hell of a boom.

"Nemesis, start laying down lead to cover me, stat," he called into comms as he scrambled over the wall.

As if the tangos had a direct line to his comms, five of them rounded the corner of the wall to shoot at him as he moved the twenty or so meters to where the boxes had landed. Under withering enemy fire, he grabbed the first box and bolted for what looked like a wadi or riverbed about fifty feet from the wall. He skidded to a stop at the top of the bank and huffed out a breath. "Water, thank fuck." He dropped the box and didn't even wait for the splash before he raced back into the gunfire to grab the next one. After he'd made multiple trips to the river to dispose of the ordnance, he raced back into the fight, firing as he ran for the wall, he took out two tangos. He felt the burn of a bullet skimming his shoulder as he dived over for cover.

"Jeep?"

"Good, Boss." He kept up a steady stream of gunfire, keeping those assholes from closing in on the walls. It was probably stupid to be here right above where a burning RPG smoldered, but someone had to hold the line on this side. It was up to him.

"They're bailing," Snow said.

"Run, ya fucking bastards," Dalton added.

He wasn't sure how long the firefight had gone on for, but he'd used three of the four magazines he'd had in the pouches of his vest. Casings littered the ground around him. He heard the engines of the trucks firing to life. "Are they making a push for the gate?"

"Negative."

"Status?" Dalton's voice crackled in his ear.

"Bullet burn, left shoulder, but I'll live."

"Clear," Mokaccino confirmed.

"Clear." Snow's confirmation that she was okay was splintered by the sound of her racking her sniper rifle, no doubt making sure she was ready should the fighters come back.

"Walking wounded," Devil-Man cursed. "Damn it, I didn't even feel that until I patted down when you asked."

"VIPs clear," Sensei said. "Although I think one of them needs to learn to use the potty and not the floor. Tell me it's safe to come out, I can't stand the smell of piss."

"Roger," Dalton confirmed. "Asses out and load into the trucks."

Jeep climbed down from where he'd set up on the wall and crossed to meet Dalton as he did the same on the other side. "Boss, there's a shit load of ammo in that building."

"I saw." Dalton poked his finger into the hole on his sleeve. "How bad?"

"A burn."

Dalton nodded. Cormack knew he trusted his guys to tell him if a wound needed attention. "You and Devil-Man take first watch. Rotate every two hours. Head on a swivel," he ordered. "I'll contact base and have them send a convoy for that shit." He nodded to the ammo house.

"Roger that."

"Sensei, I'm coming to you."

"Copy."

"It's like the fucking Alamo," Lucifer grumbled as they met near the building. He gestured for Cormack to proceed him in the door. "Rome's going to shit a brick if I come home with ouches."

"You know everyone died at the Alamo, right?" Cormack stomped on a smoldering patch on the ground, grinding his boot into the dirt floor to kill the embers. "Start on that side." He pointed to the left. "I'll go from this side, and we meet in the middle."

"Don't fucking say everyone died, asshole, Davy Crockett is a legend."

"Yup," Cormack agreed, he was a legend. "A dead one."

"Let's get this shit done, I need a drink."

"Yeah, whiskey's gonna go over really well in a Muslim country."

"Right now, I don't give a fuck." He stomped on another smoldering patch and saw Lucifer doing the same. "I nearly blew myself to fucking hell and back, I'm having a drink."

"Roger that, I might even join you."

CHAPTER TWENTY

WILLOW FELT her lips curve into a smile as she read the email from Cormack. He'd remembered. Why she'd been concerned he wouldn't just because she was now living here in Montana was beyond her. It was geeky and probably a little sad, but seeing those words, IKYAS, Sunshine, fixed the jumbled mess she'd been battling in her head. Those words reminded her what Cormack meant to her and she to him. "It's okay to reply on here?"

"Of course." Lina stood from the couch. "I'm just going to use your bathroom." She shook her head. "I swear this baby is no bigger than a freaking dot and already it's sitting on my bladder."

"Help yourself, I assume you know the way?"

"Yes, I do." Lina grabbed Willow's mug where it balanced on the couch cushion and placed it on the coffee table alongside her water bottle. "If that rings, answer it." She nodded to the phone. "The only people it will be is either Trev or the doctor with an appointment for a scan."

"You want me to answer your phone?"

"Girl, there's nothing on that cell that you can't see." She chewed on the corner of her lip and shifted from one foot to the other. "But if you don't want to need bleach for your eyes, you might want to stay out of the photos."

"Huh?" It took a heartbeat or two for the reason Lina might want her to stay out of her photos to become clear, and even then, it took the addition of the slight reddening of Lina's cheeks for it to really make sense. "Ew, I do not need to see Uncle D like that." She pointed her finger at Lina. "That's just mean."

Lina grinned at her and turned toward the bathroom. "It would be meaner if I didn't warn you and you saw something that might scar you for life."

"Just eww," she called after her retreating back. "I'm rethinking this friendship thing."

"Nopie, too bad, you said we could be friends, no take backsies."

"Fine." She made sure to say the word in a snarky tone so Lina would know she was joking. She smiled down at the phone and hit reply on the email.

Grumpy.
Yay for rich men and their planes with wi-fi. I'm muttery (and yes, I know that's not a real word, but it is now so add it to the dictionary so you don't have the red squiggles that make you crazy) that you were gone when I woke up. But I'll forgive you for it as you provided Lina who made me coffee. Even if it did come after the creepy doorbell buzzing repetitively. Remind me to whine at you for the doorbell, too, k.

She knew he wouldn't remember and to be fair, she wouldn't either, but bitching and muttering about stuff to him was normal in her world. She'd spent so long on her own only talking to him over text messages and emails that it was easier to talk this way than in person.

Lina said she'd get me a phone. It's weird not having mine at my fingertips. I don't suppose anyone picked it up when they got my stuff from the house. I'm going to have to call people soon and I don't know the numbers. Hello, Google, here I come, if not, and I'll figure it out, but I'd rather not have to fall down the rabbit hole of Google, thank you.

She stretched out her foot and scratched the puppy's belly with her bare toes. He rolled fully over onto his back and melted into the floor.

This puppy is cute. Maybe we can get a puppy?

She snapped a photo and attached it to the email without looking at any of the previous photos. She frowned at the screen and chewed on her bottom lip. Was a puppy too much too soon? Her fingers hovered over the words, and she tapped backspace until she hit P on the second puppy, then retyped out the word and the question mark again. She'd not hid anything from him before, so she wouldn't do either of them a disservice by starting now.

Is that too much too soon? I think maybe it is, but I kinda like the idea of planning for the future with you. When you come home, add that to the list of stuff to talk about along with the doorbell.

Good lord, she didn't want him to think she was a bunny boiler or moving too fast or something. But he should be used to her by now, so hopefully he would see those words for what they were. She figured he would, he was pretty good at reading her quirks and moods.

Thank you for talking to Kayce, I'll go see him later today and talk to him about working in the kitchen. I think I'd like that, as I'll be daft as a brush with nothing to do. Which you figured out already, right? That was really sweet of you, Cormack, thank you <3

It had been really sweet of him to think of how she'd spend her days while he was gone. Her belly did that flip-flop thingy it always did when he went out of his way to make sure she was looked after or that she had everything she needed. Her silly man didn't know how sweet he was. She could hear him snorting at her for calling him sweet and getting all huffy about it, but he could deal.

Lina's coming back, so I must give her back her phone. I love you, Grumpy. Be safe and I'll see you when I see you.
IBW
Sunshine.

She hit send on the email and waited for it to show in her outbox. Her finger hovered over it for a second. She glanced up at Lina as she came back from the bathroom. "Do you want me to delete it?"

"Entirely up to you." Lina stepped over the puppy and sank into the couch, tucking her feet up under her. "I don't need to know what you sent him. If you don't delete it, Dalton might read it if he knew it was there though."

"Rude."

"Yup, he can be." Lina's voice got all soft and squishy when she spoke about Dalton.

Did Cormack's do that when he spoke about her? She'd have to listen and see if she noticed a difference the next time. Or did she do it when she spoke about him? She really was an idiot when it came to people. "I'll delete it," she decided. If her pseudo uncle wanted to be an idiot, there was no way she was making it easier for him. She tapped on the message, hit the trash and then deleted it from the trash too. "Thank you for letting me use your phone."

"De nada." Lina reached for the cell as it started to ring. She frowned at the screen, then even Willow with her lack of people skills could see the recognition dawn in the other woman's eyes as she tapped answer with one fingernail. "Hello." She cocked her head to one side, obviously listening to what the person on the other side of the call had to say. "Yes, this is she." She listened to the other woman and mouthed the word, "Doctor," to Willow.

"Sure, I can do three o'clock. Thanks, Doc." She paused a second. "My husband isn't able to come today, is it okay if I bring a friend instead?"

"Super, thank you, we'll see you about three."

"Yes, see you later, Doc." She pressed end on the call and glanced at Willow. "You want to come do an ultrasound with me?"

Whoa, that was the last thing she'd expected Lina to offer. "Are you sure you want me there? You barely know me."

"Well, I'm not bringing one of the hands or the other teams." She quirked up the corner of her mouth. "Dalton would lose his shit if one of them saw me in stirrups while the doctor sticks a wand in my girlie bits, and we'd be looking for a dump site and require either bail money or shovels. Besides, you're a sister wife."

Willow spat out her coffee. "If you mean like on that show, then I have an issue with sharing."

Lina laughed out loud. "Hell no, I don't share, I mean you're a MILSO and our men are essentially deployed. While I'd love for Nemy to be here for this, deploying and missions are a fact of our lives. If I was waiting for him to be here and grounded, this baby would be two years old, and I still wouldn't have had an ultrasound."

"That makes sense." She remembered the other women and wives from when she was a kid, they'd always done stuff together when their husbands couldn't make it. This she could do for Lina and Dalton. "Okay, if you're sure?"

"Absolutely sure." Lina looked as if she was thinking for a second, then she added on, "We can grab you a cell and some stuff at the store while we're out."

Money, crap, she didn't even know if her purse had made it to Montana. "I don't think I have my credit cards. Can I borrow your cell again? I have to call my bank."

"Nope, no banks and no using cards. That's how King will look for you." Lina got to her feet and brought her water bottle to the trash can. "I'll grab some extra cash; we can sort it out with Jeep when he gets back."

"Are you sure it's safe to leave the ranch with King out there?" There hadn't been much discussing, okay, no discussing at all about what King wanted from her, and she hesitated to do something which might cause a repeat of the assholes trying to kidnap her again. She wasn't stupid, at least she liked to think that she wasn't too stupid to live like those women in the movies she couldn't stand.

"Maybe." Lina rubbed her finger under one eye, wiping away the smudged eyeliner. "We've seen no evidence that he even knows this place exists…which is why I don't want you to use your bank cards and stuff, he's smart enough to have alerts on all that stuff."

"He can reach that far into the depths of society?"

"The Organization has fingers in way more places than I'd ever want to see them," Lina muttered. "And King hates to lose."

Shit, and by managing to escape, she'd probably pissed him off. But she shrugged off the worry which niggled its way under her skin. King was hopefully a problem they could deal with when the boys got back. "Okay, but I'm paying you back for any cash I borrow."

"Sure thing, Jeep can sort it out when he gets back." She snapped her fingers for the puppy. "I'm gonna go shower. Is half an hour enough time for you to be ready to leave?"

She sniffed her armpit and wrinkled her nose. "Yes, I need a shower, too, but I can do half an hour."

"I'll pick you up outside the door."

"Thank you, Lina."

"No." Lina pulled open the door. "I really don't want to go by myself, so you're doing me the favor, not the other way around."

WILLOW CHECKED to make sure the door to the building had closed behind her and skipped down the steps to where the Hummer idled next to the steps. Getting out of the house was something she hadn't known she needed until right this minute.

"You can't leave for anything, even a doctor's appointment. Nemesis and Jeep will murder me." Kayce stood next to Lina's lowered window. "He told me to keep you out of trouble."

"From what? It's just an hour's round trip to town and back." Lina gestured to Willow to jump in. "Add in the doctor's visit and a quick stop at the store and we'll be two and a half hours tops. It's not like we're driving to Vegas for a girls' weekend booze up." She tapped her fingers on the steering wheel. "And if you mean potential danger from The Organization? Well, aside from Willow's incident, we haven't heard anything from them in months."

"Lina…"

"No," she cut him off with a slash of her hand and put the Hummer in gear. "I can't live my life worrying whether or not King or his people are sending someone after me. I refuse to live my life in fear." She reached for the door and hit the button to raise the window. "If I thought there was real danger out there, I wouldn't leave, not even for the doctor. I'd insist the doctor came here. Do you think I'd ever expose my baby to danger?"

Kayce frowned and tapped his fist on the now closed window. "Jesus, Lina, I know you wouldn't, but…"

"There's no but about it. I'm going for this ultrasound."

Willow could see that Lina was pissed as hell, if it had been her, she'd have wanted to scream at him that she was a grown ass woman who could make her own decisions. But she was so far out of her depth. What normal person had to worry about being kidnapped off the streets? "Is there something to worry about?" she asked softly, knowing that Kayce couldn't hear her through the closed window.

"Not that I know of," Lina muttered. "I'm an adult. I'm pregnant, I'm not sick or disabled and I haven't lost my mind. Too stupid to live isn't normally on my list of shit to do and I'm not about to start today." Lina hit the gas and the Hummer took off. "If you don't want to come, now is your time to say it."

There was no freaking way she was letting Lina go to this appointment on her own. None. Zero. Zilch. "Nope, you're exactly right. Pregnant doesn't mean stupid. I think we should go if you still want to, and then you can show Dalton the pictures when he gets back. That might get you out of trouble a little."

"I like your style." Lina grinned. "But Kayce is right on one point. Nemy and Jeep will ream the boys a bunch of new assholes when he finds out we've left the ranch."

"Yes, that might not be so fun."

"How much do you wanna bet that Trev is already calling and telling them we've made a break for freedom?" Lina asked. She turned right out of the ranch road and threw the Hummer into four-wheel drive.

"Then they've done their duty in reporting our break for freedom and the boys can be mad at us when they get back." She reached for the radio. "Do you mind?"

"Knock yourself out."

Flipping through the channels until she found some soft rock, she settled back into the seat. "Who knows, trouble could be fun when they get back."

"My butt may not think so," Lina deadpanned. "But I can handle his moody ass."

"Ew, that's just way too much information."

"Get used to it, I spent most of my life except for the years I was with Dalton living with the dredges of society. My mouth is dirtier than half the guys at the ranch."

"My grandmother would have washed my mouth out with soap, and then grounded me for the rest of my life."

"I'm sorry you had to deal with that."

"It is what it is." She hadn't had a bad life, just a strict as hell one. It was kind of ironic that after all the warnings about boys from the wrong side of the tracks her grams had given her growing up that here she was after running off with the one thing she'd never known she'd wanted... a former SEAL. "I try not to let it shape who I am."

"Your past shapes you, no two ways about it," Lina spoke as if she was fully aware of the struggle, and Willow supposed she was. From the little bits of information she'd been able to gather, Lina's life hadn't exactly been a piece of cake either. "It's what you make of the future that's what matters most though. So, make it count."

"That's what I'm doing."

At that moment, as if the universe was listening to their conversation, Bon Jovi started singing about how his song wasn't for the broken hearted.

"Girl, turn that tune up and sing like it's going out of style."

Yup, Willow could totally get down with that... "It's my life..."

CHAPTER TWENTY-ONE

THE SUN HAD FULLY RISEN when a platoon of Marines finally rolled into the village. Cormack rubbed his eyes, making them even grittier than they had been. This country sucked donkey balls. Sand got everywhere, from your eyes to your butt crack, and there was not a damn thing you could do about it.

"Who's in charge?"

"Dalton Knight, Nemesis Inc." He gestured to the hut where the VIPs were housed along with the village elders and the grandson he wasn't entirely sure wasn't responsible for the ammo cache in the first place. "I'll radio through for you."

"Copy that, thank you." The lieutenant took a swig of water from his camel back.

He wasn't someone Cormack had met before, but there were so many boots on the ground that there was no way he'd know everyone. He thumbed his comms. "Boss, the platoon has arrived."

"Copy, send him over." Even before Dalton had finished talking, the door of the house he was in opened and he stepped outside.

"Thanks, man." The lieutenant turned toward Dalton when Cormack pointed him out to him. He stripped off his Kevlar and swiped a hand over his sweaty hair as he walked. "Knight, good to meet you, tell me what you got?"

"Somebody fed us bad intel; it was a set-up..."

Dalton's voice cut off as the door shut behind the lieutenant and Cormack couldn't hear any more. But he agreed with Dalton's assessment. They had been told this was hearts and minds shit, they should have known better.

"You think we'll be bringing the VIPs back with us?"

"Minus the dickhead in cuffs." He turned to Mokaccino. "There's no way Nem will pass our responsibilities over to someone else, but that dude, he'll send with the Marines."

Rory shifted on his feet, obviously trying to find a more comfortable way to stand. Cormack didn't blame him, keeping watch sucked. Yes, they'd had a couple of hours sleep, but not much. When you were guarding a house full of weapons that the tangos didn't want you to have, every freaking sound was something to jerk awake for.

BY MID-AFTERNOON, they were all ready to go when the battalion finally left with the ammo, the disgraced bodyguard, and the elder's grandson on board.

"Do you think they'll have problems?"

"Nah, and they have backup from a predator drone and air support." Dalton slapped dust off his camo with his gloves before pulling them back on. "Gather your shit, I'll just grab the senator and the other bodyguard, then I'm ready to roll."

"Me, too." He wanted out of here. If they'd been staying put for another night, he'd have voiced his dissatisfaction to

Dalton, but at least his boss appeared to be as much in a hurry to get home as he was himself.

"Hey, Boss?"

"Yup?" Dalton paused outside the door to the house and glanced over his shoulder.

"We're not going on to the next village…right?"

"Hell no," Dalton muttered. "The senator has had enough of a taste of Afghanistan and wants to go directly back to the US, stat."

"Smart." He acknowledged Dalton's salute with one of his own and breathed out a sigh of relief. Going deeper into the tribal lands would be stupid. But as they were being paid to protect the senator, if he'd insisted on going, they'd have had to oblige him. He'd rather not have to fight his way out of that particular hell hole, thank you.

"Smartest shit he's said all week," Mokaccino said softly.

"Right?" Everything about this trip was off. Nothing felt right, from the short notice to the ill-experienced bodyguards to the weapons cache and the fucking RPG. He'd been a warrior for long enough to know when their luck was running out. This was one of those times and it was time to make a strategic retreat. "It's just a damn shame that platoon is going in the opposite direction."

"Yeah, agree," Rory said. "I wouldn't have minded having them at my back when we made our way back to the plane."

"Me, too." He clapped him on the shoulder. "C'mon, get moving, Nem and the others will be out in a sec, I want to be ready to go as soon as their asses hit the seats."

"WHAT THE FUCK, TREV?" Dalton's furious growl had all of them turning back from the steps of the plane to look at their boss. "Repeat that?"

"That's not good."

"Nope." Cormack scratched the back of his neck to combat the itch climbing into the back of his head. "Definitely not good."

"You better be shitting me." Dalton lifted his head and pinned him with a look.

His stomach dropped into his boots. He just knew something had happened to his sunshine girl. He took the four steps needed to stand directly in front of Dalton. "Tell me."

"Find her." Dalton's fingers were wrapped so tight around his cell phone that Cormack could see the whites of his knuckles. "Are you sure my wife is okay?" He kept his gaze on Cormack and turned the cell over, tapping speaker as he did so.

"Other than pissed as hell." Lina's voice came over the phone. "I'm fine, I swear."

"Princess…"

"I'm going to find her, I promise, I'm leaving right now."

"Your ass is not to set foot off the damn ranch again until I get there."

"Sailor…"

"Give me this, baby, I can't lose you again…" Dalton's voice broke, and he swallowed hard. "Please."

"I can find her…"

Jeep couldn't wait any longer, he needed to know what the hell was going on. Bile rose in the back of his throat as he asked the question he already knew the answer to, and he cut Lina off. "Where's Willow?"

Lina's harsh inhale was audible over the phone. "Snatched out of the passenger seat of my Hummer at a traffic light when we were on the way to the doctor for an ultrasound."

His whole world screeched to a stop. Everything happened in slow motion. The twitching in his muscles was the only warning that he was going to lose it. He spun away from Dalton and the words filtering through the phone.

This could not be happening to Willow; she was so fucking gentle and soft. What was coming for her was unacceptable. Unthinkable. He'd been around the block often enough and seen the results of kidnapped women enough to know what was in store for his sunshine.

His fists slammed into the windscreen of the truck, sending a spider web of cracks spreading out across the glass. His breathing was ragged and raw as he struggled to pull himself together. "FUCK. Fucking stupid shit. What the fuck did you leave the ranch for? Why the fuck did you take her with you?"

The voices around him were worried and pissed as hell, but he didn't hear anything they said, instead his own mind slamming him with every kind of worst-case scenario possible. Anger, fear, terror, and pain all bubbled and spat in his soul until he could take no more and he dropped to his knees, a howl of pain and rage so raw it hurt his throat escaping, but he didn't feel it.

It didn't register that he looked like a crazy madman. The hands pulling him to his feet didn't register in his brain either, except as an annoyance that he needed off him right the fuck now. He slammed off his fist upward, connecting with a jaw and sending a jolt of pain up his hand. He exploded off the ground, in his head he was fighting the people who'd taken Willow and not his friends, his brothers.

"Fuck. Ow." Lucifer's grunt finally snapped him out of the red rage that screamed for vengeance in his heart. Shit, he needed to focus, somehow he needed to get his shit together and focus on the fact that Willow was out there somewhere waiting for him to come get her.

"Stop." Dalton grabbed his fist as he lashed out once more. "Focus, breathe, brother."

"Fuck you."

"I know you want to keep punching." Dalton slammed him against the truck and got right in his face. "You want to rip the world apart and burn it to the ground until you find her."

"Yes, burn it."

"Willow needs your A-game, fucking find it, stat." Dalton jerked his chin over his shoulder. "We're getting on that plane and we're going home, and then we're going hunting," he promised. "We won't stop until we find her."

"Sunshine, Sunshine, Sunshine." He thought he'd said her name in his head until Dalton peered into his face and nodded.

"Yes, we'll get Sunshine back and put everyone involved in the fucking ground. I swear."

"Okay, deal." He shook himself. He could do exactly jack shit from here in Afghanistan, his ass needed to be in Montana.

Dalton studied him as if trying to decide if he'd lose it on the plane before he put his fingers in his mouth and whistled. "Get your asses on the plane, you, too, Senator. We need this plane in the air, stat."

"Yes, sir."

"Copy."

"I'm not sure it's safe to have him on the plane."

"Senator, with all due respect, tell the incompetent dick you have as a bodyguard to fuck off," Dalton warned. "Because I can totally leave his ass behind."

By the time the plane was in the air, Cormack had locked every emotion he had down tight. Every single one was stuffed into the metaphorical box in his head and he'd reinforced that damn thing with chains a foot wide. Willow needed his A-game and by God she was going to get it.

CHAPTER TWENTY-TWO

WILLOW'S EYES POPPED OPEN, and she came awake as she'd been knocked out...struggling and attempting to fight as best she could. She couldn't see a thing here, it was cold, dark, and she didn't know where she was. But she was a thousand percent sure it wasn't anyplace good.

Damp seeped into her bones, telling her that where she lay was wet, she already knew it was hard. The assholes, and yes this was totally a situation that deserved swearing, had chained her like a freaking dog. Her arms stretched over her head as she tugged against the bounds around her wrists, her whole body shifted, and it was then she realized her ankles had something attached to them, too. "You fucking dick-holes." If they'd used zip ties and tied her to a chair, that she'd practiced for. Over and freaking over again until she could get free in less than a minute. But shackles? Those Jeep had never shown her how to get out of. If... no... when she got out of this mess, she'd be sure to remind Mr. Prepper that he wasn't so prepped after all.

The marching band playing drums in her head made it

ache. She stared into the darkness trying to see something, anything. Even in her drowsy state she tried to keep the panic from swallowing her whole. This time there was no Cormack and his friends to come rescue her. They were out of the country. She couldn't remember much, but that she did. She leaned her head back against the metal wall at her back and reality slammed into her. She wasn't wearing her shirt. She shifted her bottom, and the rough floor under her scratched against her thighs. That was when she noticed it wasn't just her shirt that was missing.

Tears burned her eyes from the horrifying realization that she had no idea what had happened. Had she been raped? Assaulted? Every inch of her hurt. She had no idea where she was. Who were these people? Why would someone do this to her? She was nobody. Nobody. She struggled to make sense of the confusion and tried to make her brain work. She'd been at the doctor's with Lina... "Oh my God, Lina?"

She pulled on the shackles, yanking her arms and pulling her feet as hot tears rolled down her face. She had to get free, she needed to make sure Lina and the baby were okay.

"Don't make so much noise or they'll come back in here."

She screamed at the sudden, unexpected woman's voice coming from the shadows. She sounded weak, like she'd been thirsty for a while. Her voice was dry, rough like sandpaper, and Willow shuddered to repress the fear which snaked down her back.

What's going on...and what's going to happen to me?

"Hello? Who's there?" She tried to keep her voice low, but even to her own ears, her hysteria was more than clear.

"I'm Becky."

"Becky. I'm Willow. Where we are? What's happening?" Wherever here was, she shouldn't be here. Cormack would come, he had to. Her throat tightened and she swallowed hard. Working her tongue, trying to get rid of the stickiness in the back of her mouth. Had she not paid enough? All her family was dead. Aside from Cormack there was nobody who cared about her.

"You don't know where we are either, huh?" Becky's voice was hoarse. "Or who these people are?"

"No." Maybe she did, she assumed it was the man King, who the guys had said sent the men to her house. But she didn't know for sure. Trying to figure out what was happening hurt her head. It ached almost as much as her heart. Please let Lina be okay. If she concentrated on the woman who'd become her friend, maybe she could keep the panic and fear from overwhelming her. "Do you?"

"What are you talking about? Who these men are?" Becky asked. "No, I don't know."

"Are there other girls? How long have you been here?"

"Few days, I think, maybe a week. I don't really know anymore; it could be two weeks. You lose track of time in here."

"A few... what?" Her voice got pitchy with panic, and a million terrible scenarios flashed through her head. Even with her father, and with Cormack's jobs, she knew stuff like this happened overseas. But this was America, people shouldn't just get kidnapped off the streets. They just shouldn't. "Becky?"

"Yes." Shackles rattled. "I'm not going anywhere. I'm sort of attached to this place."

"What do they want from us?"

Her sigh was heavy and full of despair and sadness. "Take a guess—"

"Did they..." She swallowed hard. "Do they..."

"Did they rape me?"

"Yes." She needed to know what she was facing. Needed to prepare herself. Cormack would be looking for her. But would he find her in time?

"Yes," she answered. Willow could hear the tears in her voice. "Every time they feel like it."

"Oh my God."

"There isn't a god on the planet who can stop it."

"My man will come for me."

"They'll kill him," Becky said. "They killed a cop the day before yesterday when he came nosing around."

Bile burned the back of her throat. She debated puking all over herself, maybe that would make whoever these people were leave her alone. But her reflexes had her swallowing it down. "He's hard to kill."

"We'll see," Becky replied softly. "I hope you're right." Her voice broke on a sob. "I want to go home."

"What did they do to you?" she whispered. She chewed on the corner of her nail. She'd pay anything, give anything and everything she owned to be back hiding in Cormack's bunker with the spiders and snakes. The anxiety of not knowing what was happening, of sitting here in the dark, talking to a voice of someone she couldn't see—maybe this was a dream, a nightmare and she'd wake up instead of feeling like she was losing her grip on reality. Yep, it was official, she was completely losing it.

"What haven't they done?" Becky whispered. "When they want me, they unchain me and do whatever they want, and if I don't let them, there are consequences."

"But do what? What consequences?" Maybe needing to know what was coming was stupid. But it didn't matter; if she knew, she could do something, anything. "Tell me, please, I need to know what's going to happen to me."

"They're going to take turns with you, or even not turns, but together. Each and every single one of them are going to rape you."

No, that could not happen, she'd die fighting first.

As if Becky was reading her mind, she advised, "Don't fight them; they like it when you fight them."

"Don't fight them?" she spluttered in shock. She couldn't believe she would say something like that. "Don't fight. How can you say that?"

"Because I've tried fighting, I've tried crying, and I've tried begging. You haven't seen what they're capable of. You'll see what being here means. I'm sorry for what's going to happen to you. Believe me—you'll wish you were dead; you'll pray for it. I do."

She could feel the ice creeping along her veins. Her heart stuttered and the air froze in her lungs, making it difficult to breathe. She didn't want to die. She wanted Cormack. She wanted to go home. There had to be something she could do. She couldn't just sit here and let these people do whatever they wanted without fighting. She tugged on her shackles again, she had to get free.

She didn't even know how to respond to Becky. What was there to say? Every word Becky had said to her went around and around in her head, ramping up the terror she was struggling to suppress.

"What did you do?" Becky asked. "Before this happened?"

"I was a cook. But I'm sort of between jobs. I'd just moved from Virginia to live with my boyfriend in Montana." Calling Cormack a boy would normally be laughable, but there was nothing remotely funny about this situation. "What about you?"

"I'm a teacher. I love my job. I love the kids I teach. I'm sorry this happened to you," Becky said.

"This sucks and it's scary."

"It's okay to be scared, but I'm telling you right now, don't let them see your fear." Becky's voice was filled with sympathy. "Pretend like you never have before," she advised. "Shut your mind down, see someone else touching you in your head, and pretend as if you like what they're doing to you."

There was no way she could do that. It just wasn't possible. She glanced at where she thought the door was. *Please, Cormack.... Please come get me.*

"It stops a hell of a lot sooner if you don't fight them," Becky continued. "Because they like their girls to fight them. Okay?"

I'll never stop fighting.

But how did she know Becky wasn't one of the people who'd taken her? How did she know she wasn't sent here to screw with her mind? Not fighting just wasn't in her DNA. "Sure."

"I'm sorry," Becky said softly. "I wish I didn't have to tell you how it is. I'm sorry, it's shitty and cruel, there's no way to soften the blow, and I'm not going to give you a pack of lies that this is going to be sunshine and roses. There's no hope here. None at all."

Sunshine, Cormack called her Sunshine. She swallowed down the sob which blocked her throat. She was grateful that Becky was telling her the truth. It was giving her time to prepare mentally, not that there could ever possibly be a way to prepare for what was about to happen. "How many are there?"

"Three," Becky said. "Well, four, but one man, I don't know his name. He's different than the others."

"Different how?"

"He brings food and water, he doesn't have sex with me," Becky said. "He makes sure he isn't around when they rape me."

Oh, God, was it too much to hope for that this man might be undercover? That he might help them escape? Even as the thought entered her head, she pushed down the hope it brought. "Will he help us?"

"No, I've asked before," Becky said. "He refuses every time."

"Crap."

"I had worse words than that, but yes, crap." Metal clanged from the direction of Becky's voice, and Willow imagined that she'd scrubbed her hand over her face in frustration. "I asked him why, and he said they'll kill him if I push for it."

God, she was naive, he'd probably told her that to get her to stop asking for help. She knew she was probably being stupid. It didn't stop the flame of hope from flaring in her chest. She had to get this man to understand that letting her go was the best thing he could do for his *friends*.

"I know what you're thinking. I've tried so many times to get him to help. He always says no," Becky muttered. "He said he hates what's happening, but his hands are tied, and he can't do anything."

This man was sounding more and more like someone who was undercover. Cormack would lose his shit if he found that to be true. "Doing nothing to help you escape or to tell someone where you are doesn't make him a good person, it makes him almost as big a dick as the others."

The sound of rattling from outside stopped all conversation and all Willow could do was brace herself for whatever the door opening would bring. Somehow, some way, she would find it within herself to survive, all she had to do was hold out long enough. Cormack would come for her. She had to believe that, or she might as well give up right now. Giving up wasn't an option, it wasn't written on her deck of cards. She would survive, and Cormack would come.

CHAPTER TWENTY-THREE

HE BARELY WAITED for the plane to slow to a stop before he was out of his seat. Since they'd dropped off the senator and his one remaining bodyguard in DC and jumped onto Nemesis's plane, he'd been itching to get back to the war-room.

"Slow down, Jeep." Dalton might be telling him to take his time, but the big lug was stepping on his heels as he bitched.

"I need to see what Trev has found."

"He'll find her."

"He didn't find Lina until she wanted to come out of the woodwork." Maybe it was shitty to remind Dalton of that, but he wasn't feeling very charitable right now.

"He'll have found something by now." Dalton tried to reassure him. "Guys, you grab the gear, I'm running to the war-room with Jeep!" he yelled the order over his shoulder to the rest of the guys.

"Yes, sir."

"You got it."

The chorus of affirmative answers barely registered in his

brain. Willow couldn't have disappeared without a trace. King and his organization of fuckers were good, but Trev was better. He just had to be.

He jumped into the truck and turned the key. Thank fuck for living in a remote ass ranch where he could leave the keys in his damn truck and still find it right where he'd parked it when he got back. Although, who the hell was going to steal a truck out here? The cows? Cows stealing a truck would end up as a post on what was that app Willow liked called, Tickle Tocker or something. He gunned the engine and hit the gas.

"Wait for me, dickhead."

He glanced at the passenger door, his eyes widening when he saw Dalton running beside the truck with his fingers wrapped into the frame of the door. "Shit." He slammed on the brakes. "Sorry, Boss."

"Try not to kill me before we get to the house, okay? Lina'll be pissed."

"Yeah, sorry." As soon as Dalton's ass hit the seat, he hit the gas again. The door slammed shut just about the same time he hit the road to the ranch.

"Man, I know you're freaking out, but keep your head on straight…"

His snort cut off whatever stupid shit was going to fall out of his friend's mouth. "If you think there's any fucking way I'm not this close…" he held his thumb and forefinger a tiny piece apart, "to losing my shit, then you've forgotten the panic it is when the person you love the most is ripped out of your world, and there's fucking nothing you can do about it because you're way too many time zones away to get to her in time."

"Fuck you." Dalton slammed his hand onto the dash to prevent himself hitting the windshield as the truck took the turn into the yard as if they were racing through the streets of Fallujah to escape an RPG. "I know exactly how that feels, so don't go there."

They sped past Dalton's house and the team houses. He hit the brakes hard enough and just in time to prevent the grill of his truck from slamming into the doors of the Intel offices as they pulled to a stop. He didn't bother with mundane things like switching off the engine, as soon as the truck stopped, he pushed open the door and bolted for the building.

He ran up the steps to the locked door and slapped his palm against the scanner. "Come on, come on." He pushed the door open so hard the metal handle slammed off the bulletproof glass behind it, but he didn't notice as he raced for Trev's office.

"Tell me you found her."

"Not yet." Trev's voice was filled with sympathy as he spun around in his chair to face him. "I swear I'm working on it."

"Fuck." He'd been holding out hope that Trev had something, anything, that they could go on. "Fuck!" he screamed out the word and swiped his hand across the closest desk, sending computers and shit flying. But even breaking shit didn't help. His Willow-sized hole where his heart should be hurt like hell.

"Jesus…" Trev bounced out of his chair and across the room. His hands fisted into Jeep's flak jacket as he pushed him ahead of him and away from anymore breakables toward the door. "Stop wrecking my office."

"Get off me." His voice lowered to almost a whisper, deadly soft. It should be enough to warn Trev that he was about two seconds from getting his ass kicked.

"The more you fuck up my shit, the longer it takes to find

her." He pushed against Cormack's chest but didn't make much progress as he planted his feet and braced himself against it.

"Find her...Now..."

He went into fight mode when he took a hit to the knee, and hands banded around him from behind. "He's old, always go for the knees," Dalton told Trev. "He'll go down like a sack of potatoes."

"Bastard." Struggling against Dalton was like trying to pull a truck with wet spaghetti. It was impossible, he knew it, but his brain refused to let go of the need to hit and punch something.

"Come with me, asshole." Despite his efforts and digging his feet into the floor trying to get purchase, Dalton dragged him backward and out of the room. "Lock that door, Trev, Jeep has no access until I give it."

"Yes, sir."

"What?"

"Shut up." Dalton dragged his ass down the hall backward and hit the door to the gym with his butt. As soon as Cormack's boots cleared the door, Dalton released him and turned and locked the door. "Strip off your gear, fucker, we're sorting this shit before you go back to the war-room."

"Fuck you."

The words were barely out of his mouth when Dalton's fist connected with his eye socket in a hard as hell left hook. "Take that shit off, or I'll do it for you." Dalton placed his hand on the lock and tapped in a code.

Oh, he wanted to be that dick, did he? The asshole had just locked them into the gym. Until his asshole boss put his code back into the locking mechanism, there was no fucking way he was getting out of here until Dalton had knocked some lumps out of him. He stripped off his Kevlar, dropped his weapons on the floor and rushed Dalton.

As if Nemesis, and there was no doubt Dalton was in full-on Nemesis mode at this point, sensed him coming, he slammed his foot back and raised to knee level in a hard kick.

They'd been on this merry-go-round before, so he was able to turn his body enough to deflect the hit with his thigh rather than taking the hit to the balls Nemesis had intended. "That all you got, fucker?"

"Nope." Nemesis spun around and stepped forward with his right leg, bending slightly as he lifted the heel on his opposite leg slightly to give himself maneuverability. His hands came up, his chin tucked down, and he beckoned to Cormack with his fingers. "Bring it, asshole."

Cormack mirrored his stance. They'd both been trained in Krav Maga for long enough to be able to bounce or spring in any direction from here. He raised his hands to just under about twelve inches in front of his face to give himself a margin for error if he needed it.

The closer he got to Dalton, the more his hands contracted closer to his face, then Cormack threw the first punch, which Nemesis easily deflected.

"That all you got?"

"Hell no." He sprung forward with his fists and feet flying, landing some hits, and taking some. "Let me look for her."

"You brought her into this world and now she has to live with the fucked-up shit King does to her." Nemesis spun his foot out, aiming for his feet. "You shouldn't have touched her."

"Fuck you, I didn't tell you to not look for Lina, I…"
Punch.

His head jerked back from the force of the knuckles hitting his jaw. "My wife has jack shit to do with this."

"She let her get taken." Until the words had popped out of his mouth, he hadn't known he thought that.

"Fuck you, there was no way to know."

Kick, punch, kick.

"She worked for King; she should have known he could find her."

"Not relevant."

Nemesis lashed out with a punch, but he leaned back, almost bending double so the fist didn't connect with his nose but skimmed off his cheek instead.

"Yes, it fucking is." He retaliated with a roundhouse kick, which slipped through the space between Nemesis's lowered elbows, and he stumbled backward. There was no fucking way he wasn't taking advantage of that lapse in concentration from Nemesis, and he pushed forward. "She let my woman get taken."

"She's Eli's daughter."

"She. Is. Mine." Nemesis could mutter and bitch about it all he wanted. Willow was his, end of discussion.

Nemesis blocked all his hits and came back with a flurry of fists and feet flying of his own. "She is a kid."

Rage poured off him, how fucking dare he? "She's twenty-seven, not seven, fuck off."

"And you're old enough to be her father," Nemesis grunted when Cormack's foot connected with his knee, hard.

"But I'm not her father, I'm her man."

Nemesis managed to slip between Cormack's defenses and wrapped his hands around his throat, shoving him backward until he slammed against the wall. He lowered his face until they were nose to nose. "You got him killed."

"Asshole, do you think I knew that fucking chopper was

going to get hit by a missile? Do you think I don't kick my own ass for sending him on that fucking bird? Do you think I don't live with that every day?"

Nemesis's accusations took the rage out of him, and he deflated, sagging against the wall. If his boss hadn't had his hands wrapped around his neck, he'd have slid down the wall to land on his ass on the floor.

"Fucker." Nemesis was so mad he spat as he spoke. "You didn't tell her, did you? She wouldn't touch you if you told her."

"I am hers and she is mine." She'd promised him she was his and despite what Nemesis said, he had to believe that she meant it, or nothing was worth living for anymore.

"Not what I asked." Nemesis kept pushing. "You. Didn't. Tell. Her. You. Ordered. Her. Father. On. That. Fucking. Bird. Did. You?" Each word was punctuated by a slam of Nemesis's fist.

The accusation finally made sense in his head, is that what the man, who was not only his boss but also his friend, thought of him? Seriously? Did he not know him at all? But why Nemesis was so pissed about him and Willow being together made a fucked-up kind of sense now. "It was the first thing I told her." He might be an asshole, even the dick that apparently Nemesis thought he was, but there were a couple of things he would never, ever do and lying to Willow was at the top of that very short list. "It was the first thing I told her," he repeated.

"Oh."

Yeah, stick that in your peace-pipe and fucking smoke it. His very first email to Willow had been an apology for being the man who gave the order for Eli to take that ride back to base.

"Why the fuck didn't you tell me?" Nemesis released him

and turned to slide down the wall to sit on the floor next to him.

"You didn't ask, you just assumed." He felt around his neck, wincing at the sore spots. The corner of his mouth hurt like hell, too, and when he probed it with a finger, he saw blood when he pulled it back. That Nemesis was doing the same to his left eye, and his right one was almost closed but not bloody eased some of the sting of having his ass handed to him in a Krav Maga fight.

"I'm sorry."

He should have known that Dalton would apologize as fast as he'd made the assumption that he was a dick. But this time stung. "Why the fuck would you think I'd treat my woman with any less respect than you do yours?"

"Because I'm a goddamn idiot," Dalton said. "At least that's what my wife would have said."

"She'd be right."

"My only legitimate excuse…" Dalton trailed off. "No, scratch that, there is no legitimate excuse. I was a dick and I'm sorry."

"I get it, man, you've looked out for her since she was a kid, but…"

"But now she's yours."

"Yes, she is." He could hold a grudge and be petty as fuck about it. But they'd fought too long and too hard at each other's backs for him to do that. He held out his hand, his bruised knuckles closed into a fist. "Bros?"

"Always, man." Dalton tapped his fist off his. Then shifted his jaw from side to side. Jeep winced as he heard the audible click. "I think you knocked some teeth loose."

"You're ugly anyway, another couple of missing teeth ain't going to make any difference."

"Fucker."

The ding of the intercom cut off anything else they might have said, and like a pair of puppies, both men tilted their heads to one side to listen as Trev's voice filled the gym.

"Boss, I got something. You're gonna want to see this."

———

"Boss, you wanted me to find King's mistake," Trev spoke as soon as they opened the door to the war-room. He didn't even bat an eyelid at the state of the pair of them. Just wait until one of them dripped blood all over a keyboard or something then shit would fly. He sent a map to the main screen of the war-room. "Take a look at this."

"What am I looking at?" Dalton paused on his way to the screen to grab some tissues off Snow's desk and used one to dab at the cut over his eye.

"I searched through shit loads of intel and dummy corps, looking to see what I'm missing." Trev sounded totally disgruntled. "Of the one hundred and seventeen known organization front companies Lina says King has used in the past." He circled a map. "Twenty-five are located in the US."

"Shit." This was not what he wanted to hear. Twenty-five locations were too many to check in a short time span. Jeep clamped down on the frustration building inside him. There had to be a better way.

"Well, that's not news." Dalton studied the screen. "I don't understand what you're trying to say to us."

"It might not give us the exact location," Trev said. "But it's a baseline to start from." He flipped screens and pulled up lists of scrolling data. "Every organization King or The Organization have used in the past, I was able to plug all this data into a spreadsheet and crunch it to give me a very rough communication pattern except..." He circled one of the red pins on the map. "This one has no known communication in or out ever."

Okay, he had to admit that was probably unusual.

"Get me a street view on that location."

"Already have it, Boss." Trev flipped the screens again and zoomed in until they could all see what was happening on the ground at that location.

Cormack scowled at their comms tech. "Dude, that's under construction." He scratched his head. He had to be missing the point here, but when he saw the confused look on Dalton's face he knew it wasn't just him that was struggling to follow where their resident geek was trying to take them. "No one lives at a building site, and there's probably workers all over that place."

"I agree," Dalton said. "If that's a live construction site, then there's no way they are keeping Willow there, especially not on a weekday."

"That's why this is particularly interesting." Trev once again flipped the screen. "I had one of my hacker friends take a look at the power usage for that location."

He and Dalton exchanged glances, apparently Trev was seeing something they weren't.

"What did he find?" Dalton asked the question before he could.

Would grabbing Trev and shaking him make him spit out the intel any faster? Probably not, but it didn't stop him from fantasizing about it.

"Up until about the time when you moved from Kabul to the ranch, there was nothing to make it stand out. The usage is about average for any construction site in the US. During the workweek it's elevated, and it dies down again over a weekend or on holidays." On screen Trev shrugged. "But two days after you moved your base of operations and took Lina with you, the power usage went through the roof for every day of the week, and the construction company who was working there is now across town at this site." Trev circled a blue pin on the map.

Dalton scanned the lines on the charts and power points Trev was highlighting with his laser on screen. "That's a pretty big jump, considering nobody lives there, and the construction crew have moved sites. Would leaving shit on cause that?"

"Nope." Trev shook his head. "That's computers and internet and lights and a hell of a lot of other shit needed to power something like this room." He swept his hand in a circle to take in the whole room.

Cormack peered at the map, trying to see the area codes. Not that he knew many of them, but color him surprised when he recognized the street names. "That's just outside Billings." He pinched his fingers into his eyes. "Right under our fucking noses."

"He has balls," Trev agreed.

Dalton scowled at the map on the screen as if it was all Google's fault. "Did you verify that with your buddy?"

"Yup."

"Good." He reached for the phone on his desk and hit a button and then hit speaker. His fingers drummed on the wood as he waited for Lina to answer. "Get me all team leaders, tell them to warn their boys to get ready, we're gonna make a house call."

"You found something?"

"Trev did, but, Princess, I'm gonna need you, too."

"You always need me."

"True. But this is intel related only and you're not going

in the field." Apparently, Dalton was making sure there were no misunderstandings between him and Lina.

"I'll give you whatever I can."

"Okay, you come down with the guys, too."

"Yes, dear."

CHAPTER TWENTY-FOUR

How the hell had it come to this? Cormack stood next to one of the whiteboards. Normally, when they were mission planning, his ass would be planted in his chair so he could pull up intel and distribute it to the team leaders. He'd tried that a few minutes ago, but his leg kept jiggling and knocking off the desk and Trev had threatened to throw him out of the room if it didn't stop distracting him.

His eyes widened as the door to the war-room opened, and not just the team leaders entered, but every member of Alpha, Bravo, and Charlie teams filed into the room and found somewhere to either sit or stand.

"What's happening?"

"She's your woman, that makes her family." Kentucky Smith, the Charlie team commander, lifted one shoulder. He leaned his ass and one booted foot against the wall next to the door. "We protect family, and they all," he nodded to the men standing around the room, "want to make sure that nothing gets missed or lost in translation on this mission."

Those weren't tears stinging his sore eyes. Nope,

someone had sprayed some shit in the air. He had to clear his throat twice before he could speak. "Thank you."

Dalton stuck his fingers in his mouth and gave a sharp whistle. "Listen up, assholes." But before he could continue, the door opened again and Rexar entered the room.

"Don't even say it." Rexar took a place between Smith and the door. "I'm going, end of discussion."

"We wouldn't dream of leaving you out." Cormack nodded to Rexar. If anyone had a right to go rescue Willow, it was one of her father's teammates.

"I'm going to give it to all y'all straight," Dalton said. "This job is on US soil, hell, we aren't even leaving the state. We're going to ride almost into Billings and rip this construction site apart until we find Willow Black."

Cormack scanned the room at the mutterings from all the men. "If anyone has a problem with that or doesn't want to be involved, that's the door, feel free to leave."

"What Jeep means," Dalton cut off anything else he might have said. "Is there are no direct orders for this mission. There is no contract, no hazard pay, and no one is going to hold a grudge if you don't want to raise your weapons against US citizens."

"It's Willy." Rexar looked Cormack dead in the eye from across the room. "I'm in, zero fucks given."

The other people in the room all muttered or nodded their agreement, and after about thirty seconds Dalton glanced at his watch. "Until we go wheels up, the option to withdraw is on the table, once we're at go-time, if you're on my helos and change your mind, I'm going to assume you are a plant or King has bought you off."

"That's kinda shitty, Sailor."

"The Organization has its reach fucking everywhere,"

Dalton told Lina. "Can you swear on our baby's life to Cormack that he hasn't attempted to turn someone here?"

"I know he has," Lina answered. "I also know he didn't succeed." She flicked her thumbnail over one of her other nails. "If he had, you'd have been dead before you found me."

"I'm not saying I don't trust y'all, or for you to not trust each other." Dalton pinned each person with a stare. "I'm telling you that this rat is dangerous as all get out, and I'm fucking worried, understood?"

"Yes, sir." He did understand. He didn't like it one bit that Dalton was maybe pissing off their guys. But there was no other way to do it. Neither of them would put Willow's life at stake on the off chance there was a mole.

Dalton scanned the room one last time, then nodded at Trev.

"All communication in and out of the ranch is jammed," Trev said. "Defcon red protocols, all comms are limited to our internal radios and comms units."

"Good."

"What do we know, Trev?"

Maps, photos, and a lot of other intel started populating the big screens over Trev's desk. "The construction company is a front for a militia." Trev used a laser pointer to circle the logo. "As you can see, their company logo is a rattlesnake." He winced in Lina's direction but kept going. "The snake pinged my radar, as King calls his assassins Snakes." He shrugged. "It was a leap, but it paid off." He flipped the screens to bring up some back accounts and highlighted a payment for one hundred thousand dollars. "This payment was made yesterday from one of the other dummy corporations Lina provided us with. If I had time, I'd follow the money and see where that leads."

"We don't have any time." Cormack would love to be able to get closer to King, but Willow was more important. "Willow doesn't have that time."

"I know." Trev flipped back to the satellite view of the maps again. "If this was Iraq or Afghanistan, I'd suggest sending an armored vehicle in to draw fire to know and how many you're going to be fighting."

"But this isn't the sandbox," Rexar muttered. "And we can't use armored vehicles without drawing a hell of a lot of attention."

"I want a volunteer," Dalton said. "One of the team leaders, or you, Rex."

Those were the men he'd have picked for the job, too.

"What do you need?" Rexar straightened off the wall. "Name it and it's yours."

Cormack could see where the boss was going with this. "It's a big ask."

"We can't attack a fortified position without knowing the strength of our enemy," Smith said. "Especially if we don't want to put the hostage at risk."

"I'd do it myself." Cormack pointed to his chest. "But..." He didn't bother finishing, they all knew he had to be on the ground looking for Willow, anything else wouldn't be acceptable.

"Yeah, you have to be there when we find her," Rexar said. "I'll draw their fire," he offered. "I do have one question though."

"Shoot," Dalton replied.

"Do we want answers or blood?"

Dalton glanced at him, and Cormack drew his hand across his throat. While he was grateful to be allowed to make the decision, there was only one answer he could give. They'd taken his sunshine girl; the only acceptable price was what these fuckers prized most… their lives.

"Blood."

"Roger that."

"Okay." Trev flexed his shoulders and stretched his neck first to the left and then to the right, obviously trying to relieve the pressure which came from being hunched over a computer for way too many hours in a day. "Your wrist-computers will have a copy of the map I was able to hijack from the county archives, along with pictures of the known militia members." As he spoke, images flashed up on the screen. Information was as good as ammo, and in this instance they would take all the ammo they could get.

"Wait," one of Bravo team members spoke up as the images rolled across the screen. "Go back two shots."

"Whatcha see, Tate?"

"That's Graham Pitney."

"Who the fuck is Graham Pitney?"

"ATF," Tate said. "Or at least that's where I think he went after he got out of the Corps."

Well, if anyone would be running an undercover op in a militia it would probably be the Bureau of Alcohol, Tobacco, Firearms, and Explosives. "The ATF's running an undercover op?" A tiny spark of hope fluttered to life, but he didn't dare let it get a foot hold. "Who do we know at ATF?" he demanded the answers and he needed them stat.

"Let me see if my hacker friend knows anyone." Trev pulled up a chat box and his fingers flew over the keyboard as he sent the suspected agent's photo and name to his friend.

Dalton's hand landed on Trev's shoulder just before he hit send. "You trust this guy?"

"Yeppers." Trev nodded. "He's a brother from back in the day."

"Go ahead then."

"Would this Pitney guy have turned?" Cormack asked Tate.

Tate shook his head. "I can't see that happening. But he did save my life, so I'm kinda biased."

"What happened?"

"We were working in Ramadi." He scratched his nose. "You know the normal, one of those seize, clear, hold, build, standard operations?"

"Yes." He was quite sure most of the people in the room knew what those operations entailed.

"We rolled into town in some Bradley tanks, and as we moved into the first building, we started taking fire from an adjacent one."

"Getting caught in crossfire like that is a raw deal." He knew the deal. He'd seen it happen so many times it wasn't funny. They'd go kick in doors in a supposedly abandoned area, only for the shit to hit the fan the second their butts cleared the door. "Let me guess, as soon as you entered, the tangos in the house across the way joined in the fun?"

"Yeah, don't you know it." Tate exchanged glances with him. While he was talking to Cormack, all the others in the room could feel like he was talking directly to them and everything he said would make perfect sense. "Pits jumped into me; he most likely saved my life because if I'd walked out into that hallway, I'd probably have ended up getting hit in the crossfire."

"My buddy is tracking Pitney's cell and hitting up a buddy in ATF," Trev said. "I'll have that information for you before you go wheels up."

"Roger that."

They went over and back and over and back, dissecting all the intel Trev and his friend had been able to pull. Maps, images, drone footage, everything they needed, Trev produced as if by magic. Finally, despite the fact they hadn't had a response from the ATF, they had what they hoped was a workable plan and Dalton called it.

"Wheels up in sixty, it won't take us long to set down close enough to get to, but far enough away that we shouldn't be heard. Double plates in your vests. How copy?"

"Solid copy."

"Let's move."

HE HAD no fucking clue where the hell Rexar had produced a desert Uber from, but the dirt bike was perfect for what they needed. "Snow will be covering you from overwatch." He knew Rexar knew the details, but it kept him from losing his grip on his self-control and running into the compound, taking out everyone in his way until he found Willow.

"Yes, sir." Rexar adjusted his M-24 on his sling, securing it over his back where it wouldn't interfere with his ability to ride.

"Since when the fuck do you call me sir?"

"Since you're running the op." Rexar's teeth flashed white against his warpaint painted face.

"Don't let the boss hear you say that shit," Cormack advised. "I've already had one beating this week, I don't want another."

"The boss already heard it," Dalton whispered. "And if I think you need another beating to knock some sense into that hard head of yours, then I'll oblige you by dishing it out."

"Nemesis Six to One, confirmation of night vision," Snow called over comms.

"Fuck, that probably means they have thermal, too," Dalton muttered. "Assholes."

"You can bet on it," Cormack agreed.

"On my count." Dalton clamped his hand onto Rexar's shoulder. "Ride like you're chasing skirt."

"Fuck you." Rexar huffed out a breath. "I love you. Assholes." He kickstarted the bike, the growl of the engine shattering the night sky. He twisted the throttle a couple of times just to give their target assholes time to show themselves, and then fishtailed into motion, drawing immediate gunfire.

As soon as the assholes started firing on Rexar, the snipers from all three teams on overwatch were pinpointing the flashes and started reducing numbers and taking targets out of commission.

"Drop your weapons!" Cormack and Dalton made their way in formation down the valley and toward the compound.

"Just like being back in the 'Stans," Dalton muttered as they ducked and ran at a crouch, zig-zagging to avoid the gunfire.

"Drop your weapons." All around them the orders spilled out as the teams reported either targets captured or dead.

He and Dalton skimmed their way around the perimeter wall, looking for the entrance to the door which housed the power. According to the plans Trev's friend had provided them with, from there they could access a basement level. They had all agreed, if you were going to hold a kidnap victim anywhere, then the basement level was where her screams for help were least likely to be heard.

As they approached the corner of a building, they stacked up, ready to swivel around it when a man did just what they had been planning to and walked straight into the muzzle of Cormack's weapon. "Down! On the ground, now!"

"Who the fuck are you?"

"Your worst nightmare." He jammed the muzzle into the asshole's forehead. It was probably hot from all the firing, but he didn't give a fuck if this prick had a nice round burn imprint for the rest of his life. It would remind the asshole to not be a dick to women every fucking time he looked in the mirror. "Get the fuck down!" The asshole finally figured out that he meant what he said. "All the way, asshole, all the way down!"

As soon as the man hit the dirt, Dalton slapped zippy cuffs on his hands and feet. Once his boss was done, Cormack gripped the man by the hair and lifted his head up enough to look at him. "Where's my woman?"

"Shit."

"Where the fuck is she?" Cormack smacked the man's face into the ground, then pulled his head up again by the hair, and growled into his face. "Do you know where my woman is?"

The fucker apparently still didn't want to answer, so Cormack helped him make a decision by slamming his face into the dirt a couple of more times.

"Easy, chief," Dalton said softly. "We need him to be able to talk and not be unconscious yet."

The man mumbled something against the ground and Cormack lifted the fucker's head again. "What did you say?"

"Are you cops?"

"Fuck no, where's my woman?"

"I'm ATF."

He and Dalton exchanged glances, then peered down into the man's face. Dalton tapped through the screens on his wrist computer until he found the shot of Graham Pitney, and he shoved his arm almost under Cormack's nose.

"That him?"

"No, I don't think so." He winced as he glanced down at the battered face and squeezed his eyes shut briefly before opening them again. "Name?"

"Pitney, Graham Pitney."

"Fuck."

"Where's my woman, asshole?" Rage like he'd never felt before blasted through his veins. This fucking ATF officer knew his woman was here and didn't fucking help her escape? What the actual fuck? He balled his fist and only Dalton clamping his hand over his prevented the punch from falling.

"Easy, bro, we'll find her." Dalton clicked on his comms. "Alpha One to Bravo Four, we're in the quadrant three echo, get your ass over here and ID the potential friendly."

"Bravo Four on my way, sir," Tate replied almost immediately.

"Military?"

"Shut the fuck up, unless it's to tell me where my woman is." Cormack dropped the man's head again and pressed the muzzle of his weapon into the back of the man's neck.

"You're going to murder me?"

"I haven't decided yet, asshole."

The sound of footsteps running toward them barely registered before Dalton spun around with his weapon raised.

"Hey, Boss." Tate skidded to a stop next to them with Kentucky right on his heels.

"This your boy?" He wrapped his fingers into the man's hair and tugged his face out of the dirt so Tate could get a good look at his face.

"Tate? That you, man?"

"That's him," Tate confirmed. "Not that I could tell from his face, only his voice."

"Fucker won't tell me where Sunshine is."

"Where's the girl, Pits?" Tate crouched down onto his haunches and tilted his head, studying him like Trev did intel.

"They're in a container in the basement," Pitney finally said. "I had no warning this was going down."

"Fuck you, asshole." Cormack loosened his grip on the asshole's hair and his face once again hit the dirt. "You didn't get her out of there." He turned to go toward the door where they should have access to the basement.

"Stop," Kentucky ordered. He rolled the ATF agent over onto his back. "You said they... there's more than one girl?"

"Ah, fuck, ow." The agent covered his face with his hands, grunting and groaning as he probed his nose.

Kentucky nudged him with his boot. "Answer, fuckwad, there's more than one girl?"

"Yes, there's two."

"Fucker." Kentucky kicked him in the ribs. "You deserve a lot worse than this."

"A fucking bullet to the brain stem is what he deserves," Cormack muttered.

"Alpha One, all stations." Now that all three teams were in the field for this op, Nemesis had taken over the callsign Alpha One to avoid any confusion. All teams were Nemesis, but when they didn't want anyone to know who they were, the Nemesis part was dropped from their communications. "Be aware we have two HVPs, I repeat, two high value packages."

"Let's go."

"How many guards?" Dalton asked before he turned away from the ATF agent on the ground.

"None, I was the guard."

"If you're lying to me, I'll fuck you up," Dalton warned. He gestured to Tate and Kentucky. "Stash him, Tate. Bravo One, you're with us."

"Yes, sir."

"Copy that, sir."

"What a fucking cocksucker." Cormack took point just as he would in the field, with Dalton two steps behind him and slightly to the right, and Kentucky in a similar position but on the opposite side. In these positions each knew where the other would be without looking.

"Yeah," Dalton muttered.

Cormack felt a tap on his shoulder and Dalton's hand skimmed past his ear, pointing to the door they needed to enter. "Got it."

All around them the sounds of gunfire were tapering off. Instead of a steady barrage, it now came in sporadic bursts, telling them some pockets of militia were holding out against the stronger fire power of his teams.

They made it to the door without incident. Other than a scraggly cat scaring the shit out of them as they were on their final approach. They stacked up on the door and Cormack reached out a hand to check it.

"Locked." He reached into one of the pouches on his vest for his lock picking kit. "The son of a bitch locked it." He should have known to check the fucker for keys before they'd left him with Tate. He dropped to his knees in front of the door, if he didn't have this unlocked in ten seconds, he was putting a damn charge on it and blowing the fucker out of his way.

But as if the door was able to read his thoughts, the lock gave almost as soon as he made the first turn of the pick. "There you go."

He got to his feet and stepped aside to press his back against the wall again. Standing in front of the door as you opened it was one hell of a good way to get shot. He pulled open the door, waited a heartbeat to see if there was any gunfire, and sidestepped into the building, his weapon at ready position as he went left, Kentucky went right, and Dalton straight down the middle to clear the room.

"Fuck, it stinks," Kentucky muttered.

His eyes burned from the smell of human feces and urine, the deeper into the room they went, the stronger the smell got. Every step he took made him madder and madder. His sunshine girl didn't deserve this.

"We'll find her." Dalton's hand on his shoulder told him as he stumbled to a stop as they approached the door which the plans said led to the staircase. "You have my word."

Yeah, but Dalton couldn't promise him that she'd be in one piece.

"Keep it together, bro," Kentucky encouraged.

He pulled up his big boy panties and moved forward with the boys on his six. This staircase into the basement was a bottleneck and the position which had worried them most. But they cleared it without incident.

"Finally, something is going our way," Dalton muttered softly.

As the lights of the upper floor faded behind them, they flipped on the torches on their headgear. Night vision needed some bit of light to work and down here, there was exactly zero light. So, they had to take the chance that their headlights didn't paint a target directly on their foreheads.

They moved in formation across the basement until they made it to where the container sat right in the middle of the open space.

"Fucking locked again." He scowled at the padlock and reached for his kit again. "Bastards." But as before the lock didn't offer much resistance and gave under his pick.

"On my mark," Dalton said. He raised three fingers. "Three." He dropped one finger. "Two." And another. "One."

Cormack didn't wait for the go; he threw open the door and pushed inside. The smell made him gag, but it was the ear-splitting terrified scream from his naked sunshine girl which ripped his soul out and sent a rush of bile racing into the back of his throat. Somehow he got the words out. "Cover me. She wouldn't want you to see her like this."

"Go on." Dalton's voice was stone cold, telling him Dalton had already seen everything he needed to see.

As soon as Dalton confirmed he had his six, he raced across the container and dropped to his knees next to her. "Sunshine?"

"Jeep, turn off your light," Kentucky said softly. "We'll keep ours turned away."

"Good thinking." He snapped the switch to turn off the beam of light plunging them almost into darkness. "Sunshine. It's me."

"No, no, no, no."

He heard the rattle of chains as she shrank away from him. His heart ripped itself right out of his chest and dropped onto the floor, as if it had been stomped flat. He touched her ankle and she lashed out at him, kicking as best she could while chained to the fucking floor.

"No, no."

"Shh, Willow, baby, it's Grumpy."

"Coming in behind you to check the other girl," Kentucky's voice came through his comms telling him that the Bravo team leader didn't want to scare Willow any more than she already was.

"Look at me. Look at me, baby, it's Grumpy." He tried to hold her, but she shrieked so loud his ears were going to be ringing for a couple of days, and with how she was chained to the wall he couldn't pick her up. "Boss, toss me the fucking cutters."

"Sliding to your boots now," Dalton immediately answered. He reached down and grabbed the bolt cutters as soon as he felt it hit his boot.

"When she's free toss it over here," Kentucky said. "This girl's unconscious."

"Yeah." He had to avoid Willow's attempts at fighting him off as he tried to cut the chains holding her to the wall. He didn't dare try to cut the lock from the shackle around her neck. With how she was tossing and twisting, he might cut her skin. The fucking shackles would have to wait until she realized she was safe.

He reached up and cut the chains holding her arms over her head first, then the one at her neck. As soon as her upper body was free, his warrior queen came bolting upright, her head aiming for his face in one hell of a headbutt. If he had been just a tiny bit slower to react, his face would have had another bruise to match the ones Dalton had given him earlier.

"No." He caught her wrists as she punched out at him. "Baby, it's Cormack."

"Fuck you!" she screamed at the top of her lungs, once again trying to headbutt him. He was so fucking proud of her. His sunshine, bruised, battered, hurt, and probably more scared than she'd ever been in her life, and she was fighting him with everything she had.

"It's Cormack, hey." He couldn't get the bolt cutters near her feet when she was fighting so hard. He might hurt her. He twisted and slid them across the floor to Kentucky. "I'm gonna need those back in a few."

"Thanks."

He heard the snip of the cutters, the soft murmur of Kentucky's voice, and the whimper from the other prisoner as her bonds were cut. But he didn't have time to worry about what was happening at the other side of the container.

"Hey, hey, Willow. Look at me." He scooted closer to her. Capturing both her wrists in one hand and being careful not to twist her legs in their shackles, he tugged her into his arms. "Look at me, baby." He tucked her against him as best he could. "Look at me, it's Cormack. IKYAS, Sunshine."

All he could do was keep repeating himself over and over and hope it broke through the barrier in her brain. "It's Grumpy, IKYAS, Sunshine."

"Coming past you with the other girl," Kentucky warned.

"Becky?"

"Is that her name?"

"Grumpy?"

Relief and hope. Was she back? Did she recognize him? "Yes, baby, it's Grumpy." He pushed her hair back from her face. "Are you okay, baby?"

Her fingers wrapped into the collar of his shirt, her knuckles grazing his throat as she tugged him closer to her nose and sniffed. "Grumpy?"

His heart broke at the wistful break in her voice. "IKYAS, Sunshine, it's me, Grumpy, I swear it."

"You're saving me?"

"You bet, baby. Can I cut these chains off your legs?"

"Yes, they hurt."

"I know." He reached one hand out and made a gimme gesture. Despite having told Dalton to stay out, he knew there was not a snowballs chance in hell of that happening. His suspicion was confirmed as soon as the metal of the bolt cutters hit his hand.

She whimpered when he pulled away from her. "Cormack."

"I'm not leaving, I swear." He touched her foot with

one finger and cursed and wished a thousand deaths on the ones who'd hurt her. "I'm just going to cut the chains, okay?"

"Okay."

As soon as her feet were free, she launched herself up and thank fuck, straight into his arms.

"I'm naked."

"I know, baby. It's okay, it's okay. Let me grab my pack and I'm gonna grab the clothes I brought for you."

"You brought me clothes?"

"Well, not fancy stuff." He forced a smile to his face. "I know nothing about fancy, so I brought one of my t-shirts and some yogas." As he spoke he shuffled his ruck off his back and swung it around until he could unzip the front pocket. The second the clothes appeared, she snatched them out of his hands and scrambled into the t-shirt. Only once it was covering her from her neck almost to her knees did he see her shoulders relax.

"I want to go home."

"I'll take you," he promised. "Want me to help you get into the pants?"

"No." She jerked back from him, giving his heart another harsh stomp in the process. "I can do it."

"I'll… um… I'll just turn around." He fisted his hands where she couldn't see and squeezed his eyes shut.

"Alpha Two, All Stations," Lucifer called through comms. "Status?"

"Alpha One, Three, and Bravo Four along with the HVPs all clear," Dalton replied. By the time the rest of the team had checked in, Willow was dressed.

"I'm gonna have to pick you up, Sunshine." He hovered near her. "That okay with you?"

She lowered her head. "Yes." He could barely hear the

word, but at least she'd said it. He scooped her up into his arms before she could change her mind.

"Let's get you home." He didn't dare mention that he thought she would need to stop at a hospital first. Until they were in the fucking helo and far away from this hellhole, he was holding on tight and not letting her go.

CHAPTER TWENTY-FIVE

SHE HELD herself as still as possible. Was this some kind of messed up nightmare? Was she going to wake up and find she'd imagined Cormack and Uncle Dalton coming to get her? If that happened, she was going to insist that someone stop the world so she could get off.

"I got you, Sunshine."

That was Cormack's voice, right?

"Keep your face tucked in against me, I'll get you out of here, I promise."

"Jeep, you and Ken get the girls to the bird."

Okay, she never dreamed of Dalton's voice, so this had to be real, right? She turned her head until most of her face was against Cormack's throat.

"We're going up the stairs, hold on tight, okay?"

"Yes." She wrapped her fingers into one of the hoops on his vest. The Kevlar hurt her sore fingers, but she didn't care. The pain told her she was alive, that she'd made it. She shifted against him with each step he took. Soon, soon she'd be out of the ground and maybe then her chest would stop hurting and she'd be able to breathe.

"Alpha One, coming out of the basement." Dalton's voice came from somewhere in front of them. "How am I looking?"

"Clear."

She barely heard the word coming from close to her ear but pulled back to stare at Cormack's face. Not that she could see much. Her eyes refused to open much. Even her eyelashes hurt so much.

"It's my comms," he explained. "Snow's just telling us we're safe to come out."

"They came?"

"Yeah, baby, they all came, I brought a damn army."

She felt Cormack duck and then straighten.

"We're out," he whispered softly.

She ignored the pain and forced the eyelid which wasn't pressed into his neck to lift a little, it wasn't fully but enough that she could see it was still dark outside. "No sun?"

"Not for a couple of hours." He followed behind another man. She could tell from the shape it was Dalton.

"Alpha One to Seven, get your ass over here."

"He's calling Rexar," Cormack whispered. "Probably to cover me and Kentucky as we take you and the other girl to the choppers."

"Becky."

"Huh?"

"Her name is Becky, is she okay?"

"Yes, you told me her name is Becky." He shifted her in his arms. "Ken's got her, he'll make sure she's okay."

"'kay."

"Hey, assholes, you can't just leave me here."

She flinched away from one of the voices which would haunt her nightmares for the rest of her life. "No." She struggled against Cormack's hold. "Noooo."

"Shh, it's okay, baby. Sunshine, I got you."

"Let me go."

"I swear he can't hurt you, baby, but we got to go past him."

"Noo." She pushed against him as hard as she could, if she pushed hard enough, maybe he'd turn back. He had to understand she didn't want to be anywhere near that man. Not now, not ever.

"Tate, get the fucker out of here," Cormack growled.

"You just fucked up my op," the man's voice said. "You can't leave me here, uncuff me."

"Fuck off," Uncle Dalton's voice growled from somewhere she couldn't see. "You see that woman? Do you? You tell your fucking boss that the next time they leave the daughter of a fallen SEAL in a fucking hellhole in the ground that I'll make it my business to make fucking sure everything done to her is done to them."

"I didn't know."

"Irrelevant." Dalton's voice was followed by the sound of flesh hitting flesh. "Her father served his country with honor and respect, his kid deserved better from the AT fucking F."

"Nem is reinforcing his words with his fists."

"Alpha Seven, coming up on your six, Alpha Three."

"It's Rexar." Cormack's whisper stopped the urge to bolt and run screaming off into the sunset in its tracks.

"Willy?"

She didn't want any of them to see her like this. Could she not just drop into a dead faint or a swoon like the good southern belle she was brought up to be? "Get me out of here," she whispered to Cormack.

"Seven, you stay right on my ass and keep anyone from getting too close, got it?" Cormack ordered.

"You bet."

She shivered at the coldness in Rexar's tone. But when

Cormack started walking again, the asshole's, who'd been in the bunker or whatever the fuck it was, voice faded behind her. Only then did she risk opening her eyes again.

"Bravo One, you bring Becky and keep up."

"Yes, sir. We'll be dogging your heels all the way to our ride."

It felt like they'd been waiting forever while soft chatter filtered through Cormack's earpiece. But as most of it was in shorthand or military terms, she didn't understand all of it, just bits and pieces here and there. Cormack stumbled and she winced as he tightened his grip on her.

"Sorry, I can't see my feet, almost there."

She nodded, the top of her head rubbing off his chin. It wasn't the most comfortable to be pressed against his chest when he was wearing a full battle rattle Kevlar and all the other bits and pieces which made up his gear. But she didn't care, as much as she needed to feel him and not his gear, she'd take it over the alternative any day of the week.

"Dee, get this bird in the air, stat."

"Yes, sir," a woman's voice answered immediately. "Alpha team is coming?"

"Nope, they're finishing up here," Cormack said. "Get us to the hospital stat."

"No." She jerked out from where she'd been hiding her face. "No hospital, you promised you'd bring me home."

"I will bring you home, I swear."

"No hospital." There was no frick-fracking way she was letting a bunch of strangers touch her again. It was not happening. "I am not going to a hospital."

"I think she means it."

"Becky needs to go to a hospital," a voice she didn't recognize said and she flinched away from it as fast as she could. "I'm Kentucky, Bravo Team Leader, ma'am."

"We'll stop at the hospital and drop you guys off," Dee called from her place in front of the controls.

She twisted in his arms and looked into his face, she had to make him understand. "Please, listen to me. No... no hospitals, no questions and nobody touches me but you."

"I'm listening, Sunshine, I swear, and I hear you."

"No hospitals."

He studied her for so long that she thought he wasn't going to agree and that he'd insist on a hospital. "Okay." He nodded. "No hospitals." He sat into a seat on the helo and strapped them in. "Dee Dee, radio through to Trev and tell him I want a medic on site when we land at the ranch."

"No..."

"Shh, you have to give me something here, Sunshine. It's a medic at the ranch or the hospital."

"You're being so mean."

"Yeah, Sunshine, I know you think so." He wrapped his arms around her, rubbing one hand up and down her arm, creating both friction and heat. Oh, god, the heat, she was so cold inside she didn't think there was ever going to be a way to feel warm again.

"Take the medic," Rexar advised. He held the door of the helicopter until Kentucky and Becky were settled into a seat across from them. "He's been losing his shit since he heard you were missing. Trust him. Okay?" Rexar didn't wait for her to answer, he slammed the sliding door shut so he wouldn't be able to hear her response either.

"You said he'd come, and he did."

"Beck...Becky?" She twisted in Cormack's arms trying to see the woman who'd only been a voice in the dark. Her swollen eyes didn't help much, but she could make out a fall of what looked like red hair. She was filthy and every patch of skin she could see was covered in bruises.

"Thank you for taking me, too."

"We never leave anyone behind," the man holding her muttered. This must be Kentucky, he was as big as her uncle Dalton, but his soft voice and southern drawl belied his size.

"I…" Becky shifted, trying to pull her body away from Kentucky's. "I don't want to go to the hospital either."

"You have to, Doll." Kentucky shifted her on his lap, tucking her head back under his chin. "You have so many bruises, I can't see the pretty under all the blues and greens."

"There's people at a hospital, I don't want to see people."

"Bring her to the ranch," Cormack growled. "Medic can see both, then we'll figure shit out. It might be better to keep the authorities out of it anyway."

She felt him huff under her chest and knew he was mad and worried, but he had to understand, people touching her was not an option. It would never be an option again.

"Dee-Dee, did you get that?"

"Yes, sir," Dee-Dee replied. "Diverting now, sir." The helicopter banked hard to the right before straightening again.

"Rest, Sunshine," Cormack ordered softly. "We have about forty minutes until we get home."

"Okay." There was no way she'd sleep, but she could rest her eyes until they got there. Yes, that was what she'd do.

CHAPTER TWENTY-SIX

HE REFUSED to move and hurt her. Every time the helo swooped or banked and Willow shifted on his lap, she whimpered without opening her eyes. Rage and fury burned through him like a wildfire through an uncleared forest after a ten-year drought.

He was almost afraid to touch her, to hurt her or scare her. It would rip his soul to shreds to have her be as scared of him as she had been when he'd found her in that hellhole. "King will fucking pay for this."

"Wha…?"

"Shh, Sunshine, I'm only bitching. We'll be home in ten minutes." He lifted the hand which wasn't tucked in between her and his chest and kissed her knuckles. "The first thing I'm doing when we're on the ground is cutting those damn shackles off you."

"Yes, please, I need them off. They burn."

"I think your girl is a fairy," Kentucky said quietly in his earpiece. "Iron and metals burn her."

"You came."

His breath hitched when he glanced down at her face. She

barely even looked like herself. "I'll always come for you, Sunshine, I'd go straight through the gates of hell and shake hands with the devil himself before flattening his ass in front of the hellhounds if it meant you were safe."

"We're approaching HQ," Dee-Dee said.

"Put her down in front of the house."

"The boss's house? Not a fucking chance."

"Nope, the main HQ where the medics are." As much as he wanted to take her into his suite and to examine every single inch of her, he didn't dare. He didn't know how hurt she was and the one thing he wouldn't do was compromise her health just to satisfy his own caveman urges.

"Okay, that I can do, if the field is empty."

"Fuck, have Trev confirm with Jack that the damn bull isn't in the field." If the bull was there, he was shooting him if that fucker charged them before they made it to the gate.

"Roger."

Through comms he heard Trev confirm the field was clear just as the helo came in to hover, getting ready to land. He snapped open the straps which had held them in place as they flew. "I'm gonna stand," he warned her.

"I'm ready."

"Ken, bring Becky and follow me."

"Yes, sir."

The rotors hadn't stopped turning when the door was slid back, and he nodded to Jack. "Thanks, man."

"Go. Medic is on standby."

He was so fucking grateful that he didn't have to figure out how to open the damn door without putting her down, but couldn't find the words to voice it, so he just nodded to the foreman instead.

"Lina's holding the door open." Jack steadied him as he

stepped out of the helo, then did the same for Kentucky as soon as Cormack cleared the way for him.

He hurried as fast as he could but didn't want to jostle or shake her by running so he had to make do with a fast walk. As he approached HQ, just as Jack had said, Lina stood holding the door open for them.

"This carrying me over a threshold is becoming a habit."

"There she is." Relief at her attempt at humor made his breath hitch again. That damn lump in his throat wasn't going anywhere for the foreseeable future. He needed a time and a place where nobody could see him cry out his pain until it was out of his system. People might say SEALs and former SEALs shouldn't cry, well, fuck them and the horse they rode in on. Wounds healed but things in your memory would always be there, and sometimes the only way to deal with the memories was to cry until the river was fucking dry.

He strode through the main entrance and turned in the opposite direction from the war-rooms. "Which room?"

"This one." The medic stuck his head out the first door on the left. "I have two beds in here set up for them."

"Thanks, John." He went to the furthest bed and gently laid her onto it while someone pulled the curtain around the bed behind them.

Willow kept her fingers wrapped into the neck of his Kevlar. "You're not going to let him touch me?" Her big baby blues filled with tears, kicking his heart hard. "Right?"

"Let me get these shackles off you first." He had to avoid answering the question. He didn't know the answer. She'd refused a hospital, the medic they had on site was John. "But either way, I'm not leaving you."

She stared into his eyes as if she was trying to figure out if he meant it or not. Eventually, she nodded and released him so he could straighten. "Get them off me, please."

"You got it, Darlin'." He reached for his lock pick because as much as he wanted to take an angle grinder to the metal, he didn't dare. The sparks might damage her skin and she was hurt enough. "May I?" He nodded to the bed.

She scooted her legs over to one side, making room for him to sit down.

He sat with his back next to her knees and reached for one hand and cradled it in his palm. "Okay?"

"Just do it."

He could see where her skin was rubbed raw by the metal, but he couldn't focus on that, and he went to work. It took less than a minute to open the first lock. He winced when he saw the real damage. His girl had kept fighting and hurt herself in the process. He dropped the metal on the floor next to his boot and reached for her other hand. He heard a similar clang coming from the other bed and knew Kentucky was removing the chains from Becky, too.

It probably took him all of five minutes to get the shackles off her hands and feet then he turned his attention to the one around her neck. "Lean forward, baby."

"Fucking assholes."

"Just cut it off."

Kentucky's soft cursing and Becky's quiet reply from the other side of the curtain warned him this one might not be as easy.

He scowled at the lock. "What the hell?"

"What's wrong?" Willow bent almost double over at her waist, her face between her knees so he could see the locking mechanism at the back of her neck.

"The lock is fucked."

"You can't open it?"

"I'll get it off you, I swear." He could hear voices rising and falling and he hoped like hell that meant John and

Kentucky were figuring out a way to make that happen because he had nothing. Absolutely fucking nothing.

"Jeep, I have an idea," John called. "Wanna hear it?"

He helped Willow to straighten and glanced at her with an eyebrow raised. "Do you want to hear it?" As soon as she nodded, he swished back the curtain. "Hell yes."

"We'll put the girls under and cut the necklaces off."

Fuck, that was exactly what he didn't want to happen.

"Put me under? Under what? I'm not going under anything."

It didn't take a genius to hear the panic in her voice. "He means knock you out. Sedation. Right, John?" His voice hardened, his tone better warn the medic that his answer had better be that he'd sedate both girls and cut off the chains and not that he was going to put her under the damn building. He mentally smacked his own head for even thinking stupid shit like that.

"Yes, that's right," John answered. "It's the only way to do it without hurting or burning them. They've been hurt enough."

"Agreed." He could hear the breath catch in her throat and knew she was scared shitless. "I'll stay with you, Sunshine, I won't leave for a second."

"Swear it?"

"I swear."

"Okay."

"Willow?" Becky's voice shook as she stuck her head around the curtain surrounding her bed. "They won't hurt us?"

"Never. Cormack won't let them."

The vehemence in her voice hit him right in the feels. Un-fucking-believable. His sunshine girl was bruised, battered, and had more marks on her normally soft skin than a soldier coming out of one hell of a firefight and still she trusted him to keep her safe, just as she'd trusted that he'd come for her.

"Do it." He nodded to John and pulled Willow back against his chest. "You know he's going to have to touch you?" He wouldn't lie to her or hide it from her and damn it, his heart needed to know that she knew what would happen.

"I know, but you'll protect me."

"Always, Sunshine, I swear."

"Imma going to go get the cutter I use for taking off bandages." John turned toward the door. "I'll be back."

"I'm scared."

"I know. Me, too." He wouldn't normally admit that, but she needed to hear it. He was terrified of letting her down. What if he wasn't who she needed him to be to help her get through this? Not just the talking of the metal shackles thing, but mental shackles, too. What if he wasn't strong enough or he fucked up? Fuck, seeing the one you love going through shit you hadn't experienced and didn't understand with first-hand knowledge was going to be rough. But he would be here for as long as she let him. He silently promised her that he'd show up. He'd be there no matter what. All he could do was hope it would be enough.

Half an hour later and she was finally free of the fucking symbol of her captivity. Both he and John breathed out sighs of relief in unison.

"Check her scalp while I drop this as far away as possible."

He lifted his vest off the back of her head. He hadn't been sure the Kevlar would protect her enough. But now as he skimmed his fingers over her skin, he could see he'd been wrong. At least he thought he was. It was kind of hard to tell with all the other cuts and marks she was wearing.

"Want me to treat all her wounds while she's out?"

Fuck, he hadn't thought to ask her that before she was given the anesthetic. "I didn't ask her." If it was him, he'd want it done, but he wasn't a woman, he hadn't been... he swallowed down bile... in her situation. "Go ask Lina and Becky. I don't know what's best to do. They're women, they might be closer to reality than me."

"Good thinking." John disappeared again, only to return a couple of seconds later. "Both say do it now, so she's not embarrassed."

Okay, he could see that. He nodded his agreement.

"Whatever we see, don't lose your shit until you are out of here and far enough away that she can't hear you," John warned as he took the scissors to cut up the middle of her t-shirt.

"Yeah." He agreed to John's order, but then immediately regretted it when he saw all the welts and cuts on her back.

"It looks like she was whipped with a belt. Fucking dicks." John went to work, cleaning and treating each mark. "Your girl put up one hell of a fight."

"Yeah." He'd never been so fucking mad or so fucking proud as he'd been when he'd picked up her hand and seen her ripped and torn fingernails. "Was she raped?"

"I think not, there are signs of an attempt, but I think she somehow fought them off." John scowled. "It's probably why they went after her with the belt."

"Fuckers."

One hundred and seventy-three marks on her skin. He counted every single one of them as John cleaned and stitched and treated them. Someday, somehow, he'd make fucking King pay for each of those wounds. Every. Single. One.

CHAPTER TWENTY-SEVEN

TWO DAYS later and she was going out of her mind. Her body hurt every freaking where, and the bits that didn't hurt itched like the bites of a thousand mosquitoes. She didn't dare make a noise or she'd wake Cormack. Every time she'd opened her eyes since she'd come around from having the chains cut off, he'd been there, sitting in the chair keeping watch while she slept. This was the first time she'd seen him sleep. He'd been both her protector and her watchdog, keeping everyone except for Kentucky away from both her and Becky.

"Is it safe to come in?"

Even though it made her neck ache, her head whipped around at Lina's soft whisper, and she nodded in response. She gestured to Cormack and put her finger to her lips. "Are you okay? The baby?"

"We're both fine, I swear," Lina whispered back. "They didn't touch us, just opened the door of my fucking Hummer, pulled you out, and took off before I could do anything."

"The one called King was pissed as hell that they didn't take you, too."

"King," Lina said in a normalish tone, but lowered her

voice when Willow smacked at her arm and gestured to Cormack. "King was there?"

"Yes." She picked at a loose thread on the bed covers. "He was so mad when I screamed at him that he'd never get you through me."

"Fuck."

"Yeah, he tried that, too, but he couldn't get it up," Willow muttered. "So the coward whipped me with his belt instead."

"I'm going to kill him."

"Get in fucking line."

Oh, crap, she should have known that the slightest sound, even their whispering would wake him. You didn't spend a lifetime in war zones and not learn how to wake up when the sounds surrounding you changed. "I'm okay," she reassured him. "You saved me in time."

"Was he still there when the boys went in for you?" Lina pulled out her cell. "I'm gonna text Dalton."

"I don't know, I blacked out at some point and the next thing I knew, Cormack was leaning over me."

"Is Nem back from D.C. yet?" Cormack asked.

"No, I hope tomorrow though." Lina tapped out a message and hit send. "He had to call the Commander-in-Chief and call in a favor to shut down the stink the ATF are making over the rescue."

"Fuckers had an undercover cop in there," Cormack muttered. "He should have done something or called someone."

"He did." Willow nodded to the curtain which separated her bed from Becky's. "Ask Becky though, she probably heard more than me because I was kinda out of it."

"Becky?" Cormack got to his feet and pushed back the curtain. "What did King say?"

"He was so mad the militia didn't get both of them." She glanced at Kentucky and when he nodded encouragingly to her, she continued. "There was a lot of big fancy words that even I as a teacher hadn't heard. I'm sure some of them were French."

"Makes sense," Lina said. "He spends a lot of time in Europe."

"He told them they had one week to get who I assume is her?" She pointed to Lina. "He'd be back. To pick all of us up then."

"What was to happen then?"

"Us two were to be sold at some auction he was arranging, and he had other plans for her." Again, she gestured to Lina.

"Fuck, send that to Nem."

"Already ahead of you, Jeep." Lina turned her cell to show them she was holding the record button.

"He won't find much when he goes back there," Cormack said. "We pretty much ripped that compound apart and from what the guys have said, the ATF are crawling all over it trying to salvage something from their op."

"Yes, the one you said was ATF?" Becky said. "After he brought Willow back into the bunker, he made a call to someone and told them that they needed to move their asses or he was helping us escape."

"What happened then?" Kentucky asked.

"He swore a lot and then threw up."

"Fucker," Cormack muttered. "I'd like five more minutes with him."

"Did you hear anything else?" Lina asked Becky.

"No, you lose all sense of time in the dark, so I don't know how long it was before you all stormed in and got us out." She glanced at the man sitting on her bed. "Is it enough?"

"Yes," Cormack answered, even though Kentucky nodded. "It's enough." His cell buzzed and he checked it, his mouth tightening into a grim line, then he moved from the chair onto the side of Willow's bed. "Will you be okay if I go to the war-room?"

"Yes." She loved him. She adored that he'd kept his promise and not left her side. But now she needed space. She needed to not worry about how he'd react each time she flinched as she tried to unpack the baggage which was what had happened to her. "But, Grumpy…?"

"Yeah?"

"Shower first, you stink."

"Hey, a full week in the sandbox, getting you back, and sleeping in a chair for two days is going to raise a little sweat."

"Trev's gonna lock you out of the war-room if you head in there stinking like that," Lina interjected. "You're kinda ripe, buddy."

"Okay, okay." He kissed the top of her head and got to his feet. "I'm just at the other side of the building, if you need me, send Kentucky."

"I will."

She watched him leave and was more than a little relieved that she still could appreciate the fineness which was his butt as he crossed to the door. She'd been concerned that she'd not be attracted to him or that all men would repulse her after what happened. But that flip-flop in her belly reassured her more than all the words he'd given her could.

"Ken?" Lina switched off her cell and raised an eyelid. "Beat it, we have girlie shit to talk about."

"I… uh… yes, Mrs. Boss." He reddened. "I'll just go check on my team. Will you be okay here, Becky?"

"Yes, here is much better than there. I'll be fine."

"Okay." He hovered next to Becky's bed for a couple of seconds before he glanced at Lina. "Will you call me if she needs me, Mrs. Boss?"

Oh my lord, Mrs. Boss? She swallowed down a snicker. Wait until she told Cormack that Kentucky had called Lina Mrs. Boss, he'd hurt himself laughing.

"All day long and twice on Sunday." Lina nodded. "If she asks for you I'll call you."

"Thanks." He dipped his chin and left the room.

"Why couldn't I meet someone like him before?" Becky asked. "Why did it have to be now?"

"We don't get a choice when we meet the one meant for us," Lina said sagely. "I met Dalton when I was little more than a kid. But the second he saved me from my drink being spiked, I was his and he was mine."

"I think I'd like to hear that story someday," Becky said.

"Someday I might tell you." Lina brushed her hands together. "Don't let what happened stop you from chasing what you want," she advised. "You'll find men like ours, like Kentucky, they're a little growly, a whole lot stubborn, more than over the top protective, but if you're sassy enough and you throw enough sass back at them, the steam and the fun times between the sheets is more than worth it." She got to her feet. "But different kind of real talk for a second. Who wants a shower?"

"Me." She would do anything to be able to stand under hot water and scrub her skin raw. It would go a long way to helping her cleanse the filth from her mind. She could only imagine how much stronger that feeling was for Becky.

"Oh, God. I'd love a shower so bad."

"Then while we don't have your guard dogs to stop us, let's get you to my house where the only strange man is my puppy."

"You're springing us?"

"John said you could get out of here," Lina said. "Both the lugs who didn't move from the chairs for the last two days insisted it was too soon."

"It's like they think we're the weaker sex or something." She tossed back the covers. Lina was offering a chance to escape, and she was grabbing onto that chance with both hands and taking it. As soon as her bare feet hit the tile floor, she knew there was a problem. "Darn it, we don't have shoes."

"Yes, you do." Lina went to a locker on the far side of the room and opened it to rummage inside. "What size?"

"Eight."

"Nine for me, please," Becky added.

"Nope, nope, nope," Lina muttered. "You're a nine." More banging followed by multiple 'nopes' until finally she said, "There you are, right at the bottom, of course you'd be under everything else." She stuffed something under her armpit and backed away from the locker, keeping one hand inside until the door was almost closing on it. She whipped her hand out of the space and slammed and locked the door. "I may have made a bit of a mess," she admitted. "And every- thing will probably fall out the next time someone opens that door. But I got these..." She produced two pairs of boots from under her armpits with a flourish. "I mean they're no Louis Vuitton or Dior, but they'll get you to my house, and Amazon has been delivering some boxes. I had to guess at your size, Becky."

"You bought me clothes?"

"Of course I did." Lina handed over the combat boots.

"You can't go around in scruffy men's clothes for all of your days."

"I don't know how to thank you enough."

"We'll figure it out," Lina promised. "We'll figure out how to get you to where you need to be and make sure you're okay."

"Thank you."

"No tears," Lina said fiercely. "From either of you. You survived an asshole, so many never have a second chance at life. Grab it with both hands and run with it."

Dang it, it was so hard to be mad about her bossy tendencies when she was being so freaking nice. When she'd first met her, she'd been determined to be mad at her for hurting her uncle Dalton. Then she'd chatted and laughed with her in her and Cormack's suite and found she liked her. Now here she was again, showing why sometimes you had to look deeper than first impressions. She concentrated on tying her laces.

"Ready?" Lina glanced between them.

"Yes."

"As I'll ever be." She couldn't wait to feel the sun on her face. To even smell the cows and the horses. The smells which had been so foreign to her when she'd first come here now represented home. How stupid and sappy was that?

"Just let me do something." Lina grabbed a chart off the foot of Willow's bed and ripped out a blank page from the back. She scribbled something on the page and hung the chart back in its place. "Then let's blow this joint." Lina pulled open the door, ducked her head out then waved them on ahead of her. She paused in one spot in the hallway and looked up. "Just a sec," she said. "I'm just making sure Trev sees us on the cameras, so the boys don't freak if they come back here and find you gone."

"Yeah, Grumpy would be grumpy as all get out 'bout that."

"I'll bet." Lina waved into the camera and held up the paper. "I'm just telling him you're with me."

"Why not send him a text?"

"Where's the fun in that?" Lina smirked. "Let him work for it a little."

"You two are hilarious," Becky said from where she followed behind them. "Have you been friends long?"

"About three hours before she jumped out of my Hummer and into the asshole's van." Lina slapped her palm to the lock on the front door and pulled it open. "Go breathe the fresh air outside for two seconds flat and jump in the truck."

———

AFTER DEPOSITING Becky in the guest bathroom and handing over some Amazon packages and clean towels, she followed Lina down the hall and into a bedroom.

"You're in here, it's a guest bedroom and the bathroom is small, but it's clean." She lifted one shoulder. "I don't dare take you to your suite, as there you'd be alone and Jeep would do his nut."

"I appreciate this so much."

"I know you do." Lina walked over to the bed and pointed to a stack of folded clothes. "I grabbed some stuff from your closet, I hope that's okay."

"I think I love you."

"If it was me, I'd want my own stuff." Lina smiled at her. "Towels are on the toilet seat, and I grabbed some of your stuff from your bathroom, but there some new toiletries in the bathroom, too. Go." She made a shooing motion with her hands. "I'll be just downstairs in the living room, shout if you need me."

"Thank you, Lina. I'd hug you, but I don't know that either of us are very huggy."

"I'm not." Lina grinned at her. "But for you I might consider it." She left the room and pulled the door shut behind her.

Willow crossed the room, heading toward the bathroom when she caught sight of her reflection in the mirror over the dressing table next to the bathroom door. She stumbled to a stop and caught herself on the corner of the vanity, knocking something off it, but she didn't look to see what it was.

She studied her reflection, her gaze fixed on the stitches on her forehead, just over her left eyebrow. The eye was swollen almost shut, surrounded by blue and black smudges. She stripped off the t-shirt she wore and tentatively put her hand to her throat and the purple two-inch-wide ring which surrounded it like a necklace.

Her stomach churned and roiled when she saw the hickeys and bite marks on her chest and shoulders. Those combined with bruises and scratch marks covering almost her entire body made her want to throw up. "Assholes."

"Sunshine?" She turned and saw Cormack standing at the door watching her, he glanced between her and the mirror and blew out a soft breath. He stepped further into the room, and she backed away before he got close enough to touch her, and she turned and bolted for the bathroom, tossed the folded towels to one side, and lifted up the lid to empty the contents of her stomach.

She felt a hand gathering her hair and holding it back out of the way, and the toilet flushed, reducing the smell from the vomit. "I'm ugly."

"You will never, ever be anything but beautiful to me."

She sank onto her bottom and scooted against the bath. She dipped her head and used the curtain fall of her hair to hide her face. How could he say that? She'd seen the evidence for herself, she was ugly, and battered, and…weak.

"Stop." Cormack squatted down onto his haunches in front of her. "You are beautiful and strong. Baby, you survived. I could never think you anything but stunningly beautiful."

"You're just saying that."

He tucked his hand under her chin and lifted her face to meet his gaze. "When have you ever known me to lie?"

"You haven't that I know of," she admitted. He'd always told her the truth, even when it was something which might make her send him away.

"Then believe me now. You. Are. Beautiful." His fingers caressed the side of her face, avoiding the cuts, barely skimming over her skin as if he didn't want to hurt her.

She attempted to suck the corner of her lip into her mouth, an unconscious action she used when she was thinking, but it pulled at one of the healing cuts and she released it again. She couldn't see anything in his eyes to make her think he was trying to spare her feelings. All she could see was affection, pride, and love.

"Do you believe me?"

"I…"

He sighed. "Someday I'm going to make you believe that you are prettiest girl this side of the Mississippi."

"Just on this side?" She struggled to put a teasing tone into her voice, but she made an attempt at it.

"Well, when we're on the East Coast, then you're the prettiest girl on that side of it."

"Flatterer."

"I've been practicing." He winked at her. "Does it show?"

"Just a little."

"Come on, Sunshine, let's get you in the shower. It might help you feel better."

"I...um... can you wait outside until I'm done?" She didn't want him seeing all the marks on her skin. She knew he probably had seen them already, but she didn't know that for sure, and until she did, she was choosing to believe he hadn't seen them. She didn't even know if that made sense to anyone, but it made sense to her right then and that was what mattered.

"If that's what you want me to do." He helped her to her feet and pressed a gentle kiss to her forehead. "You tell me what you need, and I'll make sure you get it, okay?"

She nodded and watched as he left the bathroom and tugged the door shut behind him. "Cormack?"

The door opened and he stuck his head around it. "Yes?"

"Thank you."

"You are my top priority, Sunshine, everything else is about ten klicks behind you. Got it?"

"Yes."

"Good girl, now go shower and I'll go find us some food." He pulled the door shut again.

"Don't touch the stove, Cormack. I do not want any sexy firefighters invading this house and seeing me like this, you hear me?" He didn't reply, but she heard his rich laughter through the door.

"Shower, Sunshine."

"Bossy boots," she muttered to herself as she switched on the shower. But she wouldn't swap him for the tea in China. Now she just had to figure out a way to tell him that she wanted to sleep alone for a bit. Not because she didn't want him wrapped around her, but because she needed to know that she could do it. She had to know for herself that she wasn't broken, that she may be down, but there was no frick-fracking way she was out. He would need to leave for work. She had to prove to him before he did that she would be okay when he was gone. Otherwise, he'd be so worried about her that he wouldn't concentrate on what he should be doing. Keeping himself alive so he could come home to her.

CHAPTER TWENTY-EIGHT

HIS EYES POPPED OPEN, and he lifted his torso off the couch, then twisted and punched the pillow. A quick glance at the clock started the silent one-minute countdown in his head. Every night for the last three nights at exactly two thirty this happened. He swung his legs off the couch and braced his elbows on his knees, ready to bounce up the second it started.

"Three, two, one." He got to his feet just as a blood curdling scream echoed down the hallway.

"No, let me go, no!" she screamed, every word shattering another piece of his heart.

He pushed in the door and paused a second to allow his eyes to adjust to the soft light of his bedroom after the dark of the hallway and living room. Just as on the previous two nights, Willow screamed and fought the sheets she was tangled in, her eyes wide in her head and filled with raw terror. He fucking hated that she wouldn't let him hold her through this.

"IKYAS, Sunshine." He didn't dare do more than stroke one finger down the foot which stuck out the end of the covers. She launched herself up, already fighting an unseen foe. "Get off me, get off." She fought the sheets, fought herself, and him.

"Willow, Sunshine." He kneeled next to the bed, speaking to her softly. "It's me, Grumpy, you're safe, you're home with me. Sunshine." He tilted his head to one side, she seemed to be a little calmer, so he kept talking. "It's okay, baby, it's just a nightmare, you're here with me." He repeated the words a few more times before he felt the change in her body and knew the night terror had released its grip on her.

He climbed to his feet and sat on the edge of the bed. When she wrapped her arm around his waist, he sighed.

"I'm sorry."

He wrapped his fingers over hers. "No, Sunshine, no sorry needed. But you need to talk to someone. If you won't talk to me, then let me organize someone else."

"A shrink?" She pressed her forehead against his back, muffling his words. "I'm not crazy."

"No, you're not crazy, you're traumatized. Huge differ-ence." He twisted to stroke her hair. "Can I sit back and hold you?"

He held his breath until she nodded and pulled away from him, allowing him the room to scoot back against the pillow. His fingers itched to pull her against his chest, but this soon after the nightmare, he didn't dare. He had to wait for her to come to him.

She released a long breath as if she'd been holding it for too long and moved next to him, putting her head on his shoulder, her breath snuffling against his neck. "You know it's not you I'm afraid of, right?"

Un-fucking-believable, she had nightmares and she was worried he'd think she was afraid of him. "I know, Sunshine." Silent sobs rolled through her body, and he gently stroked his hand up and down her back. "Please let me find someone to help you, Sunshine, you're breaking my heart. Please do it for me."

She was silent for such a long time that he was sure that she'd refuse the offer again tonight. He froze when he heard her hiccuped, "Okay."

"Thank you, Sunshine."

She wrapped her fingers into his t-shirt and eventually her breathing evened out and she slept. First thing tomorrow he was asking Trev to find them a doctor or a shrink. Their community was vast, there had to be someone who could recommend a doc who'd like to have a patient in the back ass of Montana.

He closed his eyes and inhaled a lungful of her shampoo, having her here against his chest went a long way to soothing what raged inside him. She was here. She was safe. She was his. He would find a way to get her the help she needed.

They'd only been asleep for maybe twenty minutes when he felt her jerk against him. "You okay?"

"Yeah, I woke up before it caught me."

As tired as he was, he knew sleep was off the table for both of them. "Why don't we go to the kitchen and you can bake?" Damn it, he should have thought of this two nights ago, he was an idiot.

"Muffins?"

"Hm?"

"You want some muffins?" She was already crawling toward the end of the bed.

"I'd love muffins." He'd eat any damn thing she baked as long as it made her happy. His belly growled in agreement.

"You haven't eaten?" She sat on the end of the bed and grabbed a pair of slip-on shoes.

"Um, I did earlier."

"Not enough or your belly wouldn't be growling."

"That's not growling from hunger, that's my belly insisting you make the best muffins and telling you to hurry your pretty backside up and get it in the kitchen, stat."

"Sure, it is." She bunched her hair up into a ponytail and took the tie he offered before twisting it into a knot. "You haven't been looking after yourself."

If she thought he was putting himself before her happiness and well-being, then she'd lost her damn mind.

"I can give some to Becky before she leaves in the morning." She got to her feet and twisted her mouth. "She'll be okay in San Diego?"

"I swear." He stood off the bed. "I promise, the people we're sending her to are good people. They'll make sure she's looked after and safe. Kentucky will make sure she makes it there okay." He headed for the couch and his boots, then put them on and grabbed a tablet while she used the bathroom. He could get some work done while Willow baked.

"I think Kentucky has a crush on her." Willow tucked some loose bits of hair into the knot on her head as she entered the living room. "I'm ready."

"Then let's go find you an oven to make sing." He bit back a snicker. Kentucky having a crush on Becky, wasn't that the understatement of the year? He put his hand on the lock and waited for the click. He pulled open the door and checked up and down the hallway to check it was clear before waving her out ahead of them. "Yeah, maybe he has."

"It's kind of cute."

"I dare you to tell Kentucky that he's cute."

"He'd let me."

"What makes you say that?" He couldn't wait to hear what popped out of her mouth. Fuck, he'd missed her unique way of looking at the world.

"He's afraid of..."

"My ass, Kentucky Smith is a badass who isn't afraid of anything or anyone including me."

"He's afraid of Becky."

Whoops, he'd thought she was going to say he was afraid of him or Dalton. "Nope, he's already a goner there, I think." They walked side by side down the stairs. "I just think he'll fight it with everything that he is."

"Typical man, if he doesn't talk to her, I'm going to kick him in the balls and render them useless."

"That's the last thing I expected to come out of your mouth, Sunshine." He pushed open the swinging doors to the kitchen and let her in ahead of him after a quick glance to make sure it was clear.

"Sorry."

"Nope, what did we say about no sorries?" He went back into the dining room and grabbed a chair. "You cook, I'll work. You can pay me in muffins later."

"You want me to tell Uncle Dalton that your check comes muffin style this month?" she called from the pantry.

Even though she couldn't see him, he grinned wide. She was throwing him sass and snark and it fucking thrilled him. "Hell no, don't tell him that, he'd make it happen."

"Maybe I should talk to Lina…" She returned to the kitchen with her hands filled with supplies and dumped them on the countertop.

"Don't you dare." He hit the button on the tablet and scowled at it. He huffed out a breath and dropped it on the table. "Asshole."

"Me?"

"No, the tablet, it won't switch on."

"Is it charged?"

"Hell if I know."

"Why don't you go get another one from Trev?" He hesi-

tated long enough that she huffed at him, "Go, I'll be fine."
She waved a hand, taking in the room. "It's a kitchen, this is
my happy place."

"Are you sure?"

"Grumpy, I'm sure." She rounded the counter and came to
stand in front of him and peered up, looking into his eyes. "I
promise I'll call you the second I'm not."

He wasn't entirely sure he wanted to go. Seeing the spark
in her eyes as she planned what she was baking and the slight
humming under her breath as she wandered around the
kitchen made him want to stay longer and just see her being
her. "Um."

"Shoo, I have muffin batter calling my name."

"Okay, okay." He tapped her nose. "Far be it from me to
keep you from your batter." The corners of his lips quirked up
into a smile when she wrinkled her nose at him. "Kayce will
be here soon, just so you know, okay?" He didn't want her to
lose her mind if the door opened. He also didn't want to have
to find a new cook because if Kayce scared her, he was going
to kill him, end of discussion.

"I know." She petted his cheek. "I swear I'll be okay. I
know kitchens, I know how they work, it's my happy place,"
she reminded him. "Being in a kitchen feeds my soul."

"Okay." He believed her. "I never thought I'd be jealous
of a room though. Feed my soul." Grumbling, he turned away
to leave. She'd call him if she needed him.

"You feed my heart, the kitchen feeds my soul, and my
being in the kitchen feeds your belly."

"IKYAS, Sunshine."

"IBW, Grumpy."

He blew her a kiss as he walked out the door. Once the
doors had swung shut behind him, he pulled out his cell and
tapped through the screens until he found Kayce's number.

Text: Willow's in the kitchen baking, make some noise on approach.

Text: Copy that.

Text: Seriously, bro, if you scare her, I'll kick your ass.

Text: I promise I won't scare your woman, bro. But I will go down there and make sure she knows I'm around just in case.

Text: Thanks, man.

Text: Welcome.

CHAPTER TWENTY-NINE

SHE'D MEASURED some coffee out of the pot into a mug and added it to the chocolate batter. Her head shot up at a thump from the dining room, followed by muffled swearing. She cocked her head to one side, was that Kayce? "Hey, that you, Kayce?"

"Yeah, I stubbed my dang toe, I'll be in in a minute."

Relief zinged through her when she recognized what the muttering was, multiple languages. Stubbing your toe was usually when one learned how many languages you could actually swear in. She glanced at the batter; it could wait a second before she had to finish whipping it. She poured some coffee into another mug. "You want coffee?"

"Yes, please," Kayce grunted. "And a daily reminder to put on my boots before I walk through a place where the furniture moves all by itself in the middle of the night. I'm coming in," he warned about five seconds before the door opened.

While she was grateful for the warning, she'd been expecting him and just smiled at his disheveled hair and the t-shirt which was on backward. "Cormack called you, didn't he?"

"More of a heads up that you were here than a wakeup call." Kayce took the mug. "I'd have had to be here in an hour anyway and I wasn't sleeping, so I figured I'd see if you wanted company."

"Oh." She'd figure out later if she was going to beat Cormack or thank him for making sure she wasn't alone. She picked up the bowl and put some elbow grease into beating the batter. "Why weren't you sleeping?" As soon as the words were out of her mouth, she wanted to take them back. There were some things you didn't ask a soldier and his nightmares were usually pretty close to the top of that list.

"Sometimes with the dreams and memories I have it's easier to sleep in the daytime. The monsters can't hide in the shadows when the sun is shining."

It was strangely poetic to hear him say that. "Agree." They fell into a comfortable silence while she measured out the batter into the pans and he sipped his coffee. This was just what she needed. To move her hands, to let her brain roam free, and to just be in a space where she was herself most. She ignored the glances Kayce threw her way a couple of times. Whatever it was he was working up to saying, he'd get there when he was ready or when he figured she was. She popped the trays into the oven and set the timer, poured herself another mug of coffee and added copious amounts of caramel topping and creamer to it, then leaned against the counter almost opposite where Kayce sat.

"I'll only say one thing about what happened." He fiddled with the handle of his mug. "Don't let anyone tell you to get over it. You do shit on your time. If anyone pushes, you send them to Jeep or me. Got it?"

"Why?"

"Why what?"

"Why send them to you?"

"Because you remind me of my little sister, and I'd like to think that wherever she is she has someone to fight for her to do things on her timeline, not on the timeline those around her say shit should happen."

"Cormack wants me to see someone." It felt weird as hell to voice the words out loud. She waited for Kayce to scoff or laugh, but it didn't happen.

"That depends on you." He lifted one shoulder. "If you find the right person and you gel with them, then you aren't telling Cormack that you don't want to be the reason why he looks at you differently."

"And if I don't find someone I gel with?"

"Then it sucks, and you pull on your big girl panties and you try again and again until you find one who does." Kayce drained the mug and stood to take it to the sink. "You can let what happened break you or you can break the hold it has on you. You survived what went down, don't let those bastards define the rest of your life." He scratched the stubble on his chin. "As my grandma used to say, don't let someone who hasn't walked in your boots tell you how to tie your laces." He grabbed an apron and tied it around his waist. "Ready to work?"

"Yes." She'd have to think about what he said to make sense of all of it. But it struck a chord somewhere deep inside her. She'd figure it out later.

"Good girl. Let's cook."

SHE OPENED the door of the doctor's office and was hit with a blast of ninety-four degree heat. When people said it was cooler in the mountains, they forgot to mention that was only when you were in the shade. When you were in direct sunlight as the door of the building was, then it was hell hot and even the pavements steamed.

"Sunshine?"

"Hi?" She should have known he'd be right here waiting for her, just as he had been at every session for the last month.

"How did it go?"

"Three boxes of tissues and not five this time." It had started as a way to deflect from the raw and angry feelings the therapist pulled from her in their sessions, but sometime between the first Monday of the month and this Friday the reduction in the number of boxes of tissues required to get through each session had become a marker for the progress she was making.

"Awesome." He placed one hand on her lower back and guided her across the street to the café. "You want ice cream, pie, or a cola float?"

Doing the therapy and bringing up all the feelings and what-not, that sucked, but the favorite part of her day was when Cormack took her for a treat afterward. She'd snorted at Lina when she'd suggested that he was treating her like she did the puppy. She loved that he was wooing her, almost as if he were dating her all over again. "A cola float, please."

"Awesome, your wish is my command." He pulled open the door and pushed gently on her back, encouraging her to proceed him in the door. She led the way to the back of the room and took a seat in the booth which was rapidly becoming theirs. She scooted across the seat, leaving room for him, and then smiled when he managed to squish himself into the same seat, his thigh pressed against hers, his left arm flung across the seat behind her head, and his fingers tangling into the strands of her ponytail.

"Why do you do that?"

"Mmh, do what?"

"Play with my hair?"

"It's your hair, I like touching you." He grinned down at her. "This I can do in public without getting arrested for indecent exposure."

"Please don't get arrested for that, Uncle D would have a conniption fit."

"Is that like a shit fit?"

His eyes were laughing as he asked the question, and she huffed out a breath. "You're going to use that, aren't you?"

"Yup, totally." He laughed outright. That rich tone which told her he was genuinely amused. "It will take him at least five minutes to figure out what the big words mean."

"Please do that where I can see?" she begged him. "Please."

He swooped down and pressed a kiss to the side of her mouth. "You bet, Sunshine, that's a deal. You keep feeding me the big words and I promise to poke fun at Nem with them in your presence."

"What can I get you folks today?"

"Hi, Orla, how are you doing?" He turned that megawatt smile of his on the waitress. "My girl will have a cola float and I'll have a big slice of that rhubarb pie I saw on the counter and a mug of coffee." He glanced down at her. "Would you like anything else, Sunshine?"

"No, thank you."

"Do you want that pie hot with ice cream?"

"You'll spoil him."

"Honey, if I had a fine specimen of a man like that, I'd spoil him silly every day of the week and twice on Sunday."

"She does."

"Cormack." She could already feel the heat climbing up her face, she didn't want to draw attention to it though, so she just nudged him with her elbow in the ribs.

"Oops, sorry, that was out loud, wasn't it?"

"Um, yes, yes it was."

"You folks are good for this old woman's heart. I'll have your order ready in just a jiffy." Orla put her notepad into a pocket in her apron, smiled at them, and took off to the next table to ask for the sheriff's order on her way back to the counter.

"You're naughty."

"Did you just call me naughty?" Cormack's eyebrows almost disappeared into his eyebrows, and he twisted his face into a comical scowl.

"If the boots fit…"

"Minx."

She laughed at his indignant tone, God, she'd needed this after the heaviness of the sessions with the therapist, she needed the reminder that life was still something worth fighting for. It had taken a while to get here, but this was the path she was supposed to be on. She reached up to press a kiss to his jaw and snuggled into his side. "I love you."

"You and I are going to talk about your timing of when you say those words, Darlin'. Both times you've blindsided me when I least expect it."

"You're not going to swoon into a dead faint, are you?" She arched an eyebrow. "Do I need to call Orla back here and ask her for some smelling salts to revive you?"

"Nope, Sunshine, no fainting, I promise. Just an I love you, too."

"I know you do."

"Here you go, folks." Orla placed a plate of pie piled high

with ice cream and lashings of whipped cream in front of Cormack, and a cola float dripping with toppings and cream in front of her. "I brought you double cutlery in case you want to share."

"You're the best, tell your boss I said you should have a raise."

Orla snorted. "I am my boss, and I say I can't afford it." Her smile took in both of them. "Enjoy, folks."

"We should talk to Kayce about ordering some goodies from here." She scooped up a spoonful of fizzy melting goodness and put it in her mouth, moaning as the flavor exploded over her tongue. "Especially this homemade ice cream. The guys would be loving it." Her breath caught in her throat at the heat in his gaze.

"Yeah." He cleared his throat and then continued on. "But then Kayce may never get them to leave the dining room and Dalton will never get them on a plane to go to work."

"True."

"But it would be worth it." He grinned at her. "Talk to Kayce and bring him here to taste it."

"The locals will have a field day if I turn up here with a different hot man tomorrow, they'll be saying I'm cheating on you for sure."

"You think Kayce's hot?"

"That's what you got from what I said?"

"You mentioned hot and another man in the same sentence, of course my brain got stuck right there."

And there it was, the grumbly growly tone which sent sparks zinging through her. She'd been so worried she, no, not just her, but both of them had lost the connection they'd had. Note: Her girlie bits could confirm that was not the case. When he growled in that possessive tone, her girlie bits sat up and took notice, even if that growling was caused by her teasing him. "There is only you for me, Grumpy."

"I know." He grinned at her. "I just love when you blush as you try to figure out if I'm mad or not."

"Oh, I wasn't trying to figure that out." She willed her face to stay serious. "I was just telling my girlie bits to behave because we're in public."

His pie and ice cream filled fork flew, sending splatters of pie across the room. "Shit."

She watched the trajectory of the pie and her eyes widened as she saw where it was headed. "Oh my." She slapped her hand across her mouth and tried to stop it, but she couldn't help it and a snicker escaped just as the pie landed on the sheriff's plate, making him jerk and shove the plate skimming across his table and onto the floor. At least it hadn't landed on his head.

"You cannot say things like that to me in public. Damn it," he growled low in her ear.

"Girlie. Bits."

"Damn it, woman." He got to his feet and turned toward the sheriff whose plate he'd assaulted with pie. "I'm so sorry, sir. I don't know what happened. Let me get you a new plate."

"Boy, if I had a girl as pretty as yours whispering sweet nothings in my ear, I'd be sending my pie flying, too." The sheriff grinned at him. "Only difference is I'd have her over my shoulder and be making a beeline for the preacher to make sure nobody stole her when I wasn't looking."

She couldn't hear Cormack's response as the sod lowered his voice too much. "I'm so sorry, Orla." She winced as the older woman approached. "I think I shocked his delicate sensibilities." She scooped up the last of her float and licked it off the spoon.

"Honey, you are too good for this old woman's heart, I haven't laughed so hard in a month," Orla snickered. "His aim is pretty darn good considering he wasn't looking that way a'tall."

"I'm…"

Orla cut him off with a wave of her hand. "It's grand, y'all are more entertainment than the circus."

Cormack pulled some bills out of his pocket and handed them to Orla. "I'm covering the sheriff's lunch as well, and bring him some dessert, too."

"I'll do that, son."

"How are you doing, Sunshine?"

"Finished, it was yummy." She took the hand he held out and let him help her out of the booth. As soon as she was on her feet he grinned at her, dipped his shoulder, and tossed her over it.

"What are you doing?" she shrieked in his ear.

"Taking the sheriff's advice."

"Yeehaw, son."

She waved at the sheriff and Orla as he carried her out the door. As soon as the door shut behind them she took total and utter advantage of the position he had her in and petted his pretty butt.

"Sunshine."

Ooh, he growls. She giggled and petted him again. Laughing together, they crossed the street to the parking lot and his truck. Him growling at her and her laughing as she petted his butt. Yup, the twitching curtain brigade and gossips were going to have a field day for sure. When they reached the truck, he slid her off his shoulder and pressed her against the door, dipped his head, and captured her lips with his.

She tasted the tartness of the rhubarbs and the sweetness of the ice cream, but it was the taste which was uniquely

Cormack which made her clutch onto his arms and throw herself into the kiss.

When they pulled back, they were both breathing hard. "Marry me."

"What?" Was he insane? They were in the middle of a parking lot for heaven's sake.

He shifted her to one side and hit the locks on the truck. Pulling open the door, he leaned into the truck to search in the glovebox. "There you are."

"Cor…"

He backed out of the truck, turned, and dropped down on one knee.

Her hands flew up to cover her mouth. "What are you doing?"

He opened his hand and her breath caught in her throat. This wasn't some wild ass whim, he'd thought about this. "Please, Willow, will you do me the honor of being the sun in my sky from now until the day I die? Will you please be mine forever?"

Hot tears spilled out of her eyes and down her face. She slashed them away with the back of her hands. "Do you mean it?"

"Yes, baby. I mean it, marry me."

"Yes." She dropped to her knees next to him, her arms around his neck as his wrapped around her back, holding her to him as he peered into her face.

"Really?"

"Yes." He pulled one hand back and held out the ring to her. "This was my grandmother's ring. It came with her from Ireland. It's been in our family for over five hundred years."

"It's beautiful." It was stunning with the intricately woven band of Celtic knots and the hands holding the diamond.

"If you don't like it, we can go pick something different."

"No, don't you dare, I love it." If he tried to take it back now, she was going to give those ladies she could see twittering across the street something to really talk about by getting to her feet and booting him in the balls.

"This is a Claddagh ring." He pointed out the hands holding the heart shaped diamond in place. "The hands represent that I'll always be your friend." He kissed one finger on her left hand. "The crown over the diamond says I'll always be loyal and true to you." He pressed another kiss to her fingers. "And the heart represents the love I have for you." He picked up her left hand and placed the ring on her finger with the heart facing out and pressed a kiss to that finger, too. "Wearing it this way says your heart is forever taken."

"It is." She swiped away the happy tears which didn't want to stop falling and kissed him softly on the lips. "It's yours forever."

He helped her to her feet and helped her into the truck. He caressed her cheek with his hand. "I love you, Sunshine."

"I love you, too." She leaned her head against the headrest and turned to watch him getting behind the wheel. "Soooo, when are you going to tell Uncle D and Rexar?"

"Never. Montana is a no wait state. They don't need to know."

Was he serious? He couldn't be serious.

"I'm kidding, baby." He turned on the truck and hit the aircon so they didn't die of heat stroke. "Imma going to stop at the store and grab some good whiskey. Tonight, we celebrate and we tell them."

"Yes. Let's do that." She settled into the seat, and once he pulled out of the lot, she placed her hand on his thigh, his fingers immediately covering hers. She wouldn't care if there was a thousand miles of highway between here and the ranch, her heart was happy. Her soul at peace. They could take all week to get home and she wouldn't notice the length of the ride, only the person she shared the truck with. This was what hopes and dreams were made of. If anyone ever offered you your heart's desire, grab it with both hands and hold on tight. She planned on doing that for as many lifetimes as possible.

MUSHOLOGUE

He took his hand from where it rested on Willow's fingers on his thigh and dropped a gear. The truck turned in under the high gate made of massive timber beams with Nemesis Ranch branded into it along with an anchor on each side. She'd said yes. Holy fucking shit, they were getting married. Married.

He pulled the truck into his parking space outside their building and lifted her hand to his lips, pressing a soft kiss to her knuckles. "Ready?"

"Yes."

He felt his eyes crinkle at the corners as he smiled at how the word escaped in a breathless rush. "Wait for me to get the door." He jumped out of the truck and went around to help her out. He reached past her and shut the truck door. She launched herself at him the second his hands were free, only his fast reflexes kept him from dropping her.

She wrapped around him like a monkey, her legs crossing behind his back. Instant arousal and fiery heat blasted through him. That his woman who'd been hurt so badly could trust him enough to not only cover his face in kisses from her soft lips, but to agree to spend the rest of her life with him was beyond erotic and something he hadn't dared hope for.

Innocence was always going to be a word he would associate with Willow. He adored how she looked at the world. And loved how her mouth touching his brimmed with heat. He hadn't expected the relentless coaxing and testing of his patience. The ravenous dominance which hammered at his willpower demanded he take over the kiss. But he refused to rush her, instead, he gave her time, gave her a chance to get accustomed to the taste and the feel of him again, to experience how his body hardened under hers.

Somehow, he managed to walk and kiss her at the same time. He totally ignored the catcalls and whistles from the hands working in the corral. With each exquisitely tender caress of her lips, anticipation and urgency built until she was squirming against him. Damn, he wished his hands were free so he could tighten her against him. But he didn't dare until they were in the privacy of their suite where he could take this gentle but mind-blowing kiss to an exploring all of her she was comfortable with.

"Hurry, Grumpy," she whispered against his mouth.

"I'm going to eat you up like candy," he promised, nipping at her lips. He climbed the stairs with her still wrapped around him.

"I think you're just planning on soft and slow," she accused him. "But I need you to remind me who we are when we set fire to the sheets."

"Oh, baby, I promise we will send the whole damn bed down in flames, never mind the sheets." He made short work of the lock on their suite door and strode down the hall and lowered her to the bed. He followed her down and kissed her deep and messy before pulling back to peer into her eyes. "Promise you'll tell me if you need to stop."

"I swear. I swear, hurry."

His chuckle was dark and deep. "Sunshine, fast is the last thing on my mind." He stripped her t-shirt off over her head and lowered the cups of her bra. His head lowered, his lips seeking one plump nipple.

Willow arched against him as the heat of his mouth surrounded the sensitive tip. Her fingers curled, digging into the back of his head as she held him against her.

"Oh, God, Cormack." Her fingers fisted into his hair as he sucked at the hard point of her nipple. His tongue licking at it, his teeth scraping it. He sucked and nipped, tormenting, torturing, as she pushed to hold him to her.

Perspiration dampened his brow and desire rushed through him with a force he'd never felt before. He could feel the pulse and throb of blood in his dick as she arched against him.

He was on fire. If he was the kindling, she was the spark which made him go boom. Flames of need and desire were racing across his flesh, aching and throbbing between his thighs. When he slid his leg between hers, his heavy muscles shifting her legs apart, he groaned at the heat of her pressing against him. He could come from just this tiny bit of contact alone. But he wouldn't, she had to come first. She'd asked him to remind her of the fire and boom, the accelerant was about to fan the flames.

She urged him on, arching into his mouth as she writhed and pushed against him. His lips moved from one peaked nipple to the other. Licking, sucking, and biting gently until she was whining at him to do something. By the time he pulled back to pop the button on her jeans and draw them down her legs, he had to work hard to find some self-control somewhere. He stepped back and swept his eyes from the top of her head to the soles of her feet.

"Fuck, Sunshine, you're beautiful." He made short work of stripping off his clothes and reached for her again.

"No."

He froze and slowly lifted his hands. It would kill him, but if she needed to stop, then he'd find a way to make it happen. "Talk to me, Sunshine. Do you need me to stop?"

"No more teasing, please. Take me."

"Not until you're ready."

"I'm ready, please."

"No, baby, you're not ready until you're screaming my name." He rubbed the swollen knot of her clit with his thumb as he kissed her slow and deep.

When he lifted from her lips, his mouth roamed down her body, raining kisses and sucking up marks on her skin. Her legs parted for his shoulders, and when his tongue licked through the heavy juices built along the folds of her sex, if his hand hadn't been flat on her tummy, she'd have lifted off the bed.

Sensual, wicked, engulfing, his tongue licked slow and easy through her slit, then his lips captured her flesh, giving a suckling kiss before doing the same on the other side.

"Cormack…"

He smiled against her. "You'll have to give me more, Sunshine, louder."

"Cormack, please."

His tongue licked around her clit; his teeth scraped over the hood. All the while his fingers played, circled, and pressed at her entrance.

"You're teasing me," she moaned as her fingers pulled on his hair and she fought to hold him in place while he sucked and licked at her clit. "You're killing me, Grumpy."

"Not killing," he whispered against her sex. "Loving you.

Fuck, baby, you taste like summertime apple pie and cinnamon ice cream."

"Soap." She arched her hips, pushing against his mouth.

"There is no soap on the planet that tastes like this." He pushed his tongue deep into her pussy, licking and sucking, before pulling back to blow on her clit. "That's all you, Sunshine. So sweet and hot I want to eat you up."

He loved how she clenched and melted around him when his tongue thrust inside her.

"Cormack, please."

"Louder, Sunshine." He sucked hard on her clit, scraping it with his tongue, then licking around it. Giving her more, wanting more from her. He used his mouth and fingers, combining the overload on her senses, until she finally came chanting his name.

"Cormack. Cormack. Cormack."

"You're so beautiful, my sunshine." He rose between her thighs and crawled onto the bed next to her, pausing to gather her in his arms and rolling onto his back. "Come here, baby. Come on, Sunshine love. You take me now."

"Mmh huh?"

"You're in control, baby." He nudged her gently, encouraging her to take what she wanted, what she needed.

"But…"

He cupped her face in his hand and drew her down to press a kiss to her mouth. "Baby, I need you in control, because if I miss a cue from you and I didn't stop when you needed me to, I'd hate it and it would kill me to scare you."

"I love you."

"I know you do; I love you, too." She watched as she lifted her hips and positioned herself over the swollen head of his dick. His breath caught in his throat when she gripped him and sank down to slide him between the lips of her sex to nudge against the entrance of her pussy.

Her eyes slamming shut and her gasp of pleasure as she began to sink down him on with a slow rocking motion was an image he wanted seared into his memory forever.

With each shift of her hips, he could feel her muscles melting around him against the width of his flesh. The folds of her pussy gleamed with her juices as his aching heavy shaft parted them.

"Hold on to me, baby." He tangled his fingers with hers, first one hand and then the other as her hips lifted. Moans ripped from them both as she sank down again to take more of him.

"So beautiful," he murmured. "There you go, love. Take what you need. I've never seen anything so damned sexy in my life as the sight of you sinking onto my dick."

Her hips rocked and rolled, his dick sinking deeper inside her. He raised his knees behind her back, his feet planted wide on the bed to give her support and the ability to take more of him if she needed it. Emotions and sensation that he hadn't known existed wrapped around them, blowing his mind.

Nothing existed but them, her taking him, his dick stretching her as she cried out his name, begging for more. Deeper. Harder. She sped up, taking more of him, all of him. Fuck, with each clench she was burning him alive.

"So beautiful." His hands gripped her hips as he tried to slow the pace a little, but she was having none of it. She lifted almost off him until only the head of his dick stretched the lips of her pussy, and in one hard stroke she dropped onto him, taking all of him down to the root.

His cock throbbed inside her clenching pussy. Aching and

pulsing in rhythm with their ragged breaths, he nearly came from that alone. Almost. But he fought it back, she needed to come first.

Her lashes lifted until she could look down at him. Her face was flushed, her lips swollen and damp from their kisses. She was the goddess who'd captured his heart, and there was no way in hell he was ever letting her go.

She clenched and released her muscles around his dick. Her hips shifted and rolled as her moans filled the room. She leaned over him to hover her lips over his mouth. "Help me," she whispered. "Help me make love to you."

God, did she have any idea how close he was to losing it? She untangled her fingers from his and pulled one of his hands and pushed it under her butt.

"Please, Grumpy, help me."

He peered into her eyes looking for any hesitation or fear, but all he found was love, trust, and need. He nodded and cupped her bottom with both hands, lifting her almost off him, then pushed his hips up to meet her flesh as he lowered her again.

It didn't take him long to make her scream. Her nails dug into his shoulders as he began to thrust, to move. Willow's knees pressed against his sides. Her muscles strained as she lifted when he did.

Each time she sank onto him ripped another cry from her and a grunt from him and sent them both flying higher. Heat whipped through him as he pushed her onward, giving and taking. It seared him from the inside out, and finally when he thought he could hold back no more, she shattered over him, crying his name.

Her orgasm called to every cell in his body and sent ecstasy racing down his back and wrapping around his front.

It stole his breath, blanked out his mind, and all he could do was thrust hard and deep one last time as his body tightened and his release tore through him.

They were still fighting for breath when she collapsed onto his chest, and he enfolded her into his arms. "IKYAS, Sunshine."

"IBW, Grumpy."

She lay against his chest, her ear over his heart, and he silently thanked any God that would listen that he'd found her again. That she was his, and he was hers, forever.

Logan glanced at his watch and strode down the corridor to the war-room door and knocked. He didn't bother to wait for an answer but pushed it open and glanced inside. "You wanted to see me, Boss?"

"Yes, Sensei, get your ass in here stat."

"Boss, I have to be standing at the altar with Jeep in thirty minutes, and you have to be dressed in a damn monkey suit to walk Willow down the aisle about five minutes after that…"

"This won't take long," Nemesis reassured him. "Trev, put that intel on the screen."

"You got it."

"I know you asked for some leave, but I'm asking if you can do a job first." Nemesis shrugged. "Normally, this would fall to Jeep, but as you know he's going on his honeymoon tomorrow, and both he and my wife both threatened to chop off my balls if I interfered with that."

He'd asked for leave as he was bored shitless here in Montana. "I can move it around. I'm just meeting some buddies in the Caribbean for some scuba diving."

"Perfect, let me give you some intel. You know we've

been chasing a lead on how to find more information on that fucker King's organization?"

"Yeah."

"We finally have what may be viable intel."

"Go on."

"We have had a request for security from Gideon Holdings International in Dubai." Nemesis pulled up information on the company.

"What connects this to King? Did Lina confirm it?"

"Lina wasn't aware of this one," Nemesis admitted. "But money, bro, money connects it to The Organization, but we haven't found anything concrete to link it to King."

"Okay." He could see that. They usually followed the money; Trev and his hacker buddies were shit hot at following the money. If they said it was connected to The Organization at least... then it was. "What do you want from me?"

"I want your ass on a plane to Dubai to follow up," Nemesis said. "They would prefer if it was today, but I told them you weren't available until the day after tomorrow."

"I can leave as soon as Jeep and Willow say I do."

"Nope, there will be a boat load of beer and whiskey flowing tonight," Nemesis said. "You can wait a day."

"Did they say what they want the security for?"

"Some vague ass shit that we can't be sure if it's a set up or not." Nemesis handed him a file. "My guess is they're looking to see our strengths and weaknesses."

"Okay." He flipped through the file and closed it again. There would be plenty of time to go through the intel once the wedding was done. "Am I flying solo?"

"Hell no," Nemesis growled. "Alpha and Bravo teams will travel with you."

"Roger that." He glanced at the clock on the wall. "Boss, you better move your ass or shit will fly."

"Fuck." Nemesis's eyes widened as his cell started ringing on the desk. "I'm on my way, Princess, I swear." He hit end on the call and gestured to the other two. "Come on, boys, let's get Jeep and Willow married so my wife will stop hassling me about a damn monkey suit."

"Roger that, Boss." He followed Dalton and Trev out the door. Excitement bubbled in his belly. Love, weddings, and babies were so not his jam... missions, however, were, and he couldn't wait to get started on this one.

He made his way back to Alpha team's house and into the dining room where he'd told Jeep to wait for him when Dalton had pinged his cell.

"You're here."

"Did ya think I'd done a runner with your rings?"

"If you had, you'd have had to deal with Willow and Lina." Jeep got to his feet and rubbed his hands down his thighs. "Me, too."

"You look like a man who's nervous."

"My girl wants perfect; we're giving her perfect." Jeep huffed out a breath. "Nobody better fuck up her perfect day."

"You're getting married, too, you remember that, right?"

"Of course, I do, dipshit." Jeep tugged on the bow tie at his neck and clapped Logan on the shoulder. "Thank you for standing up with me."

"Where the fuck else would I be?" Logan glanced at his watch. "Time's up, buddy, if you planned on running, you missed your window."

"The only place I'm running is out there." Jeep jerked his chin toward the double French doors which led into the small garden attached to the house.

They walked between the rows of chairs to the flower covered archway the boys had built yesterday, and Logan took his place next to Jeep. This was as close as he was ever getting to a wedding, so he might as well enjoy the day.

He glanced back toward the door they'd come through and grinned at their friends and loved ones who'd gathered to share the day with Jeep and Willow. Thank fuck they'd decided they wanted to be married fast and not to plan a huge shindig, or they'd have had to set up in the corral or in a field to fit everyone. He spotted Orla from the café and the sheriff whom Jeep and Willow insisted had to be there. Apparently, without those two, the wedding wouldn't be happening today at all. Rexar and his momma sat in the same row the two women were chattering away as Rex and the sheriff rolled their eyes while they couldn't see.

The soft music playing in the background changed to the wedding march and Jeep's head whipped around to look at the door, ignoring the preacher he'd been chatting to.

"I'm happy for you, bro, you two are made for each other."

"And that's why you're standing here and not Dalton."

He snickered at the eat shit tone in Jeep's voice. "He's walking your bride down the aisle, remember?"

"Ye…" Jeep cut off whatever it was he'd been going to say as Lina appeared in the doorway. Her hair was pulled up in some sort of complicated twist with something sparkly which caught the sunlight as she walked fast down the aisle. Her floor-length dress was a deep purple to match the flowers which covered the archway.

"Don't faint," he whispered to Jeep. "I forgot the smelling salts."

"Fuck off, asshole," Jeep replied and the people in the

front rows all laughed, and Logan grinned at his teammates. That was ten bucks Rory owed him, he'd be sure to collect that later.

He knew the second Willow appeared in the doorway as Jeep gasped, and Logan turned his attention back to what he should be doing, supporting his friend.

His eyes widened when he caught sight of Willow waiting in the doorway with Dalton.

"Fuck, she's beautiful," Cormack whispered softly.

"You're a lucky man, bro."

Willow's dress was simple, nothing like the elaborate ones he'd seen at other weddings he'd attended. It fit her like it had been made especially for her, a sweetheart neckline, and he only knew it was called sweetheart as he'd overheard Lina telling Dalton as they drove back from the airport after a trip to NYC to purchase the dress, a fitted waist, and then it fell straight to the floor.

Out of the corner of his eye he saw Jeep move, but he wasn't fast enough to catch him as he took off down the aisle to meet his bride.

"You were meant to wait for me to bring her to you." Dalton's face darkened.

"Nemy." Lina's voice was filled with warning and Dalton schooled his face to smile down at Willow.

"Be happy, little one."

"I will."

"Keep her happy, or I'll shoot you."

Jeep offered his hand to Dalton. "I swear, her happiness is my number one goal."

"Be nice, Uncle D, or we're going back down the aisle and Uncle Rex can walk me all the way up."

"No, we're not." Jeep looked panicked and Logan

clamped down on the inside of his cheek to stop himself from laughing out loud. Apparently, normal wasn't in the wheelhouse for weddings either. Jeep slid his arm around her waist and tugged her into his side. "Ready, Sunshine?"

"Ready."

Logan didn't hear what the preacher had to say, he was way too busy looking at how Jeep and Willow appeared to not see anyone else. Their focus was on each other. They breathed in unison, they smiled simultaneously. Damn it, he had something in his eye, but he didn't dare to draw attention to it by swiping at them now.

"I believe you have written your own vows." The preacher's words were his cue to dig into his coat pocket for the rings Jeep had given him this morning.

"Yes." Jeep took the ring from him and cupped Willow's face in his hand. "Willow, from the very first email you have brightened my world. You took this sailor and guided him home time after time with your beautiful smile and your wonderful soul." He picked up her hand and rubbed his finger over her engagement ring. "I promise to always be your friend. I swear I will always be loyal. My heart is yours until the end of time. I love waking up wrapped around you, even if you insist I hog the blankets, know it's just because I love being as close to you as I can possibly be. I swear to you that you will always be my first thought when I wake and my last as I fall asleep. IKYAS, Sunshine, because just as you are mine, I am yours, if you'll have me?" His voice cracked on his last word. He pressed a kiss to each of her fingers and slid the ring on to nestle next to the Claddagh.

"Yes, I'll have you and I'm keeping you forever." Tears ran freely down Willow's face. She swiped them away with the back of one hand and took a deep breath. "I love you,

Cormack. I will never know why I answered that email you sent. I just know that doing so changed my world, changed my life. It brought me you. I didn't even know someone who could make my heart this happy existed, then you arrived with your teasing and laughter and showed me a whole new world. You saved me when I didn't know it was possible. You loved me when I didn't think I deserved it. I may be the sun in your sky, but you are the moon in mine. I promise I'll be true; I swear I'll always love you. IBW, Grumpy. I'll always be your home, just as you are mine, if you'll have me?"

"Yes, for always." Cormack held his hand out while Willow pushed the black wedding band past his knuckle.

The preacher glanced between them and waited for Cormack to nod. "Cormack Ford, Willow Black. By the power vested in me by God and the state of Montana, I now pronounce you man and wife. Cormack, you may kiss your bride."

Cormack barely waited for the preacher to finish giving him permission, he already had Willow in his arms and was kissing his wife for the first time.

Logan put his fingers to his mouth and whistled along with the catcalls and Hooyahs coming from the guests.

"Ladies and gentlemen!" the preacher boomed as soon as the kiss ended. "I present to you, Mr. and Mrs. Cormack Ford."

He followed behind them as they walked hand in hand down the aisle. Even a loveaphobe like him could admit it was a beautiful ceremony. The band was already tuning their instruments for the dancing to come, and the scent of barbecue wafted in from the other side of the house. Seeing his friend this happy almost made him wish he was of a different mindset. But he knew better than to want to inflict anyone with his lousy genes. So nope, dinner, dancing, send

Cormack and Willow off on their honeymoon. Then his ass was going back to work.

Thank you for reading Cormack and Willow's story, I hope you enjoyed the ride as much as I enjoyed writing it. Watch out for Logan's story later this year.

FOLLOW ME ON SOCIAL MEDIA:

Facebook: https://www.facebook.com/authorbellastone
Instagram: https://www.instagram.com/bellastoneauthor/
BookBub: https://www.bookbub.com/authors/bella-stone
Amazon: https://www.amazon.com/Bella-Stone/e/
B09FBQKBZG
Binge Books: https://bingebooks.com/author/bella-stone
Goodreads: https://www.goodreads.com/author/show/
17126278.Bella_Stone

BOOKS BY ANNABELLA STONE

DELTA FORCE: TEAM PANTHER
Jonah's Compass
Tied Up In Steele
Malik's Redemption
Micah's Promise
Christmas - Panther Style
Grif's Salvation
Jason's Justice

TAGS OF HONOR: RED SQUADRON
Zenko
Noble
Don't Let Go
Drax
Roman
Saxon
Reese

. . .

TASK FORCE AMBRA
Salvation's Sinner
Redemption's Rebel

GHOST PROTECTORS
To Love A Ghost
To Claim A Ghost

SHORT STORIES
They Won't Ask If We Don't Tell (Delta Force Team Panther)

Made in the USA
Las Vegas, NV
24 November 2024

12574186R00174